# the perfect wife

(a jessie hunt psychological suspense—book 1)

blake pierce

ISBN: 978-1-64029-662-6

# CHAPTER ONE

Jessie Hunt, exhausted and sweaty, dropped the last of the packing boxes on the dining room carpet. She could already feel her muscles starting to cramp up and knew she was going to be in serious pain tomorrow.

But as she looked over at Kyle, she couldn't help but smile. They were officially moved in. The wide grin on his face told her he was thinking the same thing. His shirt was drenched but she didn't care as he came over and wrapped her in a bear hug.

"We live here now," he whispered in her ear, before gently kissing her neck. "I think we're entitled to a celebratory drink, don't you?"

"Definitely," she agreed.

"Champagne? Beer?"

"Maybe a beer," Jessie suggested, "and a Gatorade chaser. I feel like my whole body might seize up at any second."

"I'll be right back," Kyle said and headed for the kitchen.

Jessie moved from the dining room to the den and plopped down on the couch, feeling her perspiration-soaked shirt press against the sheet covering the furniture. It was late August and even in the coastal Orange County community of Westport Beach, the weather was hot and sticky. The temperature was easily in the low nineties.

Of course, that was nothing compared to what it was like back in downtown Los Angeles, where they'd lived until this morning. Surrounded by the asphalt and concrete and shiny skyscrapers, Jessie would often walk out of their condo into the late summer heat to face temperatures above one hundred. In comparison, this felt like a respite.

She reminded herself that this was exactly the sort of perk that would justify moving away from the familiar life she'd grown to love in the city. She'd be trading in the excitement of the busy LA streets for cool ocean breezes. Instead of hip, new restaurants, they'd visit seaside cafes. Instead of taking the metro or an Uber to a gallery opening, they'd check out a yacht race in the harbor. And of course, there was all the extra money. It would take some getting used to. But she'd promised her husband she would embrace their new life and she intended to keep her word.

1

Kyle walked into the room, holding beers and Gatorades. He had peeled off his wet shirt. Jessie pretended to be oblivious to her husband's impressive abs and chest. How he managed to maintain that physique while working those crazy hours at the firm was beyond her. But she wasn't complaining.

He came over, handed her the drinks, and sat down beside her.

"Did you know there was a wine fridge in the pantry?" he asked.

"Yes," she said, laughing incredulously. "Didn't you notice that when we looked at the house the last two times?"

"I just assumed it was another cabinet so I never actually opened it until just now. Pretty cool, huh?"

"Yes, pretty cool, pretty boy," she agreed, marveling at how his short blond locks stayed perfectly coiffed, no matter how disheveled the rest of him got.

"You're the pretty one," he said, brushing Jessie's shoulder-length light brown hair out of her green eyes and staring at her with his own penetrating blue ones. "It's a good thing I got you out of LA. I was tired of all those fedora-wearing hipsters hitting on you."

"The fedoras weren't a great call, I have to say. I could barely see any of their faces to decide if they were my type."

"That's because you're an Amazon woman," he said, pretending not to get jealous at her gentle teasing. "Any guy under six feet tall has to crane his neck to look up at a tall drink of water like you."

"Not you, though," Jessie murmured softly, suddenly forgetting her aches and pains as she pulled him close toward her. "I'm always looking up at you, hot stuff."

Her lips were just brushing against his when the doorbell rang.

"You've got to be kidding me," she groaned.

"Why don't you answer it?" Kyle suggested. "I'll find a fresh shirt to throw on."

Jessie walked to the front door, beer in hand. It was her little rebellion against being interrupted mid-seduction. When she opened the door, she was greeted by a perky redhead who looked to be about her age.

She was cute, with a little button nose, gleaming white teeth, and a sundress that was just tight enough to prove she never missed a Pilates class. In her hands was a tray of what looked to be homemade brownies. Jessie couldn't help but notice the massive wedding ring on her finger. It gleamed in the late afternoon sun.

Almost without thinking, Jessie found herself profiling the woman: early thirties; got married young; two, maybe three children; stay-at-home-mom but had lots of help; nosy but not in a malicious way.

2

"Hi," the woman said in a chipper voice. "I'm Kimberly Miner from across the street. I just wanted to welcome you to the neighborhood. I hope I'm not disturbing you."

"Hi, Kimberly," Jessie replied in her friendliest, new neighbor voice. "I'm Jessie Hunt. We actually just finished moving our last box in a couple of minutes ago so this is great timing. And this is so sweet of you, literally! Brownies?"

"Yep," Kimberly said, handing over the tray. Jessie saw her pointedly pretend not to eye the beer in her hand. "They're kind of my specialty."

"Well, come on in and have one," Jessie offered, even though it was the last thing she wanted right now. "I'm sorry the place is such a mess, as are Kyle and I. We've been sweating all day. He's actually looking for a new shirt right now. Can I offer you something to drink? Water? Gatorade. A beer?"

"No thanks. I don't want to impose. You probably don't even know which box has your glasses yet. I remember the move-in process. It took us months. Where are you coming from?"

"Oh, we just lived up in DTLA," Jessie said and seeing the confused look on Kimberly's face, added, "Downtown Los Angeles. We had a condo in the South Park district."

"Oh wow, city folk," Kimberly said, giggling a little at her own joke. "What brought you to Orange County and our little community?"

"Kyle works for a wealth management firm," Jessie explained. "They opened a satellite office down here earlier in the year and it recently expanded. It's a big thing for them because PFG is a pretty conservative operation. Anyway, they asked him if he'd help run it. We figured it was a good time to make a change since we're thinking about starting a family."

"Oh, with the size of this house, I assumed you already had kids," Kimberly said.

"Nope—just being optimistic," Jessie answered, trying to hide the sudden embarrassment she was surprised she felt. "Do you have any children?"

"Two. Our daughter is four and our son is two. I'm actually going over to daycare to pick them up in a few."

Kyle arrived and wrapped one arm around Jessie's waist as he extended the other to shake Kimberly's.

"Hello," he said warmly.

"Hi, welcome," she replied. "My goodness, between the two of you, your future children are going to be giants. I feel like a munchkin next to you both."

3

There was a brief awkward silence as both Jessie and Kyle wondered how to respond.

"Thank you?" he finally said.

"I'm sorry. That was rude of me. I'm Kimberly, your neighbor from that house," she said, pointing across the street.

"Nice to meet you, Kimberly. I'm Kyle Voss, Jessie's husband."

"Voss? I thought it was Hunt."

"He's Voss," Jessie explained. "I'm Hunt, at least for now. I've been procrastinating on doing the paperwork to change it."

"I see," Kimberly said. "How long have you been married?"

"Almost two years," Jessie said sheepishly. "I have *real* problems with procrastination. That might explain why I'm still in school."

"Oh," Kimberly said, clearly relieved to move away from the delicate last name topic. "What are you studying?"

"Forensic psychology."

"Wow—that sounds exciting. How long before you're officially a psychologist?"

"Well, I got a little delayed," Jessie said, sharing the obligatory story from every cocktail party they'd attended for the last two years. "I started out in child psychology when we were undergrads at USC—that's where we met. I was even doing an internship for my master's when I realized I couldn't handle it. Dealing with children's emotional problems was too much for me. So I switched."

She pointedly neglected to include some of the other details of why she'd dropped out of the internship. Hardly anyone knew about them and she certainly wasn't going to share them with a neighbor she'd just met.

"So you find dealing with the psychology of criminals less disturbing than children?" Kimberly asked, dumbfounded.

"Weird, huh?" Jessie conceded.

"You'd be amazed," Kyle piped in. "She has this knack for getting in the heads of bad guys. She's going to be a great profiler eventually. Any potential Hannibal Lecters out there better look out."

"Really," Kimberly said, sounding properly impressed. "Have you had to deal with serial killers and stuff?"

"Not yet," Jessie admitted. "Most of my training has been academic. And with the move, I had to change schools. So I'm going to do my practicum at UC-Irvine starting this semester. This is my last one so I'll graduate in December."

"Practicum?" Kimberly asked.

4

"It's a little like an internship, only less involved. I'll be assigned to a prison or a psychiatric hospital, where I'll observe and interact with inmates and patients. It's what I've been waiting for."

"The chance to stare the evildoers in the eye and see into their souls," Kyle added.

"That might be overstating it just a bit," Jessie said, giving him a playful punch in the shoulder. "But eventually, yes."

"That is very exciting," Kimberly said, sounding genuinely intrigued. "I'm sure you'll have some great stories to tell. Speaking of, you said you two met at school?"

"Freshman year dorm," Kyle said.

"Oh," Kimberly pressed. "Bonded while doing laundry, that sort of thing?"

Kyle glanced over at Jessie and before he even said a word, she knew he was going to dive into their go-to cocktail party story.

"Here's the abridged version," he began. "We were friends but started dating midway through the first semester after she got stood up by some jerk. He got kicked out of school, not for bailing on the date I assume. Still, she dodged a bullet in my opinion. We broke up junior year, got back together as seniors. We dated for a year after that before moving in together. We did that for a year before getting engaged. Then we tied the knot ten months after that. It'll be two years of wedded bliss in October."

"So you're college sweethearts. That's so romantic."

"Yeah, it sounds that way," Kyle said. "But it took a while to win her over. And the whole time I was beating the competition off with a stick. As you can imagine, pretty much every guy who saw her was immediately smitten with Ms. Jessica Hunt. And that's just looking at her. Once you get to know her, you're even more besotted."

"Kyle," Jessie said, her face turning red. "You're embarrassing me. Save some of it for October."

"You know," Kimberly said with a smile, "I just remembered I need to get my kids now. And I suddenly feel like I'm interrupting a happy couple's plan to christen their new house. So I'm going to go. But I promise to introduce you around. We have a really friendly neighborhood. Everyone knows each other. We have weekly street barbecues. Kids have sleepovers all the time. Everybody belongs to the local yacht club, even if they don't have a boat. Once you're settled in, you're going to find this is a great place to live."

5

"Thanks, Kimberly," Kyle said, walking her to the door. "We look forward to meeting everyone. And thanks so much for the brownies."

After she left, he closed the door and made a big display of locking it.

"She seemed nice," he said. "Hopefully everyone's like that."

"Yeah, I liked her," Jessie agreed. "She was a little nosy, but I guess that's just how people are down here. I suppose I should get used to not having any anonymity anymore."

"It is going to be an adjustment," Kyle agreed. "But I think that long term, we'll prefer knowing our neighbors' names and being able to leave our doors unlocked."

"I noticed you locked it just now though," Jessie pointed out.

"That's because I was thinking about what Kimberly said about christening the new house," he said as he approached her, pulling off his second shirt in ten minutes. "And I don't like any interruptions when I'm christening."

*

Jessie lay in bed later that night, looking up at the ceiling, a smile on her face.

"At this pace, we'll have those extra bedrooms filled up in no time," Kyle said, seemingly reading her thoughts.

"I doubt we'll be able to keep up that pace once you start up at the office and my new semester begins."

"I'm game to try if you are," he said, sighing deeply. She could feel his whole body relax beside her.

"Aren't you nervous at all?" she asked.

"About what?"

"All of this—bigger salary, new town, new house, new lifestyle, new people, new everything."

"It's not all new," he reminded her. "You already know Teddy and Melanie."

"I've met Teddy three times and Melanie once. I barely know him. And I can only vaguely remember her. Just because your best friend from high school lives a few blocks over doesn't mean I'm suddenly at ease with our new life."

She knew she was picking a fight but she couldn't seem to stop herself. Kyle didn't take the bait. Instead, he rolled over onto his side and ran a finger lightly along her right shoulder, next to the long, pinkish moon-shaped scar that ran five inches from her upper arm to the base of her neck.

6

"I know you're apprehensive," he said tenderly. "And you have every reason to be. Everything is new. And I know that can be scary. I can't tell you how much I appreciate the sacrifice you're making."

"I know it'll be good in the end," she said, softening. "But it's just a lot to handle all at once."

"That's why seeing Teddy and Mel tomorrow will help. We'll reestablish that connection and then we'll have folks in the neighborhood to reach out to as we find our bearings. Even knowing two people will make the transition easier."

He yawned deeply and Jessie could tell he was about to crash. That big yawn usually meant he'd be fast asleep in sixty seconds or less.

"I know you're right," she said, determined to end the night on a good note. "I'm sure it will be great."

"It will," Kyle agreed lazily. "I love you."

"I love you too," Jessie said, unsure if he'd heard her before he drifted off.

She listened to his deep breaths and tried to use them to help her fall asleep. The silence was unsettling. She was used to the comforting sounds of downtown as she slipped into sleep.

She missed the honks from the cars below, the shouts of finance guys drunkenly leaving bars echoing among the high-rises, the beeping sound of trucks backing up. They'd served as her white noise for years. Now all she had to replace them was the soft whir of the air filter in the corner of the bedroom.

Every now and then she thought she heard a distant creaking sound. The house was more than thirty years old so some occasional settling was to be expected. She tried taking a series of deep relaxing breaths, both to drown out other sounds and to relax herself. But one thought kept nagging at her.

*Are you really sure it will be great here?*

She spent the next hour turning over her doubt and pushing it guiltily away before she finally gave in to her fatigue and settled into a fitful slumber.

# CHAPTER TWO

Despite the endless shouting, Jessie tried to fight off the headache nibbling at the edges of her skull. Daughton, the sweet-natured but shockingly loud three-year-old son of Edward and Melanie Carlisle, had spent the last twenty minutes playing a game called Explosion which largely consisted of him yelling "boom!"

Neither Melanie ("call me Mel") nor Edward ("Teddy" to his friends) seemed at all bothered by the intermittent screams so Jessie and Kyle acted like it was normal too. They were sitting in the Carlisle living room, catching up before a planned walk down to the harbor for brunch. The Carlisles lived only three blocks away from there.

Kyle and Teddy had been chatting outside for the last half hour while Jessie reacquainted herself with Mel in the kitchen. She only vaguely remembered her from their one previous meeting but after only a few minutes, they settled into a comfortable vibe.

"I'd ask Teddy to grill but I don't want you guys to get sick your first week down here," Mel said snarkily. "We're much safer going to the waterfront to eat."

"Not the best cook ever?" Jessie asked with a little grin.

"Let's just put it this way. If he ever offers to cook, pretend you have an emergency to attend to. Because if you eat anything he's made, you really will have an emergency on your hands."

"What's that, hon?" Teddy asked as he and Kyle came inside. He was a paunchy, doughy-looking guy with receding blond hair and pale skin that looked like it would burn after five minutes in the sun. Jessie also sensed that his personality was much the same—doughy and malleable. Some deep instinct she couldn't describe but had learned to trust over the years told her that Teddy Carlisle was a weak man.

"Nothing, sweetie," she said casually as she winked at Jessie. "Just giving Jessie here some essential Westport Beach survival info."

"Right," he said. "Make sure to warn her about the traffic over by Jamboree Road and the Pacific Coast Highway. It can be a bear."

"That was next on my list," Mel said innocently as she got up from the kitchen barstool.

As she went into the living room to collect Daughton's toys from the floor, Jessie couldn't help but notice that in her tennis skirt and polo top, her petite frame was all sinewy muscle. Her calves bulged and her wiry biceps flexed impressively as she swept up about a dozen Matchbox cars in one swift motion.

Everything about her, including her short black hair, her boundless energy, and her take-no-prisoners bark of a voice projected tough, no-nonsense New York chick, which was exactly what she'd been before moving west.

Jessie liked her immediately, though she couldn't understand what drew her to a schlub like Teddy. It ate at her slightly. Jessie prided herself on reading people. And this hole in her informal profile of Mel was mildly unsettling.

"We ready to go?" Teddy asked. He too was dressed smartly in a loose button-up shirt and white slacks.

"Just collect your son and we'll be all set," Mel said sharply.

Teddy, apparently used to her tone, went off to find the "Explosion" machine without a word. A few seconds later, they heard screeching as he came back holding Daughton, who was struggling mightily, upside down by his ankles.

"Daddy, stop!" the boy screamed.

"Put him down, Edward," Mel hissed.

"He talked back," Teddy said as he lowered his son to the floor. "I just needed to remind him that sort of thing isn't okay."

"But what if he slipped free and cracked his head?" Mel demanded.

"Then he'd have learned a valuable lesson," Teddy replied casually, apparently in no way troubled by the prospect.

Kyle chuckled appreciatively and only stopped when Jessie shot daggers at him with her eyes. He tried to turn the laugh into a cough but it was too late and he shrugged at her apologetically.

As they headed off to the harbor, down the well-maintained trail that ran parallel to the main road, Jessie looked at how she and Kyle were dressed compared to their counterparts. Even Daughton, who had his father's pale skin but his mother's dark hair, had on ironed shorts and a collared shirt. Kyle was in board shorts and a T-shirt and Jessie had thrown on a breezy peasant dress at the last minute.

"Are you sure we're dressed properly to have brunch at your club?" she asked Mel apprehensively.

"Oh, don't worry about it. You're our guests. The dress code policies don't apply to you. Only members get lashes for inappropriate attire. And since Daughton's little, he'd only get a grazing from a hot poker." Mel must have seen the look in Jessie's eyes because she immediately put her hand on her wrist and added, "I'm kidding."

Jessie smiled tightly at her inability to loosen up. Just then, Daughton ran past her with an impressive "boom" that made her jump.

"He's got a lot of energy," she said, trying to sound admiring. "I'd like to bottle it."

"Yeah," Mel agreed. "He's a piece of work. But I love him. It's weird how stuff that annoys other people is charming when it's your kid. You'll see what I mean when it happens to you. Assuming that's what you want, I mean."

"It is," Jessie said. "We've talked about it for a while. There have just been some…hiccups along the way. But we're hoping the change of scenery will help."

"Well, I should warn you. The topic is likely to come up often among the women you'll be meeting today. They love to talk about kids and everything kid-related. You'll probably get asked about your plans. But don't sweat it. That's kind of the default, go-to conversation around here."

"Thanks for heads-up," Jessie said as they reached the end of the path.

She stopped for a moment to take in the view. They were at the edge of a cliff overlooking Balboa Island and Promontory Bay. Beyond that was the Balboa Peninsula, the last chunk of land before the Pacific Ocean. The deep blue water extended as far as she could see, eventually merging with the lighter cerulean sky, dotted with a few puffy white clouds. It was breathtaking.

Closer in, she saw the busy marina, with boats moving in and out in some unspoken system that was far more organized and beautiful than the freeway. People, small as ants from up here, were wandering around the pier complex and its many shops and restaurants. It looked like there might be a farmer's market taking place.

The trail had given way to a huge rock staircase that led down to the complex. Despite the wooden railings on either side, it was mildly daunting.

"The trail picks up again about fifty yards ahead and winds down to the harbor," Mel said, sensing Jessie's reticence. "We could go that way instead of the steps but it takes another twenty minutes and the view isn't as nice."

"No, this is fine," Jessie assured her. "I just haven't been keeping up with my Stairmaster routine and suddenly I'm regretting it."

"Your legs only ouch at first," Daughton said as he leapt in front of her and took the lead.

"Nothing like being shamed into action by a toddler," Jessie said, trying to chuckle.

They started down the long flight of steps, Daughton first, followed by Mel, Jessie, and Kyle, with Teddy bringing up the rear. After a minute Daughton had gotten well ahead of them and Mel rushed down to catch up to him. Jessie could hear the guys talking behind her but couldn't really catch what they were saying. And with the tricky steps, she was hesitant to turn around to find out.

About halfway down, she saw a college-age girl walking up the stairs, wearing only a bikini and flip-flops, with a beach bag flung over her shoulder. Her hair was still wet from the water and beads of sweat were trickling down her exposed, tan skin. Her curves were impressive and the swimsuit barely contained them. She looked like she might burst out at various places any second. Jessie tried not to stare as they passed and wondered if Kyle was doing the same.

"Damn fine ass on that one," she heard Teddy say a few seconds later.

Jessie stiffened involuntarily, not just at the crudeness but because the girl would have almost certainly been close enough to hear it. She was tempted to turn around and give him a scowl when she heard Kyle's voice.

"Right?" he added, snickering like a schoolboy.

She stopped in her tracks. As Kyle reached her, she grabbed his forearm. Teddy stopped too, a surprised look on his face.

"Go ahead, Teddy," she said, putting a plastic smile on her face. "I just need my man for a sec."

Teddy gave Kyle a knowing expression before moving on without comment. When she was sure he was out of earshot, she turned to her husband.

"I know he's your friend from high school," she whispered. "But do you think you could not act like you're still there?"

"What?" he asked defensively.

"That girl probably heard Teddy and his leering tone. Then you go egging him on? Not cool."

"It's not that big a deal, Jess," he insisted. "He was just making a little crack. Maybe she was flattered."

"And maybe she was creeped out. Either way, I'd rather my husband not reinforce the 'woman as sex object' meme. Is that a reasonable request?"

"Jeez. Is this how you're going to react every time a girl in a bathing suit walks by?"

"I don't know, Kyle. Is that how *you're* going to react?"

"You guys coming?" Teddy shouted up at them. The Carlisles were a good fifty steps farther down the stairs.

"Coming," Kyle yelled back before lowering his voice. "That is, if you're still cool with it."

He moved on before she could reply, taking the steps two at a time. Jessie forced herself to take a long, slow breath before following him, hoping she could exhale her frustration along with the air in her lungs.

*We're not even fully moved in and he's starting to turn into the kind of asshole I've tried to avoid my whole life.*

Jessie tried to remind herself that one lame comment while under the influence of a high school friend didn't mean her husband was suddenly becoming a Philistine. But she couldn't shake the uncomfortable feeling that this was only the beginning.

# CHAPTER THREE

Five minutes later, with Jessie still silently seething, they walked into the lobby of the Club Deseo, getting some much-needed air-conditioned relief from the already warm day. Jessie looked around, taking the place in. She couldn't help but think that the name, which according to Teddy meant "Club of Wishes," was a little grandiose, considering what was in front of her.

She'd almost missed the club's entrance, a large, unmarked, weathered oak door attached to a modest-looking structure on the quieter edge of the harbor. The lobby itself was nondescript, with a simple hostess stand currently manned by a gorgeous, industrious-looking brunette in her early twenties.

Teddy leaned over and spoke to her quietly. She nodded and indicated for the group to pass through a small hallway. It was only when another, equally beautiful young blonde woman asked her to put her purse in a basket that Jessie realized the hall also doubled as a classy metal detector.

Once through the hallway, the woman returned her bag and indicated that she should follow the others through a second wood-paneled door that seemed to blend into the wall beside it. If she'd been alone, she might have missed the door completely.

After they stepped through that second door, all the modesty of the building's lobby quickly faded away. The cavernous circular room she was staring at had two levels. The top, where she was, had tables encircling and looking down on the lower level, which was accessed by a wide staircase.

The lower level had a small central dance floor surrounded by multiple tables. The entire place looked to have been designed using repurposed wood from old sailing vessels. Planks right beside each other, which comprised the walls, had different grades and colors. The hodgepodge shouldn't have worked but somehow did, giving the space a nautical vibe that felt reverential, not shticky.

At the far end of the room was the most impressive feature. The entire ocean-facing side of the club was comprised of a massive glass window, half of which was above water, half below. Depending on where one sat, the view could be of the horizon or schools of fish swimming below the surface. It was incredible.

They were led to a large table on the lower level, where a group of about fifteen people awaited them. Teddy and Mel introduced them around but Jessie didn't even try to remember the names. She learned that there were four couples, with about seven children split among them.

Instead, she smiled and nodded politely as each of them pummeled her with more information than she could process.

"I'm in social media marketing," someone named either Roger or Richard told her. He fidgeted constantly and picked his nose when he thought no one was looking.

"We're choosing wall rugs right now," said the woman next to him, a brunette with blonde streaks in her hair who may or may not have been his wife but who definitely had eyes for the tan guy across the table.

It went on like that. Mel introduced someone. Jessie made no serious attempt to remember their name but instead tried to glean something about their true nature based on their looks, body language, and speaking style. It was a kind of game, one she employed often in uncomfortable situations.

After the introductions, two more pretty young girls swept in and collected all the kids, including Daughton, to take them to Pirate's Cove, which one of the wives told her was the name of the youth fun zone. Jessie assumed it must have been pretty great because every child left without even a hint of separation anxiety.

Once they were gone, the meal proceeded much as Mel had warned her. Two women who were either twins or looked so similar that they might as well have been, told a story about a religious summer camp that was primarily about the terrible singing voice of the praise leader.

"She sounded like she was about to give birth," one of them said as the other cackled appreciatively. To the extent that she paid any attention, Jessie got lost as they interrupted and spoke over each interminably.

A guy with a shock of long curly hair and a bolo tie he was way too enamored with recounted the particulars of a hockey game he'd attended last spring. But there was nothing memorable about it. The entire five-minute story was comprised of who scored goals when. Jessie kept waiting for a twist, like when an octopus was thrown on the ice or a fan jumped the wall. But there was no twist.

"Anyway, it was an awesome game," he finally concluded, which she knew was her cue to smile appreciatively.

"Best. Story. Ever," Mel said dryly under her breath, giving Jessie her only happy moment so far and something close to a second wind.

Much of the conversation was consumed with discussion of various upcoming club events, including the Halloween Bash, the Bringing the Boats in Party (whatever that was) and the Holiday Ball.

"What's the Bringing in…" she started to ask before being cut off by the woman two seats down shrieking when a waiter accidentally knocked a glass of water over, getting a few drops on her.

"Bitch," she muttered way too loud after the server had left. Soon thereafter, all the men got up, kissed their wives, and said goodbye. Kyle gave Jessie a perplexed look but followed suit.

"I guess I'll see you later?" he asked more than said.

She nodded politely, though she was equally confused. It felt like they were in that scene from *Titanic*, when all the menfolk left after dinner to discuss business and politics over brandy in the smoking room.

Jessie watched as the guys wandered among the tables until they reached an ornate wooden door in the corner of the room with a muscular, humorless man standing in front of it. He looked like a bouncer at a nightclub, only he wore a tuxedo. As the guys from their table approached, he stepped aside to let them pass. He seemed to give Kyle a skeptical glance until Teddy murmured something to him. The bouncer nodded and smiled at Kyle.

The rest of the brunch went by in a whirlwind. As Mel had promised, the conversation centered around children and children-to-be, as at least two of the women in the group were clearly pregnant.

"I'm just gearing up to bitch-slap the next barista who gives me a dirty look when I'm breastfeeding," one named either Katlyn or Kaitlyn said. "I was way too accommodating after Warner was born."

"Threaten to sue," Brunette with Blonde Streaks said. "I did that and got a hundred-dollar gift certificate as an apology. The best part was that no one had done anything wrong. I just complained about an 'environment of discomfort.'"

Jessie was the only non-mother at the table but tried to join in the discussion, asking polite questions about the local elementary school ("a dump") versus the private one they all seemed to send their kids to.

As Jessie listened to the disagreements about the top daycare and preschool options and the general consensus about the best supermarket, she felt her mind wander. She pinched herself under the table a few times as opinions were voiced on good churches, the best local gym, and where to find a great dress for the Holiday Ball.

But eventually, she gave up trying to keep track of who was saying what, or even offering bland affirmations, and settled into the role of passive observer, as if she were watching the social behavior of some unusual species in the wild.

*Is this the life I've committed to? Lunches with ladies that focus on which gym has the best spinning class? Is this the world Kyle has been jonesing to become a part of? If so, just kill me now.*

At some point, she realized Mel was tapping her on the shoulder to let her know brunch was over and that she needed to collect Daughton. Apparently Teddy and Kyle would be meeting them in the lobby.

Jessie nodded, said gracious goodbyes to the women whose names she couldn't remember, and blankly followed Mel to Pirate's Cove. She felt disoriented and exhausted and wanted nothing more than to go home, take a bath, have a glass of wine, and go to sleep. She glanced at her watch and was stunned to discover that it wasn't even 1 p.m.

*

She didn't get to decompress until hours later. After the walk back to the Carlisle house and the obligatory hangout there for a while, they finally headed back home. But not before a pit stop to Costco for essentials. Jessie imagined the disapproving faces of her brunch companions.

Later that night as she washed her face while Kyle brushed his teeth, they had recovered enough to debrief the day a bit.

"What happened in the secret room you went off to?" she asked. "Did they make you strip to your undies and give you ten lashes?"

"I was actually a little worried about what was behind that door," Kyle admitted as they moved into the bedroom. "But it turned out to be essentially a really well-appointed sports bar. They had games on the TVs, a waiter walking around taking drink orders, and a few guys changing into or out of golf attire."

"So no smoking room with brandy?" she asked, wondering if he'd get the reference.

"Not that I saw, although I did notice Leonardo DiCaprio wandering aimlessly through the dressing room."

"Nice job, husband," Jessie said appreciatively as she got into bed. "You've still got it."

"Thank you, wife," he replied, sliding under the covers next to her. "Actually, I heard there was a cigar room in there somewhere but I didn't go looking for it. I think it's hidden away in some corner that's exempt from the club's 'no smoking' rules. But I bet I could have gotten a brandy if I'd asked."

"Meet anyone interesting?" she asked skeptically as she turned off the bedroom light.

"Surprisingly, yes," he said. "They were all pretty cool. And since two of them were looking for potential investments, that made them interesting to me. I think that club could be a real resource for business leads. You?"

"Everyone was very nice," Jessie said hesitantly, hoping the darkness of the room hid her furrowed brow. "Very friendly with all kinds of offers of help with anything I need."

"Why do I hear a 'but' in there?"

"No. It's just that not once in the time I was with them alone did one of those women talk about anything other kids, school, or family. No mention of their jobs or current events. It just felt very provincial."

"Maybe they just wanted to avoid controversial topics at a brunch with someone new?" Kyle suggested.

"Jobs are controversial these days?"

"I don't know, Jessie. Are you sure you're not reading too much into an innocent gathering?"

"I'm not suggesting they're Stepford Wives or anything," she insisted. "But other than Mel, they were relentlessly narcissistic. I'm not sure that any of them ever give more than a passing thought to the world outside their windows. I'm just saying that after a while, it started to feel a little...claustrophobic."

Kyle sat up in bed.

"That phrasing sounds familiar," he said, concern in his voice. "Don't get pissed at me. But the last time you talked about feeling claustrophobic was when—"

"I remember the last time," she interrupted, annoyed. "This isn't the same."

"Okay," he replied delicately. "But you'll understand if I ask if you're comfortable with your meds these days. Is the dosage still working? Do you think maybe you should schedule an appointment with Dr. Lemmon?"

"I'm fine, Kyle," she said, getting out of bed. "Not everything is about that. Can't I express some reservations without you jumping to conclusions?"

"Of course," he said. "I'm sorry. Please come back to bed."

"I mean, seriously. You weren't there. While you were off chilling with the boys, I had a plastic smile on my face while these women talked about shaking down coffee shops. That's not a medication issue. It's a 'these chicks are awful' issue."

"I'm sorry, Jess," he repeated. "I shouldn't have assumed it was the meds."

Jessie looked at him, torn between wanting to forgive him and wanting to rip him a little more. She decided not to do either.

"I'll be back in a few minutes," she said. "I just need to decompress. In case you're asleep when I get back, I'll say goodnight now."

"Okay," he said reluctantly. "Goodnight. I love you."

"Goodnight," she said, giving him a kiss despite her lack of enthusiasm at that moment. "I love you too."

She left the bedroom and wandered the house, waiting for her frustration to dissipate as she moved from room to room. She tried to put his dismissiveness out of her head but it kept sneaking back in, riling her up despite her best efforts.

She was just calming down enough to head back to bed when she heard the same distant creaking noise from the other night. Only tonight it wasn't so distant. She followed the sound until she found what she thought was the source—the attic.

She had come to a stop in the upstairs hallway right below the attic access door. After a moment's hesitation, she grabbed the string to the door and yanked it down. The creaking definitely sounded more pronounced.

She clambered up the access ladder as quietly as she could, trying not to think about how this sort of decision always ended badly in horror movies. When she got up the stairs, she pulled out her phone and used the flashlight feature to search the space. But apart from a few aged, empty cardboard boxes, the space was empty. And the creaking had stopped.

Jessie carefully climbed back down, replaced the ladder, and, too amped to sleep, resumed her restless wandering. Eventually, she found herself in the bedroom they anticipated using for the baby, when and if one ever joined them.

It was empty now but Jessie could picture where the crib would go. She imagined it against the far wall, with a mobile dangling above it. She rested her back against the wall and slid down so that she was sitting with her knees in front of her face. She wrapped her arms around them and hugged tight, trying to reassure herself that life in this new strange place would be better than it seemed so far.

*Am I reading this all wrong?*

She couldn't help but wonder if maybe her meds did need to be tweaked. She wasn't sure if she was being too hard on Kyle or if she was judging the Club Deseo women too harshly. Was the fact that Kyle was adjusting so easily to this place and she wasn't a reflection of his adaptability, her brittleness, or both? He already seemed at home, as if he'd lived here for years. She wondered if she'd ever reach that point.

She wasn't sure if she was just nervous because her last semester of classes started up tomorrow and she'd have to dive back into the world of studying rapists, child predators, and murderers. And she wasn't sure if that creak she kept hearing was real or in her head. At this moment, she wasn't sure of much of anything. And it scared her.

## CHAPTER FOUR

Jessie was short of breath and her heart was palpitating. She was late for class. This was her first time on the campus of the University of California at Irvine and finding her classroom had been daunting. After running the last quarter mile across campus in the sweltering mid-morning heat, she barreled through the door. Her forehead was beading with sweat and her top felt slightly damp.

Professor Warren Hosta, a tall, thin, fifty-something man with narrow, suspicious eyes and a lone, sad tuft of grayish-black hair on top of his head, had clearly been mid-sentence when she burst in at 10:04 a.m. She'd heard rumors about his impatience and generally churlish demeanor and he didn't disappoint. He stopped and waited for her to find her seat, staring at her the whole time.

"May I resume?" he asked sarcastically.

*Great start, Jessie. Way to make a first impression.*

"Sorry, Professor," she said. "The campus is new to me. I got a little turned around."

"I hope your skills at deduction are stronger than your sense of direction," he replied superciliously before returning to his lecture. "As I was saying, for most of you, this will be your final course before securing your master's degree in Forensic Psychology. It will not be a walk in the park."

Jessie unzipped her backpack as quietly as possible to pull out a pen and notebook but the sound of the zipper passing along every tooth seemed to resonate in the room. The professor glanced at her out of the corner of his eye but didn't stop speaking.

"I will pass out the syllabus momentarily," he said. "But in general, this is what is expected of you. In addition to the standard course work and associated exams, those of you who have yet to complete one will submit and defend your thesis. In addition, everyone—completed thesis or not—will have a practicum. Some of you will be assigned to a correctional facility, either the California Institute for Men in Chino or the California Institute for Women in Corona, both of which house a number of violent offenders. Others will visit the high-risk unit at DSH-Metropolitan, which is a state hospital in Norwalk. They treat patients commonly referred to as 'criminally insane,' although local community concerns prevent them from accepting patients with a history of murder, sex crimes, or escape."

20

An unspoken current of electricity passed through the room as the students all glanced around at each other. This was what they'd been waiting for. The rest of the lecture was fairly straightforward, with a description of their course work and details on writing their theses.

Luckily, Jessie had completed and defended hers while at USC, so she didn't pay much attention to that discussion. Instead, her mind returned to the odd brunch at the yacht club and how, despite everyone's warmth and generosity, she'd felt unsettled by it.

It was only when talk returned to the practicums that she really focused back in. Students were asking logistical and academic questions. Jessie had one of her own but decided to wait until after class. She didn't want to share it with the group.

Most of her classmates clearly wanted to work at one of the prisons. The mention of a community ban on violent offenders at the Norwalk hospital seemed to limit its popularity.

Eventually Professor Hosta signaled the end of class and folks started to file out of the room. Jessie took her time returning her notebook to her backpack while a few students asked Hosta questions. It was only when they were all gone and the professor himself was starting to walk out that she approached him.

"Sorry again for the late arrival, Professor Hosta," she said, trying not to sound too obsequious. Over the course of just one class, she'd gotten the strong sense that Hosta despised spineless groveling. He seemed to prefer inquisitiveness, even if it bordered on rudeness, to deference.

"You don't sound very apologetic, Ms...." he noted with a raised eyebrow.

"Hunt, Jessie Hunt. And I'm not really," she admitted, deciding in that moment that she'd have more success with this guy if she was straightforward. "I just figured I needed to be polite in order get an answer to my real question."

"Which is...?" he asked, his eyebrows raised in intrigued surprise.

She had his attention.

"I noticed you said that DSH-Metro doesn't accept patients with a history of violence."

"That's correct," he said. "It's their policy. I was basically quoting from their website."

"But Professor, we both know that's not entirely accurate. The Norwalk hospital does have a small section cordoned off to treat patients who have committed some horrifically violent crimes, including serial murder, rape, and assorted transgressions against children."

He stared at her impassively for a long moment before responding.

"According to the Department of State Hospitals, DSH-Atascadero up in San Luis Obispo handles those cases," he replied stone-faced. "Metro deals with nonviolent offenders. So I'm not sure what you're referencing."

"Of course you are," Jessie said more confidently than she'd expected. "It's called the Non-Rehabilitative Division, or NRD for short. But that's just the boring term they use for public consumption. Internally and within criminal justice circles, NRD is known as the 'high-risk' unit at DSH-Metro, which I happened to notice is the term you used to describe it in class."

Hosta didn't respond. Instead, he studied her inscrutably for several seconds before finally allowing his face to break into a slight grin. It was the first time she'd seen anything close to a smile from him.

"Walk with me," he said, motioning for her to exit the room. "You win the special prize, Ms. Hunt. It's been three semesters since a student last picked up on my little bit of verbal trickery there. Everyone is so turned off by the community standards bit that no one wonders what the reference to 'high-risk' is all about. But it's clear that you were familiar with NRD long before entering class today. What do you know about it?"

"Well," she began carefully, "I did the first several semesters of my study at USC and NRD is kind of an open secret there, what with them being so close."

"Ms. Hunt, you are dissembling. It is *not* an open secret. Even within law enforcement and the psychiatric community, it is a tightly guarded one. I'd hazard that fewer than two hundred people in the region are aware of its existence. Less than half of them know the full nature of the facility. And yet, somehow, you do. Please explain yourself. And this time, let's drop the careful coyness."

Now it was Jessie's turn to decide whether to be forthcoming.

*You've come this far. May as well take that final leap.*

"I did my thesis on it," she said. "It almost got me kicked out of the program."

Hosta stopped walking and looked briefly stunned before regaining his composure.

"So that was you?" he asked, sounding impressed as he started back down the hall. "That thesis is legendary among those who have read it. If I recall, the title was along the lines of 'The Impact of Non-Rehabilitative Long-Term Incarceration on the Criminally Insane.' But no one could figure out who the real author was. After all, there is no official record of 'Jane Don't.'"

"I have to admit I was pretty proud of that name. But using a fake one at all wasn't my decision," Jessie admitted.

"What do you mean?" Hosta asked, clearly intrigued.

Jessie wondered if she was skirting the edge of what she was allowed to discuss. But then she remembered the reason she was assigned to work with Hosta in the first place and decided there was no reason to be coy.

"My faculty adviser submitted the thesis to the dean," she explained. "He promptly brought in several law enforcement and medical folks I'm not allowed to mention other than by the charming term 'The Panel.' I was questioned for nine straight hours before they determined that I was sincerely writing an academic paper and not secretly some reporter or worse."

"That sounds exciting," Hosta said. He seemed to mean it.

"It sounds it. But at the time, terrifying was a more appropriate word. Eventually they decided not to arrest me. After all, they had the off-book, secret psychiatric lockup, not me. The school agreed that I hadn't done anything technically wrong and agreed not to dump me, although everything about the thesis was declared classified. The department determined that my interrogation by authorities could serve as my thesis defense. And I signed several documents promising not to discuss the matter with anyone, including my husband, or face potential prosecution, although for what charge they never said."

"Then how is it, Ms. Hunt, that we are having this conversation?"

"I received a...let's call it a special dispensation. I was permitted to continue to pursue my degree and set a specific condition. But in order to complete it, my new faculty adviser would have to be made at least superficially aware of what I'd written. The powers that be looked at the faculty at every university in Orange County and determined that you alone met their requirements. The school has a master's program in Criminal Psychology, which you direct. You have a relationship with NRD and have done field work there. You even have it as a practicum option set up there in rare instances where a student expresses interest and shows promise. You're my only option for fifty miles in any direction."

"I suppose I should be flattered. And what if I decline to be your faculty adviser?" he asked.

"You should have received a visit from someone representing The Panel to address all this—how it would be in your best interest, etc. I'm surprised you haven't. They're usually pretty thorough."

Hosta thought for a second.

"I have received several emails and a voice message recently from someone named Dr. Ranier," he said. "But the name wasn't familiar so I ignored them."

"I recommend you return the message, Professor," Jessie suggested. "It's possible that it's a pseudonym, maybe for someone you already know."

"I'll do that. In any case, I gather that I won't have to jump through all the usual bureaucratic hoops to get you authorized to do your practicum at NRD?"

"Doing it there was the specific condition I mentioned earlier. It's the reason I agreed without much fuss to their non-disclosure agreement," Jessie told him, unable to keep the excitement out of her voice. "I've been waiting almost two years for this."

"Two years?" Hosta said, surprised. "If you completed your thesis that long ago, shouldn't you have your degree by now?"

"That's a long story I'll share some other time. But for now, can I assume I have your authorization do my practicum at DSH-Metro, specifically in NRD?"

"Assuming your story checks out, yes," he said as they reached his office door. He unlocked it but didn't invite her in. "But I have to pose the question I raise with any student who requests to do their field work there—are you sure you want to do this?"

"How can you ask me that, given everything I've told you?"

"Because it's one thing to read about the people being held at that facility," he answered. "It's quite another to interact with them. It gets real very fast. I gather from the redactions in your thesis that you know about some of the inmates being housed there?"

"A few; I know that the serial rapist from Bakersfield, Delmond Stokes, is being held there. And the multiple child murderer who was captured last year by that retired lady cop is there as well. And I'm pretty sure Bolton Crutchfield is being held there too."

Hosta stared at her, as if deciding whether or not to say what he was thinking. Finally he seemed to make a decision.

"That's who you want to observe, isn't it?"

"I have to admit, I'm curious," Jessie said. "I've heard all kinds of stories about him. I'm not sure how many of them are true."

"One story I can assure you is true is that he brutally murdered nineteen people over half a dozen years. Whatever else is truth or legend, that is a fact. Don't ever lose sight of it."

"Have you met him?" Jessie asked.

"I have. I interviewed him on two occasions."

"And what was that like?"

"Ms. Hunt, that's a long story I'll have to share some other time," he said, turning her own words back on her. "For now, I will reach out to this Dr. Ranier and check your bona fides. Assuming that goes without incident, I'll contact you to set up your practicum. I know you'll want to start soon."

"I'd go tomorrow if I could."

"Yes, well, it might take a bit longer than that. In the meantime, try not to bounce off the walls. Good day, Ms. Hunt."

And with that he shut the door to his office, leaving Jessie in the hall. She turned to leave. Looking around the unfamiliar hallway, she realized she'd been so immersed in the conversation that she hadn't paid attention to anything else. She had no idea where she was.

She stood there for a moment, imagining herself sitting face to face with Bolton Crutchfield. The thought both excited and terrified her. She had wanted—no, needed—to talk to him for a while now. The possibility that it might soon happen made her tingle with anticipation. She needed answers to questions no one even knew she had. And he was the only one who could provide them. But she wasn't sure if he would. And even if he was willing, what might he demand in return?

# CHAPTER FIVE

Jessie was so keyed up that she called Kyle on the way home from school, even though she knew he was always crazed during the day and almost never answered. This time was no different but she couldn't help leaving a message anyway.

"Hey, babe," she said after the beep. "Just wanted to let you know my first day of class went extremely well. The professor's a character but I think I can work with him. And I'm hoping to start my practicum soon, maybe this week if everything pans out. I'm actually a little giddy. I hope your day is going well too. I thought I'd make a special dinner for us tonight, especially now that we actually found the boxes with all the pots and pans. Give me your ETA for tonight and I'll prep something nice. We can open one of those bottles of wine we've been saving and maybe get started on expanding our little family unit. Okay, talk soon. I love you."

She made a stop at Bristol Farms on the way home and splurged on a few branzino fish, which she planned to stuff and cook whole. She found some nice-looking broccolini and grabbed that too. As she was headed to the checkout she saw some fingerling potatoes and snagged them as well.

She was tempted to find something decadent for dessert but knew Kyle had been working out aggressively and wouldn't have any of it. Besides, they had some Italian ice in the freezer that would work just fine. By the time she checked out, she had the whole menu mapped out in her head.

*

Jessie stared at the untouched plates of food on the dining room table, then checked her phone for the third time in the last five minutes. It was 7:13 and still nothing from Kyle.

He had texted her soon after she left the voicemail, saying the dinner plan sounded great and he anticipated being home by 6:30 that night. But almost forty-five minutes had passed and he still wasn't here. Worse, he hadn't reached out to her at all.

She had set everything up so that dinner would be hot and on the table waiting for him at 6:45, just in case he ran a little late. But he hadn't shown up. She'd texted him twice and left a voicemail in the intervening time. And still, she'd heard nothing from Kyle since that first text. Now the fish lay on the table, mostly cold, staring back at her with unsympathetic eyes.

Finally, at 7:21, he called. From the noise in the background, she knew even before he spoke that he was at a bar.

"Hey, Jess," he shouted to be heard over the music. "Sorry for the late call. How are you doing?"

"I was worried about you," she said, trying to keep the frustration out of her voice.

"Oh, sorry," he said, sounding only mildly remorseful. "I didn't mean to worry you. Something came up last minute. Teddy called around six and said he had some more potential clients for me. He asked if I could meet him and these guys at a bar called Sharkie's in the marina. I figured I can't really pass up these kinds of opportunities when I'm the new guy in the office, you know?"

"You couldn't have called to let me know?"

"My bad," he yelled. "Everything was so rushed that it slipped through the cracks. I was only able to sneak away to call you now."

"I made a big dinner, Kyle. We were going to celebrate tonight, remember? I opened a hundred-dollar bottle of wine. It was supposed to be a romantic evening."

"I know," he said. "But I can't bail on this. I think I can lock down both of Teddy's friends as clients. And we can still try a little baby-making when I get home."

Jessie sighed deeply so that she could keep her voice calm when she responded.

"It'll be late when you get back," she said. "I'll be tired and you'll be half-drunk. It's not how I envisioned this going."

"Listen, Jessie. I'm sorry that I didn't call. But do you want me to just bail on an opportunity like this? I'm not just doing shots here. I'm conducting business and trying to make a few new friends while I'm at it. Are you going to hold that against me?"

"I guess I'm learning what your priorities are," she replied.

"Jessica, you are always my top priority," Kyle insisted. "I'm just trying to balance everything. I guess I screwed up. I promise I'll be home by nine, all right? Does that fit into your schedule?"

He had sounded sincere until that last line, which dripped with sarcasm and resentment. The emotional wall Jessie had erected between them was slowly crumbling until she heard those words.

"Do whatever you want," she replied brusquely before hanging up.

She stood up and caught a glimpse of herself in the dining room mirror. She was wearing a blue satin evening gown with a plunging neckline and a long slit down the right side that started at her upper thigh. Her hair was up in a casual bun that she had hoped to undo as part of a post-dinner seduction. The heels she wore pushed her from her normal five feet ten inches to well over six feet tall.

Suddenly it all felt so ridiculous. She was playing some sad game of dress-up. But when it came down to it she was just another pathetic housewife waiting for her man to come home and give her life meaning.

She grabbed the plates and walked to the kitchen, where she dumped both meals into the trash, whole fish and all. She changed out of the dress and switched to sweats. After that, she came back down to the dining room, grabbed the open bottle of Shiraz, poured a glass full to the brim, and took a gulp as she made her way into the living room.

She plopped down on the couch, turned on the TV, and settled in for what appeared to be a marathon of *Life Below Zero*, a reality series about people who voluntarily lived in remote sections of Alaska. She justified it by telling herself this would help her appreciate that there were people who had it far worse than she did in her fancy house in Southern California with her expensive wine and her seventy-inch flat-screen television.

Somewhere around the third episode and a half empty bottle she drifted off.

*

She was awakened by Kyle gently shaking her shoulder. Looking up through blurry eyes, she could tell that he was half-loaded.

"What time is it?" she mumbled.

"A little after eleven."

"What happened to being home by nine?" she asked.

"I got held up," he said sheepishly. "Listen, babe. I know I should have called earlier. That wasn't cool. I really am sorry."

"Okay," she said. Her mouth was fuzzy and her head hurt.

He ran a finger along her arm.

"I'd like to make it up to you," he offered suggestively.

"Not tonight, Kyle," she said, shrugging his hand away as she got up. "I'm not in the mood. Not even a little bit. Maybe next time you can try not to make me feel like sloppy seconds. I'm going to bed."

She walked up the stairs and, despite the urge to glance back to see his reaction, kept going without another word. Kyle said nothing. She crawled into bed without even turning off the light. Despite the headache and the cottonmouth, she was asleep in less than a minute.

*

Jessie felt a prickly branch scratch her face as she ran through the dark woods. It was winter and she knew that even barefoot, her footsteps, clomping on the fallen, dried leaves covering the snow were loud; that he would likely hear them. But she had no choice. Her only hope was to keep moving and hope he couldn't find her.

But she didn't know the woods well and he did. She was running blindly, completely lost and looking for any familiar landmark. Her little legs were too short. She knew he was catching up. She could hear his heavy footsteps and his even heavier breathing. There was no place to hide.

# CHAPTER SIX

Jessie sat bolt upright in bed, waking just in time to hear her own scream. It took a moment to orient herself and realize she was in her own bed in Westport Beach, wearing the clothes she'd drunkenly fallen asleep in last night.

Her whole body was covered in sweat and her breathing was shallow. She thought she could actually hear the blood rushing through her veins. She reached her hand up to her left cheek. The scar from the branch was still there. It had faded and could be mostly hidden with makeup, unlike the longer one along her right collarbone. But she could still feel where it protruded from the rest of her skin. She could almost feel the sharp sting even now.

She glanced over to her left and saw that the bed was empty. She could tell Kyle had slept there because of the indentation on his pillow and the jumble of sheets. But he was nowhere to be found. She listened for the sound of the shower but the house was silent. Glancing at her bedside clock, she saw that it was 7:45 a.m. He would have already left for work by now.

She eased out of the bed, trying to ignore her throbbing head as she shuffled to the bathroom. After a fifteen-minute shower, half of it spent just sitting on the chilly tile, she felt ready to face getting dressed and going downstairs. In the kitchen, she saw a note propped up on the breakfast table. It read "Sorry again about last night. Would love a rain check when you're willing. I love you."

Jessie set it aside and made herself some coffee and oatmeal, the only thing she felt capable of keeping down right now. She managed to finish half a bowl, tossed the rest in the trash, and made her way to the front sitting room, where a dozen unopened boxes waited for her.

She settled into the love seat with a pair of scissors, rested her coffee on the end table, and pulled a box toward her. As she absentmindedly went through the boxes, crossing off items as she located them, her minded drifted to her NRD thesis.

Had it not been for their fight, Jessie would have almost certainly told Kyle about not just her impending practicum at the facility, but about the aftermath of her original thesis as well, including her interrogation. That would have been a violation of her NDA.

He obviously knew the broad strokes, as she'd discussed the project with him as she'd researched it. But The Panel had sworn her to secrecy about it afterward, even from her husband.

It had felt weird hiding such a huge part of her life from her partner. But she'd been assured that it was necessary. And other than some general questions about how the whole thing had gone, he didn't really press her on the subject. A few vague answers left him satisfied, which had been a relief at the time.

But yesterday, with her enthusiasm for what she'd be doing— visiting a mental hospital for killers—at an all-time high, she was prepared to finally loop him in, despite the prohibition and its consequences. If their fight had one positive outcome, it was that it stopped her from telling him and putting both their futures at risk.

*But what kind of future is it if I can't share my secrets with my own husband? And if he seems oblivious to me keeping them?*

A slight ripple of melancholy washed over her at the thought. She tried to push it out of her head but couldn't quite sweep it away.

She was startled by the ring of the doorbell. Glancing at her watch, she realized that she'd been sitting in the same spot, lost in her glumness, hands resting on an unopened packing box, for the last ten minutes.

She stood up and walked to the door, trying to shake the gloom out of her system with each step. When she opened the door, Kimberly from across the street stood before her with a cheery smile on her face. Jessie tried to match it.

"Hello, neighbor," Kimberly said enthusiastically. "How goes the unpacking?"

"Slowly," Jessie admitted. "But thanks for asking. How are you?"

"I'm good. I actually have a few ladies from the neighborhood at my place right now for mid-morning coffee and wondered if you wanted to join us."

"Sure," Jessie replied, happy for an excuse to get out of the house for a few minutes.

She grabbed her keys, locked up, and walked over with Kimberly. When they arrived, four heads turned in their direction. None of the faces looked familiar. Kimberly introduced everyone and led Jessie over to the coffee station.

"They don't expect you to remember their names," she whispered as she poured them cups. "So don't feel any pressure. They've all been where you are now."

"That's a load off," Jessie confessed. "I have so much bouncing around in my head these days, I can barely remember my *own* name."

"Totally understandable," Kimberly said. "But I should warn you, I mentioned the whole FBI profiler thing so you may get a few questions about it."

"Oh, I don't work for the FBI. I haven't even gotten my degree yet."

"Trust me—that doesn't matter. They all think you're a real-life Clarice Starling. My over/under on serial killer references is three."

Kimberly had underestimated.

"Do you sit in the same room as these guys?" asked a woman named Caroline with hair so long that some strands reached her backside.

"It depends on the rules of the facility," Jessie answered. "But I've never interviewed one without an experienced profiler or investigator with me, taking lead."

"Are serial killers all as smart as they seem in the movies?" a mousy woman named Josette asked hesitantly.

"I haven't interviewed enough to say definitively," Jessie told her. "But based on the literature, as well as my personal experience, I'd say no. Most of these men—and they are almost always men—are no smarter than you or me. Some get away with it for a long time because of sloppy investigating. Some manage to evade capture because they choose victims no one cares about—prostitutes, the homeless. It takes a while for people to notice those folks are missing. And sometimes they're just lucky. Once I graduate, my job will be to change their luck."

The women politely pummeled her with questions, seemingly uninterested in the fact that she had not even graduated, much less formally taken on a profiling case.

"So you've never actually solved a case?" asked one particularly inquisitive woman named Joanne.

"Not yet. Technically, I'm just a student. The pros handle the live cases. Speaking of professionals, what do *you* do?" she asked in the hopes of redirecting her.

"I used to be in marketing," Joanne said. "But that was before Troy was born. He keeps me pretty busy these days. It's a full-time job all on its own."

"I'll bet. Is he somewhere napping now?" Jessie asked, looking around.

"Probably," Joanne said, glancing at her watch. "But he'll be up soon for snack. He's at daycare."

"Oh," Jessie said, before broaching her next question as delicately as possible. "I thought most kids in daycare had working moms."

"Yes," Joanne said, apparently not offended. "But they're so good over there that I couldn't *not* enroll him. He doesn't go every day. But Wednesdays are a challenge, so I usually take him then. Hump days are hard, right?"

Before Jessie could respond, the door from the garage opened and a burly thirty-something guy with a shock of unruly red hair burst into the room.

"Morgan!" Kimberly exclaimed happily. "What are you doing home?"

"I left my report in the study," he replied. "My presentation is in twenty minutes so I have to get back fast."

Morgan, apparently Kimberly's husband, didn't look at all surprised to see half a dozen women in his living room. He barreled through them, offering general greetings to the group. Joanne leaned over to Jessie.

"He's some kind of engineer," she said quietly, as if it was some kind of secret.

"For whom? One of the defense contractors?" Jessie asked.

"No, for some real estate outfit."

Jessie didn't understand why that merited such discretion but decided not to pursue it. Moments later, Morgan blasted back into the living room with a thick ream of paper in his hand.

"Nice to see you, ladies," he said. "Sorry I can't stick around. Kim, remember I've got that thing at the club tonight so I'll be back late."

"Okay, sweetie," his wife said, chasing after him to secure a kiss before he rushed out the door.

When he was gone, she returned to the living room, still flushed from the unexpected visit.

"I swear he moves with such purpose, you'd think *he* was a criminal profiler or something."

The comment sent the group into a wave of giggles. Jessie smiled, not sure exactly what was so funny.

*

An hour later, she was back in her own sitting room, trying to find the energy to open the box in front of her. As she carefully sliced through the tape, she went over the coffee outing. There was something odd about it. But she couldn't quite place what.

Kimberly was a sweetheart. Jessie genuinely liked her and especially appreciated the effort she was making to help the new girl. And the other women were all nice and personable, if a little bland. But there was something…mysterious about their interactions, as if they were all in on some shared secret that Jessie wasn't privy to.

Part of her thought she was paranoid to suspect such a thing. It wouldn't be the first time she'd incorrectly jumped to faulty conclusions. Then again, all of her instructors in the Forensic Psych program at USC had praised her for her intuitive sense. They didn't seem to think she was paranoid so much as "suspiciously inquisitive," as one professor had called her. It had sounded like a compliment at the time.

She opened the box and pulled out the first item, a framed photo from her wedding. She stared at it for a moment, looking at the happy expressions on her and Kyle's faces. On either side of them were family members, all beaming as well.

As her eyes drifted over the group, she suddenly felt the melancholy from earlier rise up again inside her. An anxious tightness gripped her chest. She reminded herself to take deep breaths but no amount of inhaling or exhaling calmed her down.

She wasn't sure exactly what had brought this on—the memories, the new environment, the fight with Kyle, a combination of all of it? Whatever it was, she recognized one fundamental truth. She was unable to control this on her own anymore. She needed to talk to someone. And despite the feeling of acute failure that began to overwhelm her as she reached for the phone, she dialed the number she had hoped she'd never have to use again.

## CHAPTER SEVEN

She made an appointment with her old therapist, Dr. Janice Lemmon, and just knowing that going would necessitate a visit back to her old stomping grounds set her at ease. The panic had subsided almost immediately after she scheduled the session.

When Kyle came home that night—early even—they ordered takeout and watched a cheesy but fun movie about alternate realities called *The 13th Floor*. Neither of them formally apologized but they seemed to have rediscovered their comfort zone. After the movie, they didn't even go upstairs to have sex. Instead, Kyle just climbed on top of her right there on the couch. It reminded Jessie of their newlywed days.

He'd even made her breakfast this morning before he headed out for work. It was awful—burnt toast, runny eggs, and undercooked turkey bacon—but Jessie appreciated the attempt. She felt a little bad about not telling him her plans for the day. But then again, he hadn't asked so she wasn't really lying.

It wasn't until she was on the freeway the next day, in sight of the downtown Los Angeles skyscrapers, that Jessie truly felt the gnawing pit of nervousness in her gut subside. She had made the midday trip from Orange County in under an hour and got into the city early just so she could walk around a bit. She parked in the lot near Dr. Lemmon's office across from the Original Pantry at the corner of Figueroa and West 9th.

Then she got the idea of calling her former USC roommate and oldest college friend, Lacey Cartwright, who lived and worked in the area, to see if she could hang out. She got her voicemail and left a message. As she started down Figueroa in the direction of the Bonaventure Hotel, Lacey texted her to say she was too busy to hang out that day but that they'd hook up the next time Jessie was around.

*Who knows when that will be?*

She put her disappointment out of her head and focused on the city around her, taking in the bustling sights and sounds that were so different from her new living environment. When she hit 5th Street, she made a right and continued ambling.

This reminded her of the days, not so long ago, when she would do this exact thing multiple times a week. If she was struggling with a case study for class, she'd just step outside and stroll along the streets, using the traffic as white noise as she turned the case over in her mind until she found a way to approach it. Her work was almost always strongest if she'd had time to wander around downtown and noodle with it a bit.

She kept the imminent discussion with Dr. Lemmon at the back of her head as she mentally revisited yesterday's coffee at Kimberly's house. She still couldn't pin down the nature of the mysterious secretiveness of the women she'd met there. But one thing did jump out at her in retrospect—how desperate they'd all been to hear the details of her profiling studies.

She couldn't tell if it was because the profession she was entering seemed so unusual or simply that it was a profession at all. Looking back, she realized that none of the women worked.

Some used to. Joanne had been in marketing. Kimberly said she used to be a real estate agent when they lived in Sherman Oaks. Josette had run a small gallery in Silverlake. But they were all stay-at-home moms now. And while they appeared happy with their new lives, they also seemed hungry for details from the professional world, greedily, almost guiltily devouring any morsel of intrigue.

Jessie stopped, realizing she had somehow arrived at the Biltmore Hotel. She'd been here many times before. It was famous for, among other things, hosting some the early Academy Awards in 1930s. She'd also once been told it was where Robert Kennedy was assassinated by Sirhan Sirhan in 1968.

Back before she decided to do her thesis on NRD, Jessie had toyed with the idea of profiling Sirhan. So she'd shown up one day unannounced and asked the concierge if they gave tours of the hotel that included the site of the shooting. He was perplexed.

It took a few embarrassing moments for him to understand what she was after and several more for him to politely explain that the assassination had not occurred there but at the now-demolished Ambassador Hotel.

He tried to soften the blow be telling her that JFK had gotten the Democratic nomination for president at the Biltmore in 1960. But she was too humiliated to stick around to hear that story.

Despite the shame, the experience taught her a valuable lesson that had stuck with her ever since: Don't make assumptions, especially in a line of work where assuming wrong might get you killed. The next day she changed thesis topics and resolved to do her research from then on *before* she showed up at a location.

Despite that debacle Jessie returned often, as she loved the old-fashioned glamour of the place. This time, she immediately settled into her comfort zone as she meandered through the halls and ballrooms for a good twenty minutes.

As she passed through the lobby on her way out, she noticed a youngish man in a suit standing nonchalantly near the bellhop station, perusing a newspaper. What drew her attention was how sweaty he was. With the air-conditioning blasting through the hotel, she didn't see how that was physically possible. And yet, every few seconds, he dabbed at the beads of perspiration constantly forming on his forehead.

*Why is a guy just casually reading a paper so sweaty?*

Jessie moved a little closer and pulled out her phone. She pretended to be reading something but put it in camera mode and tilted it so she could watch the guy without really looking at him. Every now and then she took a quick photo.

He didn't seem to actually be reading the paper but rather using it as a prop while he intermittently looked up in the direction of the bags being placed on the luggage cart. When one of the bellhops began pushing the cart in the direction of the elevator, the man in the suit put the newspaper under his arm and ambled along behind him.

The bellhop pushed the cart into the elevator and the suited man followed and stood on the other side of the cart. Just as the doors closed, Jessie saw the suited man grab a briefcase from the side of the cart that wasn't visible to the bellhop.

She watched the elevator slowly go up and stop at the eighth floor. After about ten seconds, it began to descend again. As it did, she walked over to the security guard near the front door. The guard, an amiable-looking guy in his late forties, smiled at her.

"I think you've got a thief working the hotel," Jessie said without preamble, wanting to give him the situation fast.

"How's that?" he asked, now frowning slightly.

"I saw this guy," she said, holding up the photo on her phone, "swipe a briefcase from a luggage cart. It's possible that it was his. But he was pretty sneaky about it and he was sweating like a guy who was nervous about something."

"Okay, Sherlock," the guard said skeptically. "Assuming you're right, how am I supposed to find him? Did you see what floors the elevator stopped on?"

"Eight. But if I'm right, that won't matter. If he's a hotel guest, I gather that's his floor and that's where he'll stay."

"And if he's not a guest?" the guard asked.

"If he's not, I'm guessing he'll be coming straight back down on the elevator that's returning to the lobby right now."

Just as she said that, the elevator door opened and the sweaty, suited man stepped out, newspaper in one hand, briefcase in the other. He began walking to the exit.

"I'm guessing he's going to stash that one somewhere and start the whole procedure over again," Jessie said.

"Stay here," the guard said to her, and then spoke into his radio. "I'm gonna need backup in the lobby ASAP."

He approached the suited man, who saw him out of the corner of his eye and picked up the pace of his stride. So did the guard. The suited man broke into a run and was just pushing his way out the front door when he collided with another security guard running in the opposite direction. Both of them sprawled out on the ground.

Jessie's guard grabbed hold of the suited man, lifted him up, yanked his arm behind his back, and slammed him against the hotel wall.

"Mind if I look in your bag, sir?" he demanded.

Jessie wanted to see how it would all play out but a quick glance at her watch showed that her appointment with Dr. Lemmon, set for 11 a.m., was in five minutes. She'd have to skip the walk back and catch a cab just to make it in time. She wouldn't even have the chance to say goodbye to the guard. She worried that if she tried, he'd insist that she stick around to give the police her statement.

She barely made it and was out of breath and just sitting down in the waiting room when Dr. Lemmon opened her office door to invite her in.

"Did you run here from Westport Beach?" the doctor asked with a chuckle.

"Actually, I kind of did."

"Well, come in and get comfortable," Dr Lemmon said, closing the door behind her and pouring them both glasses of water from a pitcher filled with lemon and cucumber slices. She still had the same awful perm that Jessie remembered, with tight little blonde ringlets that bounced when they touched her shoulders. She wore thick glasses that made her sharp, owl-like eyes appear tinier. She was a small woman, barely over five feet tall. But she was visibly wiry, probably a result of the yoga she'd told Jessie she did three times a week. For a woman in her mid-sixties, she looked great.

Jessie sat down in the comfy easy chair she always used for sessions and immediately settled back into the old vibe she was used to. She hadn't been here in a while, well over a year, and had hoped to keep it that way. But it was a place of comfort, where she'd struggled with, and intermittently succeeded in, making peace with her past.

Dr. Lemmon handed her the water, sat down across from her, picked up a legal pad and pen, and rested them on her lap. That was her sign that the session had formally started.

"What are we discussing today, Jessie?" she asked warmly.

"Good news first, I guess. I'm doing my practicum at DSH-Metro, NRD Unit."

"Oh wow. That is impressive. Who's your faculty adviser?"

"Warren Hosta at UC-Irvine," Jessie said. "Do you know him?"

"We've interacted," the doctor said cryptically. "I think you're in good hands. He's prickly but he knows his stuff, which is what matters for you."

"I'm glad to hear that because I didn't have much choice," Jessie noted. "He was only one The Panel would approve in the area."

"I guess that in order to get what you want, you have to color inside their lines a bit. This is what you wanted, right?"

"It is," Jessie said.

Dr. Lemmon looked at her closely. An unspoken moment of understanding passed between them. Back when Jessie had been interrogated about her thesis by the authorities, Dr. Lemmon had shown up at the police station out of the blue. Jessie remembered watching as her psychiatrist spoke quietly to several people who'd been silently observing her interview. After that, the questions seemed less accusatory and more respectful.

It was only later that Jessie learned Dr. Lemmon was a member of The Panel and was well aware of the goings-on at NRD. She had even treated some of the patients there. Looking back, it shouldn't have been a surprise. After all, Jessie had sought this woman out as a therapist precisely because of her reputation for expertise in that area.

"Can I ask you something, Jessie?" Dr. Lemmon said. "You say working at NRD is what you want. But have you considered that the place may not give you the answers you're looking for?"

"I just want to better understand how these people think," Jessie insisted, "so that I can be a better profiler."

"I think we both know you're looking for much more than that."

Jessie didn't respond. Instead she folded her hands in her lap and took a deep breath. She knew how the doctor would interpret that but she didn't care.

"We can come back to that," Dr Lemmon said quietly. "Let's move on. How's married life treating you?"

"That's the main reason I wanted to see you today," Jessie said, happy to change subjects. "As you know, Kyle and I just moved from here to Westport Beach because his firm reassigned him to their Orange County office. We've got a big house in a great neighborhood within walking distance of the harbor…"

"But…?" Dr. Lemmon prodded.

"Something just feels a little off about the place. I've been having trouble nailing it down. Everyone has been incredibly friendly so far. I've been invited to coffees and brunches and barbecues. I've gotten suggestions for the best grocery stores and daycare options, should we eventually need one. But something just feels…off-kilter. And it's starting to affect me."

"In what way?" Dr. Lemmon asked.

"I find myself feeling down for no good reason," Jessie said. "Kyle came home late for a dinner I made and I let it weigh me down much more than I should have. It wasn't that big a deal but he was so nonchalant about it. It just ate at me. Also, just unpacking boxes seems daunting in a way that's outsized for the task at hand. I have this constant, overwhelming sense that I don't belong, that there's some secret key to a room everyone else has been in and no one will give it to me."

"Jessie, it's been a while since our last session so I'm going to remind you of something we've discussed before. There doesn't have to be a 'good reason' for these feelings to take hold. What you're dealing with can appear out of nowhere. And it's not a shock that a stressful, new situation, no matter how seemingly picture-perfect, could stir them up. Are you taking your medication regularly?"

"Every day."

"Okay," the doctor said, making a note on her pad. "It's possible that we may need to switch it up. I also noticed you mentioned daycare might be necessary in the near future. Is that something you two are pursuing actively—kids? If so, that's another reason to switch your meds."

"We are trying…intermittently. But sometimes Kyle seems excited by the prospect and then he gets…distant; almost cold. Sometimes he says something and I wonder 'who is that guy?'"

"If it's any reassurance, all of this is very normal, Jessie. You're in a new environment, surrounded by strangers, with only one person you know well to cling to. It's stressful. And he's feeling a lot of those same things, so you're bound to butt heads and have moments where you don't connect."

"But that's the thing, Doctor," Jessie pressed. "Kyle doesn't seem stressed. He obviously likes his job. He has an old high school friend who lives in the area so he's got that outlet. And all signs indicate that he's totally psyched to be there—no adjustment period necessary. He doesn't appear to miss anything from our old life—not our friends, not our old hangouts, not being in a place where stuff actually happens after nine at night. He's completely adjusted."

"It might look that way. But I'd be willing to bet he's not as sure of things on the inside."

"I'd take that bet," Jessie said.

"Whether you're right or not," Dr. Lemmon said, noting the edge in Jessie's voice, "the next step is to ask yourself what you are going to do about this new life. How can you make it work better for you as an individual and as a couple?"

"I'm really at a loss," Jessie said. "I feel like I'm giving this place a shot. But I'm not like him. I'm not a 'dive right in' kind of gal."

"That's certainly true," the doctor agreed. "You're a naturally wary person, with good reason. But you may have to turn the volume down on that a smidgen to get by for a while, especially in social situations. Maybe try to open yourself up a little more to the possibilities around you. And perhaps give Kyle the benefit of the doubt a bit more. Are these reasonable requests?"

"Of course they are, when you ask in this room. Out there it's different."

"Maybe that's a choice you're making," Dr. Lemmon suggested. "Let me ask you something. The last time we met, we discussed the source of your nightmares. I gather you're still having them, yes?"

Jessie nodded. The doctor continued.

"Okay. We also discussed you sharing that with your husband, letting him know why you wake up in a cold sweat several times a week. Have you done that?"

"No," Jessie admitted guiltily.

"I know you're concerned about how he'll react. But we talked about how telling him the truth about your past might help you deal with it more effectively and bring the two of you closer together."

"Or it could tear us apart," Jessie countered. "I understand what you're saying, Doctor. But there's a reason so few people know about my personal history. It's not warm and fuzzy. Most people can't handle it. You only know because I did research on your background and determined that you had specific training and experience with this kind of thing. I sought you out and let you into my head because I knew you could handle it."

"Your husband has known you for almost a decade. You don't think he can handle it?"

"I think a seasoned professional like you had to use every ounce of restraint and empathy you had not to run out of the room screaming when I told you. How do you think a regular dude from suburban Southern California is going to react?"

"I don't know Kyle so I couldn't say," Dr. Lemmon replied. "But if you're planning to start a family with him—spend the rest of your life with him—you might want to consider whether you can realistically wall off a whole chunk of it from him."

"I'll take it under consideration," Jessie said noncommittally.

She could sense that Dr. Lemmon understood that she wasn't going to engage on the topic anymore.

"So let's talk medication," the doctor said, changing subjects. "I have a few suggestions for alternatives now that you're planning to get pregnant."

Jessie stared at Dr. Lemmon, watching her mouth move. But try as she might, she couldn't concentrate. The words drifted by as her thoughts returned to those dark woods from her childhood, the ones that haunted her dreams.

# CHAPTER EIGHT

Jessie lay in bed, tangled up in the sheets, trying to ignore the sunlight poking at her eyes through the open slit in the bedroom curtains.

It was her first Saturday morning in this house and she wanted it to be a lazy one, just her and Kyle, casually opening boxes, sipping coffee, making love. Yesterday had been a good day. Professor Hosta had sent her an email letting her know she'd get to visit NRD for the first time next week. She'd had a great run all the way down to the harbor and back. It was the first chance she'd gotten to really get some exercise and clear her head since they'd moved and she felt energized and hopeful. Kyle didn't have to go into the office so they had the whole weekend free.

She heard movement and reluctantly opened her eyes. Kyle was walking into the room with a coffee mug in each hand. She stretched happily and sat up.

"My hero," she said as she took the one he handed her.

"Is that all it takes these days?" he asked.

"Ten thousand years ago I would have expected you to bag an elk or something. But these days, a strong cup of coffee makes you a mighty fine provider."

"Well, I'm happy to meet my marital obligations."

"There are a few other marital obligations I expect you to meet today, mister," Jessie said, shimmying close to him.

"Oh yeah?" he said, playing dumb. "Like what?"

"Like ravaging me...once I've brushed my teeth; like finally unpacking that box of china in the dining room; like having your way with me again; like taking me to lunch and a movie to get out of this heat—maybe back in the old neighborhood; like coming back home for a quickie before ordering takeout and cuddling up on the couch to binge the rest of *Killing Eve*. How does that sound for a perfect Saturday?"

The look on his face suggested he didn't consider it a perfect plan.

"The first part sounds good," he said carefully. "But maybe we can rethink the evening plans."

"Oh, is that show too scary for you, big man?" she asked, trying to keep her voice playful even though she sensed he was about to make that impossible.

"I think I can handle it," he said, not playing along. "But maybe we do that another night. And maybe we have lunch around here."

"But you know how I love the theater near LA Live."

"Yeah, but that's a long way to go for a movie. I think we should find a theater near here that can become your new favorite. After all, this is home now. You promised me you'd give Westport a real chance."

Jessie, irked, was about to respond when she heard Dr. Lemmon's voice in her head, reminding her to give Kyle the benefit of the doubt. Besides, she could tell he wasn't done. Reluctantly, she bit her tongue as he continued.

"Also, I was hoping we could go to the club tonight. There were some other people who were excited to meet us and a bunch of them are going to be there this evening. It seems like the perfect chance to get to know some new people."

"Why does all the social stuff we do have to center around this club?" Jessie asked. "We're not even members there. Can't we just join a book club or something?"

"I'm happy to join a book club too, Jess," Kyle said, frustratingly calm. "But I don't see the harm in going back to Club Deseo. The whole point of being here, at least partly, is to become part of a community. I felt really isolated in the city. Seeing friends was a challenge. Meeting new ones was even harder. There's a ready-made community here, with people who are opening their arms to us. Our neighbors might actually become our friends. And a lot of them go to this club. It's a social hub. Why would we intentionally cut ourselves off from that?"

"I'm not saying we have to cut ourselves off," Jessie insisted. "But do we have to jump into the deep end right away? What if they turn out to be assholes?"

Kyle looked hard at her and she could tell he was the one now struggling to keep his cool.

"If they're assholes, we bail, Jess," he said, his voice more composed than his face. "But I'm not asking to jump into the deep end. I just want to dip my toes in the water. Can we please try that?"

Kyle was doing that thing that Jessie found both endearing and infuriating. He was being reasonable and level-headed as she became less so. She knew it was what made him so good at his job. No matter how scary the financial markets got, he always stayed cool and collected. His clients loved that. The same quality helped balance out her volatility and passion. But sometimes she just wanted him to lose it a little.

"Yes," she finally said, accepting that what he was asking for—going out to a country club dinner with his wife to meet new people—was not unreasonable. "We can try that."

*

Within seconds of arriving that night, Jessie knew she had misjudged the evening.

For starters, she was horribly underdressed. This was clearly a formal event. All the men were in suits and every woman wore an evening gown. Kyle had on a sports coat so he could fake it and get by. But she was wearing a loose sundress with a shawl in case the air conditioning was blasting. The other women wore heels. She was in sandals.

"We should leave," she whispered aggressively to Kyle as they waited to be seated. "I feel like a pauper at the ball."

"We're fine," Kyle whispered back. "No one said anything about dressy attire. And Teddy put us on the invite list so we're not going to be kicked out. Just own it, woman. You look better in that dress than any of these women do in their fancy get-ups."

He squeezed her hand supportively and she leaned into him, using his physical presence as invisible protection from the discomfort she felt. Teddy caught sight of them from across the darkened dining room and waved warmly as he walked over. Jessie looked around for Melanie but didn't see her. With the lights so low, it was hard to distinguish anyone among the assembled.

"Hi guys," Teddy said as reached them. "Perfect timing; the Agenda is about to start. Jessie, Mel is waiting for you down in the Hearthkeepers' Sanctuary. I'll walk you both over and she'll show you where to go from there."

"Agenda? Hearthkeepers?" Jessie repeated skeptically. "Those are some fancy words there, Teddy. I feel like I need a glossary of terms. Is this not just dinner at the club?"

"It is," he assured her, seemingly oblivious to her tone. "But they have these traditions here. It's not a big deal, really. The ladies just want to welcome you to the community. We have a similar thing planned for Kyle. And then we'll all meet up again to eat afterward."

"What's the guys' group called?" Jessie asked snarkily as they walked down the long stairwell to the lower level. "The Hunter-Gatherers?"

45

Kyle gave her a glare that indicated he wasn't amused.

"Actually, we're called the Oath Minders."

"Oh, that's much better," Jessie replied, trying to keep her voice sincere and not quite succeeding.

Teddy led them through the throng of people milling about in the dim light of the first floor, all sipping champagne and munching on hors d'oeuvres served by impossibly beautiful nymphettes in tight, black cocktail dresses. There wasn't a child in sight. Jessie wondered if the Pirate's Cove was packed or if they were all being kept home tonight.

Finally they made it through the crowd to a small alcove at the edge of the room, where Teddy abruptly stopped. Before them stood another gorgeous girl, who wasn't holding an appetizer or drink tray. She seemed to almost be standing guard.

Teddy leaned in and whispered something to her. She nodded and did something behind her back with her hand that Jessie couldn't quite see. Suddenly, a panel of the wall quietly slid back, revealing a darkened stairwell.

"This is where we part ways," Teddy said. "Mel will meet you down below for the Agenda. We'll all regroup back up here in a little bit for dinner."

"See you soon," Kyle said, leaning in to give her a goodbye peck on the cheek.

"What the hell is this?" Jessie whispered in his ear when he was close. "I feel like I'm about to be ritually sacrificed."

He pulled back a bit and she could tell he was trying to stifle a smile. He leaned back in and kissed her again, this time full on the lips. Then he wrapped her up for a hug.

"You are a piece of work, Jessica," he whispered back, his hot breath warming her ear. "Turn off your forensic Spidey sense for a little bit. Has it ever occurred to you that this is how folks around here keep things from getting too boring? They don't have nightly shootouts outside their condos. They don't have homeless guys chasing them down the street with used syringes. Maybe this is how they keep things interesting. I find it almost…charming."

He pulled back and she was able to see the twinkle in his eye. It gave her confidence that he was more amused than impressed by this spectacle, and that, at least, was reassuring. She smiled tightly and turned to go down the darkened stairs as the panel slid back into place behind her. It clicked and she heard a locking sound. There was nowhere to go now but down.

With each step, the crowd noise above dissipated. Soon there was silence. As she reached what she hoped was the bottom, a new sound emerged. It was music, the soothing instrumental kind one heard while getting a massage at the spa. A dim flickering light in the distance guided her.

When she finally reached the last step, she saw that she was in what looked like a large, extremely well-appointed dungeon. Torches were attached to the rustic, stone walls. The art on the walls was comprised of paintings of grotesque-looking women and odd, abstract sculptures that seemed to sprout right out of the rock.

There were elegant, old-fashioned chairs scattered through the room. Some were occupied by women in fancy dresses, sipping their drinks. Other ladies stood in small groups, chatting quietly. When Jessie's sandal flopped on the stone floor as she took her last step, they all turned and stopped speaking. Despite the absurdity of the situation, Jessie felt a chill run down her spine.

After a long, awkward second, she saw Melanie step out from behind two much taller women and rush over to her. She too was in an evening gown that flattered her diminutive frame. Her short dark hair was pulled back in a tight knot.

"You must be freaking out," Mel muttered when she got close. "I know I would be. The first time I came down here, I thought they were going to bring out a manacled virgin or something. The only the thing that kept me calm was knowing that with my history, it couldn't be me."

Jessie smiled despite her discomfort.

"What is this place?" she asked.

"It's called the Sanctuary," Melanie explained. "And the name applies. There are separate facilities down here, a private spa among them. Only club members and interviewees are allowed down here."

"I thought this whole place was 'the club.'"

"Upstairs is more for show. Imagine this area as being the good stuff behind the pay wall."

"Wait, did you say interviewees?" Jessie asked, only now processing that part of Mel's earlier comment. "Is this some kind of interview?"

"Yes," Melanie said, surprised. "This is your membership interview to join the club. It means you passed the initial background and financial checks and your application was preliminarily approved. Now you have the interview. Kyle is going through the same thing with the Oath Minders. Didn't he tell you any of this?"

"No," Jessie said, feeling the anger rise inside her. "He didn't."

"Oh, Melanie," called out a tall, angular brunette in the back of the room. "It's time to question the candidate."

"Of course," Mel replied before turning to Jessie and quietly saying, "Just be enthusiastic, respectful, and demure. They may try to rattle you. It's like highbrow hazing. Just stay cool."

Then she was gone, retreating back into the sea of gowns. The tall woman stepped forward so that she was only a few feet away. Up close, her features were even more pronounced. Every part of her face seemed carved from stone. Her nose and chin ended in sharp points. Her thin torso looked half-starved. Her dark eyes blazed in the candlelight. She seemed like she belonged in a royal European court more than an Orange County social club. The murmuring stopped and the spa music cut out.

"I am Marguerite Brennan, President of the Club Deseo Hearthkeepers. Jessica Madeline Hunt, you have been nominated for membership and submitted your bona fides. We have now reached the time of questioning. Are you prepared?"

Jessie looked around at the serious, unsmiling faces and decided this wasn't the time to crack wise. She was pissed that Kyle had applied to this club without discussing it with her first. She felt sandbagged. But that was something to address with him privately later.

"I am," she replied, mustering up what she hoped was the appropriate deference.

"Then let us begin. Do you believe that your marriage is the most important thing in your life?"

The question was complicated and intrusive. And it was clear what the right response was supposed to be. Jessie decided that she could honestly answer it, as at least most of the time it was.

"Yes," she said.

"Do you plan to have children?" Marguerite asked, her tone so uncurious that Jessie thought she might as well be asking if she planned to have chicken for dinner tonight.

She opened her mouth, about to respond to what she considered a private matter with a snarky retort about how few folks ever truly plan such a thing. But at the last minute she thought better of it.

"Yes," Jessie said, again deciding there was no harm in answering truthfully.

"Is loyalty a priority to you?"

"Absolutely," Jessie said without hesitation.

"Is discretion a priority for you?" Marguerite asked.

That question could be interpreted many ways. But considering that she was "applying" to join a secret club, Jessie decided to go with the safe answer, even though she sensed that Marguerite might be setting a trap for her.

"Yes."

"Have you ever been unfaithful to your husband?" Marguerite inquired emotionlessly.

*I guess we've gotten to part two of the Q&A session.*

"Have *you*?" Jessie blurted out before she could stop herself.

Marguerite stared daggers at her and she happily stared back. She wasn't going to be cowed by some SoCal royalty wannabe.

"I am already a member," Marguerite replied, her tone all pique. "So my indiscretions or lack thereof are not a matter for discussion at this time. So let me repeat the question. Have you—"

"No need to repeat, Marguerite. And it's not really your business. But since I already said loyalty was a priority for me, no."

Marguerite paused briefly, her thin lips pursing into something between a smile and a grimace.

"When did you lose your virginity?" she asked slowly. She seemed borderline reluctant to ask, as if worried how Jessie might react.

"Definitely not your business," Jessie replied, getting into the groove now. "I'm willing to go with the teen years, but that's as much as I care to share."

She heard soft murmuring and knew that her answers were no longer hitting the bull's-eye. She saw Mel in the back, biting her lip nervously. Marguerite stared at her humorlessly before asking what Jessie suspected was the final question.

"How many people have you had sex with?"

Jessie could feel her skin tingling with righteous resentment. She wanted to say "none of your goddamn business, cyborg lady." But she knew Marguerite was testing her, trying to upset her. She wouldn't fall prey to this amateur's machinations. After all, she'd dealt with far more cunning manipulators.

"Oh my," she said, adopting a tenor of faux embarrassment, "such a penetrating question in so public a venue. I think I'm going to have to refer you back to my earlier answer about the value of discretion and just say—that information dies with me."

She smiled sweetly and waited for the axe to fall.

# CHAPTER NINE

Later that night, as they were getting into bed, Kyle asked her again.

"You couldn't tell whether they were impressed or annoyed by your answers?"

"The woman's face was an emotionless mask," Jessie said for what she was pretty sure was the third time. "I'm not sure she had the ability to be impressed or annoyed. They let us stick around for dinner, so it couldn't have been that awful."

"That could have just been politeness," he replied, "not wanting to toss us out on the pier. That would have looked bad."

He sat quietly in bed, his eyes darting back and forth without seeing. He was clearly anxious. Part of her wanted to ease his discomfort and part of her wanted to lash out for how he'd surreptitiously applied to join the club. She'd been holding back all night and wasn't sure she could do it any longer.

"Kyle, I wasn't about to share details of my sexual history with a dungeon full of strangers. I figured you'd get that without me having to say it. Did *you* answer that question?"

"They never asked," he said. "Couldn't you just have given a safe answer?"

She stared at him, dumbfounded.

"What's the safe answer, sweetie? Ten? Five? Three? No one but my darling hubby? I would think you'd be more offended on my behalf."

"You seem offended enough for the both of us," he muttered under his breath. That was the last straw.

"You know what offends me?" she demanded. "That you applied to join this place without discussing it with me first. That I got blindsided by the 'double double toil and trouble' brigade at some adult sorority pledge event."

"I didn't sign us up," he insisted, sounding genuinely insulted. "Teddy told me he did it as a surprise. And I didn't know anything about the interviews. I thought we were just going to meet some new people at dinner. I can't believe you think I would do that on my own. I mean, really?"

"You don't seem all that broken up about it," she said, still pissed but backing down slightly now that she was uncertain what was true.

"I'm not. I thought it was a nice gesture. He's trying help us fit in. Maybe he was a little rash doing it without telling us. And he definitely should have warned us about what we were in for. But the truth is I'd like to join this club. And I probably would have talked to you about applying sooner or later anyway. So I'm not going to pretend to be upset that he jumped the gun a bit."

"I was interrogated, Kyle," she reminded him.

"It sounds like you held your own just fine."

"That's not the point," she said, getting out of bed as she felt her blood rise.

"What are you doing?" he asked.

"I don't feel like going to sleep right now. And since I don't want to lie here seething in the dark next to my currently thoughtless husband, I'm going to go read for a while."

"Oh come on, Jessie," he said. "It's not that big a deal."

"The fact that you think that is all the more reason I don't want to stick around. I'll come back to bed later. Don't wait up."

Despite her best effort to leave the room with dignity, she slammed the bedroom door as she left. The second she did it, she felt like she'd lost the high ground, suddenly a petulant child throwing a tantrum. But it was done so she doubled down by stomping down the stairs too.

\*

Jessie woke up with a start. Glancing at her watch, she saw that it was after 1 a.m. She must have drifted off while reading. She sat upright on the sitting room couch she'd slumped into and tried to blink herself awake.

She'd been resting at an awkward angle and her neck ached. She stood up to try to stretch out the kink. After a few minutes of that, she decided to go back to the bedroom. She had just started up the stairs when the groaning sound she'd heard on previous nights echoed through the otherwise silent house.

This time, it didn't sound like it was coming from the attic but from somewhere on the first. She stepped back down and tried to pinpoint the source of the noise, circling the entire first floor and finally arriving in front of the living room fireplace, which seemed to be the origin point.

But once she came to a stop, so did the groaning. She stood there for at least a minute, waiting, listening. But nothing happened and she began to feel silly.

*What is wrong with me?*

She turned to head for the stairs when she noticed she'd left a sitting room table lamp on. She walked over to turn it off when she noticed the half-open curtain and moved to the window to close it.

From her vantage point, she had a clear view of Kimberly Miner's house across the street. It looked as quiet as one would expect in the middle of a Saturday night. The only lights on were one in the kitchen, which must have been accidentally left on, and another dull one in the hallway stairwell that led from the first to the second floor.

Jessie had just started to pull the curtain shut when she caught movement out of the corner of her eye. A young woman was walking up the stairs of the Miner house, facing the window. She looked to be in her early twenties. She was blonde, with a trim, athletic figure and a tan that covered her entire body. Jessie knew this because she was completely naked.

The woman reached the top of the stairs and receded into the darkness. About thirty seconds later, a second figure emerged from the first floor, lumbering up the stairs. It took a second for Jessie to realize who it was until she saw the wild red hair. It was Kimberly's husband, Morgan. He too was completely naked.

Jessie leaned closer to the window to make sure she wasn't imagining things. As she did, she bumped the table lamp. It swayed for an interminable second before falling, hitting the wall hard as it fell and landing on the floor with a surprisingly loud thud.

Jessie saw Morgan's head pop up at the sound. Realizing that she would be visible with the open curtain and light from the lamp, she dropped quickly and heavily to the ground. With her heart thumping, she lay there on her stomach, as if about to do a pushup, for a good ten seconds before poking her head up again.

Morgan was apparently unconcerned with the sound because he continued up the stairs and soon disappeared after the girl into the darkness. Jessie stood there for a long time, staring at the now empty stairwell.

*Did I really just see that? Am I still sleeping?*

Eventually, she closed the curtain, returned the lamp to the table, turned it off, and headed back to bed, befuddled, exhausted, and not one hundred percent sure she was in her right mind. She tried to get to sleep but questions kept popping up, keeping her awake.

*Should I tell Kimberly this? What if I'm wrong? Am I putting a marriage at risk? Worse, what if I'm right? If what I saw was real, what the hell is going on in this neighborhood?*

## CHAPTER TEN

The next morning, Kyle was already showered and dressed when she woke up, feeling drained and out of sorts.

"Are you leaving?" she asked sleepily as she sat up in bed. "Isn't it Sunday?"

"It is but I got called in for an emergency all-hands meeting. One of our investors filed for bankruptcy on Friday and we only just found out. We're having a strategy session at nine."

"Oh," she said. "Will you be gone all day?"

"I hope not but I can't make any guarantees. I know we're a little churned up right now, you and I. Maybe we can hash it out this evening?"

"Okay," Jessie said, still a little discombobulated.

"I love you," he said as he leaned over and gave her a kiss on the forehead before heading out.

"I love you too," she said to the now empty room.

She listened to him hurry down the stairs, heard the garage door open and the car start. The garage door closed again as the sound of his engine faded into the distance. As she sat in bed, trying to get her bearings, the events of the night before leaked back into her brain: the club interrogation, the argument that night, her going downstairs, the weird naked hallway sighting from across the street.

*Was that real? Or just part of my dream?*

It wouldn't be the first time her memory had played tricks on her. But this wasn't a memory from her childhood. It was from last night. And it involved total strangers. She could have sworn she saw it.

Jessie resolved to go over Kimberly's house this morning to suss out the situation. She didn't want to jump to conclusions or make accusations. But if she'd really seen Morgan and some girl running naked up the stairs, that might be something his wife would want to know.

She got up, took a quick shower, got dressed, and drove over to the doughnut shop down the street, where she got a dozen. She returned home, made herself some coffee, then walked across the street and knocked on the Miners' front door. Kimberly opened it almost immediately. She was wearing a robe and had her hair in curlers.

"Hello, neighbor," she said cheerily. "This is a pleasant surprise on a Sunday morning. How are you?"

"I'm good," Jessie replied, trying to match Kimberly's energy. "I just wanted to thank you again for your hospitality the other day. I brought you all some doughnuts to let you know much I appreciate how welcoming you've been."

"That is so sweet. Come on in," she said, opening the door and leading her down the hall. "You know, I'm sorry I couldn't make it to the club last night for the big event. We had a prior commitment."

"Oh, I didn't realize you were members."

"Of course," Kimberly said. "Most folks around here are. We've just been so busy lately that we haven't had much of a chance to stop by. How'd it go?"

"Good, I guess."

Jessie followed her into the kitchen and saw the whole family, including Morgan, sitting at the breakfast table munching down. He was completely dressed, even wearing a sport jacket and slacks, and looked completely normal. Jessie was having increasing trouble believing her own recollection of last night.

"We're already eating," Kimberly said. "We've got church in a bit. But we'll save these for later. In fact," she said, addressing her family, "you all really have to go. I'll meet you there."

"You heard your mother, kids," Morgan said, standing up and bringing his plate into the kitchen. "Hurry up. We need to stop at the drugstore for Mikey's prescription on the way in."

He tossed the plate into the sink, kissed Kimberly on the cheek, and nodded at Jessie.

"Nice to see you again," he said, sounding for all the world like a pleasant, slightly harried husband and father.

The kids, despite being only four and two, took their plates into the kitchen too before shuffling into the living room to shove on loafers or fancy flats.

"We'll see you there," Morgan said to his wife before turning to the kids. "I'll be in the car. I leave in sixty seconds, with or without you."

Jessie watched as the two kids scrambled desperately to get their shoes on and rush out the door. Less than minute later the madness had been replaced by something resembling calm.

"Ah, listen to that silence," Kimberly said with a blissful smile. "It's a rarity these days."

"I'll bet," Jessie agreed.

"So what's up, neighbor? I have to get ready soon but it looks like you came over for more than just a doughnut drop-off. Care to share?"

"You know, I thought I had something to discuss. But now that I think about it, I guess I don't. I'll let you finish getting ready. We can talk some other time."

"You sure?" Kimberly asked as she removed he robe to reveal a tank top and yoga pants below.

Jessie was about to reply when she heard someone come down the stairs. She glanced over and saw the same young woman she thought she'd imagined from the night before. She was dressed now, in a T-shirt and sweatpants with a duffel bag flung over her shoulder. But it was definitely her.

"Jessie, this is Rachelle, our sometime nanny. Rachelle, this is Jessie, our new neighbor from across the street. She brought doughnuts, so dig in."

"Thanks but I can't," Rachelle said casually. "I'm going to the beach later and I don't want a belly lump. I'll just have granola."

She ambled into the kitchen, nodding at Jessie as she passed by. Jessie nodded back, desperately pretending like everything was cool. She looked over at Kimberly, who seemed to be amused at the notion that one doughnut would make Rachelle fat but oblivious to the fact that the nanny was scampering around the house naked with her husband last night.

"This girl thinks anything other than a celery stick is going to make her blow up," she said with just the slightest edge in her voice. "Super healthy body image, right, Rachelle?"

"Right, Mrs. M," Rachelle replied cluelessly, her head now in the fridge. "I actually have to head out soon to meet my friends. Do you mind if I take a bowl to go? I'll bring it back next time I come by."

"No problem," Kimberly said.

Rachelle filled a bowl with granola and milk, grabbed a spoon, and headed out the front door, shouting a casual "later" as she left.

"She's an eating disorder waiting to happen," Kimberly said ruefully once the younger girl was gone.

Jessie stood there as her neighbor removed the curlers from her hair and debated whether to say anything. Then, deciding that she would want to know, she spoke.

"Kimberly, you know I said I wanted to discuss something?"

"Uh-huh," Kimberly said vaguely, as she looked at her hair in the hall mirror.

"Well, I feel a little uncomfortable saying this. We don't really know each other very well. But I feel like I have an obligation."

Kimberly heard the seriousness in her voice and turned to look at her.

"I'm not under arrest for some forensic-y thing, am I?" she asked, forcing a smile but clearly unsettled.

"It's nothing like that. It's just…last night I was having trouble sleeping. I glanced out my window and I saw something…unusual."

"You were spying on my house?" Kimberly asked. Her tone was light but the panic in her eyes was clear.

"Inadvertently. And I saw your nanny…I saw Rachelle walking up the stairs… nude. And forgive me, but I saw your husband go up after her. He was naked as well."

Kimberly stared at her without speaking for a good five seconds. When she finally spoke, it was slowly and with a coldness that was new to Jessie.

"I think you made a mistake," she said. "Just because someone sleeps in the nude doesn't mean something untoward is going on."

"They weren't sleeping, Kimberly."

"Were they having sex?" she demanded.

"No."

"Were they even together? Couldn't one of them have gone upstairs and the other have followed soon after, not even realizing the first person was up there? Did they acknowledge each other? Are you sure Morgan even saw her?"

"No," Jessie said, surprised at the cross-examination. "I mean, it was kind of far away. But they went in the same general direction in the same general timeframe."

"Upstairs, you mean? Where all the bedrooms are?" she asked sarcastically. "So she could have gone to her room and him to ours. Did you see him go into her room?"

"It was dark. I couldn't see that far. And I had just woken up."

"So are you now saying you're not certain of what you saw?" Kimberly asked, her eyes blazing. "Because this is quite a thing to lay on a wife and mother if you're not certain."

"Kimberly, I'm certain that I saw them both walk up the stairs, naked, one soon after the other. That's all I'm saying."

"That's all you're saying. Just that bit?" Kimberly replied, her disdain evident. "What if I told you that Rachelle sleeps in the nude and that we're okay with it because our kids are too young to be bothered by it? And what if I told you that Morgan has a thyroid condition that makes him very warm at night and he sleeps in the nude too so he doesn't overheat? And what if I told you that he is a sleepwalker? Could you see if he was awake or if he was even aware that Rachelle was anywhere near him?"

"I couldn't tell any of that," Jessie said, not sure what else to say.

"Well, now that I've shared all kinds of personal details about my family life to ease your concerns that my husband isn't cheating on me, do you feel better?"

"I was just trying to help," Jessie said lamely.

"How did that go for you? Working out well?"

"I'm sorry, Kimberly. It's just...if it was me I'd want all the information."

"I already *had* all the information, Jessie. You didn't tell me anything I didn't already know, except that you're not the person I thought you were. Please leave."

Jessie, bewildered, walked toward the front door. As she opened it, she turned to try one more time. Kimberly was right behind her with the box of doughnuts, which she tossed at her. One of them shot out of the box and hit Jessie in the chest before falling to the ground. The jelly filling exploded, getting all over the floor and her shoes.

"Kimberly, please give me a chance to—"

Her neighbor slammed the door in her face. The fallen doughnut, now crushed, smeared on the front step. Jessie thought it looked almost like blood.

\*

Still stunned and confused, Jessie called Kyle at work. He sounded harried so she tried to explain quickly. When she was done, he didn't respond for so long that she thought the line had gone dead.

"Kyle, are you there?" she asked.

"I'm sorry. I'm just trying to wrap my head around why you would go over to our neighbor's house after only living here for days and tell her you think her husband is having an affair. She brought us brownies. You brought her allegations of infidelity. Does that seem like a fair trade?"

"I was hoping you'd assume the role of supportive husband here," Jessie said quietly.

Kyle sighed deeply.

"I want to, Jess. But you're making it kind of hard. I've got a work emergency. And you call me to tell me you blew up our relationship with our neighbor. And from what she says, you may have had the whole thing wrong."

"I don't think so. It felt like she was covering to me."

"Jessie, what are you talking about? Covering? This isn't a case to be solved. It's a real-life family."

"I know that, but—"

"Listen," he interrupted. "Even if it's true and he is screwing the babysitter, why is it our concern? Maybe she's nailing the gardener. Maybe they've got an open marriage. We don't know about their lives. And as far as I'm concerned, her explanation sounded convincing, especially since you're not even sure you were awake."

"I am sure."

"Really?" he asked. "You told me you switched up your meds recently, right? Are you certain that couldn't be messing with you?"

"That's not a side effect of it."

"I thought different drugs affected people differently. And you've been taking this for a couple of days. Can you tell me, without a shadow of a doubt, that this might not be a chemical thing?"

Jessie didn't respond. The truth was she wasn't sure about anything anymore. She doubted the medication had any unusual effect on her. But was she positive? No. She had seen something last night. But had she just misinterpreted something innocent? Had she let her permanently suspicious mind take her to the darkest possible conclusion rather than one that was more innocuous? She just wasn't sure.

"I don't know," she admitted.

"Listen, honey," he said, his voice immediately softer. "I want to help you with this. And maybe we can smooth things over. But for now, while my business is in a mini-crisis, can I just ask you not to alienate any more neighbors today? Is that a reasonable request?"

"It is," she said.

"Thank you. I'll see you tonight. I love you."

"I love you too," she said, then hung up. She walked upstairs and crawled into bed, where she spent most of the next two days.

# CHAPTER ELEVEN

She would have stayed in bed even longer if not for the practicum. But Tuesday was the day she was supposed to meet Professor Hosta at DSH-Metro in Norwalk to visit NRD. It was the first thing in forty-eight hours that got her excited enough to shower.

As she made the forty-five-minute drive, she unsuccessfully tried not to think about the last two days. Kyle had gone over to the Miner house in the hope of calming things down with Kimberly. But she wasn't interested and told him not to expect any more brownie deliveries.

Despite that, they had somehow been accepted into Club Deseo. Between the resentment of a current club member and Jessie's own combative responses to her grilling, she'd been sure they'd get rejected. But somehow, they'd gotten in.

She was tempted to tell Kyle she didn't want to accept it, especially after the interrogation by Marguerite Brennan. These weren't people she wanted to hang around with. But she knew how important he felt it was for work. He'd already locked in multiple clients through the place. And after blowing up things with their neighbor, she didn't feel like she was in a position to be giving ultimatums. So she held her tongue.

It wouldn't be official until the fall, when they were formally presented with their invitation. But they were provisional members until then, which allowed them access to the club without a chaperone.

In recognition, Teddy had given Kyle a new money clip. It was ridiculous—gold and oversized with a "$" symbol on it that looked like something Gordon Gekko would own circa 1987. Despite how silly Kyle looked when he pulled it out of his pocket, Jessie said nothing. She didn't want to bring him down when he was clearly so happy.

In fact, Kyle was giddy, already planning golf outings and how to maximize the upcoming autumn parties to his business advantage. He seemed largely oblivious to Jessie's blues. Either that or he hoped that by refusing to acknowledge them, they'd go away on their own. It was as if their disagreements of recent days were all water under the bridge. He seemed to hold no grudge, which made Jessie feel even guiltier for clinging to hers.

As she pulled into the hospital parking lot, she tried to push all those thoughts out of her head. She would need to have complete focus if she was going to effectively interact with the patients here, especially in the NRD unit.

Professor Hosta was waiting by his car and waved for her to pull up next to him. She rolled down her window when she got close.

"Good to see you, Ms. Hunt," he said. "There's a security gate for NRD access and they have a separate entrance. You'll need to follow me this time. We'll get you your own pass for future visits."

He got in his car and led the way. After a brief conversation with the security guard at the gate, they were allowed to pass. As she drove by, Jessie noticed the guard was armed.

They parked in a nondescript, dusty dirt lot at the back of the facility and walked to the door of another gate that surrounded the entire building, at which Hosta swiped a card. It buzzed and they passed through a small, undernourished garden courtyard, which led to the actual exterior doors of the building. It also required a pass card swipe. The same process was repeated at a set of interior doors before they finally entered the actual lobby area of the unit.

Once inside, they both had to turn over their personal items and go through a full body millimeter wave scanner like the ones airport security used as an alternative to metal detectors. Then both were patted down by additional security, also armed. Only then did they get their stuff back.

"So, they're pretty casual here then?" Jessie said acidly when the process was finally complete.

"Don't joke about security in this place, Ms. Hunt," Hosta said humorlessly. "Since NRD became operational seven years ago, they've only had two incidents. But combined, they resulted in the death of four guards and one inmate. They take precautionary measures deadly seriously here and so should you."

"Got it," Jessie said. She hadn't heard about the incidents but that was no surprise. Since hardly anyone was aware this place existed, it wasn't like there would be news reports about security breakdowns. She couldn't help but wonder who the inmate who'd died was but forced herself not to ask.

"We're going into the prep area, where you'll meet our security liaison," Hosta said. "Just to give you a sense of how vital folks here feel about taking precautions, the officer in charge is a former Army Ranger. You'll get further instructions in there. Please remember, you are only the second student allowed in this unit. It is an enormous privilege which can be revoked at any time. If that

61

happens, you risk failing your practicum and not getting your degree. Is that clear?"

"Yes, Professor."

"All right. Let's go in."

He nodded at one of the security guards, who buzzed them through an area marked by a sign with the bland title "Transitional Prep." Apparently not even Hosta's pass card could get them into every part of the facility. Once inside, Jessie was surprised at their liaison. They were met by a woman with dark blonde hair pulled back into a tight bun. She looked to be about Jessie's age, maybe a few years older.

She was shorter than Jessie, about five foot seven and clearly well-built, even with the security uniform hiding it a bit. Her shoulders were broad and Jessie noticed that her exposed forearms were rippled with muscle even without flexing. She guessed the woman weighed about 140 pounds, though she doubted any of it was fat.

The woman was attractive despite a thick scar under her left eye and pockmarks on her face and neck that stood out against her tan skin. They looked less like acne remnants than small burn marks, as if someone had put out cigarette butts on each individual spot. Jessie wondered if that was how she got them. Her eyes were gray and alert. She stepped forward and extended her hand.

"Hello, Ms. Hunt," she said. "I'm Officer Katherine Gentry. I'll be your security liaison for this visit."

"Nice to meet you," Jessie said, reaching down to shake her hand. Gentry's grip was firm but not intimidating.

"Good to see you again, Professor," Officer Gentry said, nodding at Hosta.

"And you too, Officer," he replied. "I've told Ms. Hunt that you'll be giving her the lowdown on what to expect."

"That's right. Here's how it will go. Both of you will change into facility scrubs. Ms. Hunt, you will also wash off all your makeup using the cleanser you'll find in there. I'd recommend not wearing any for future visits. You should also remove your wedding ring. There are changing rooms connected to this area. After that, we'll enter the unit. Since this is your first visit, Ms. Hunt, you'll just be observing. It can take some time to get comfortable with the procedure and the environment here."

"I'm not okay with that," Jessie interjected, ignoring Hosta's surprised expression, which she caught out of the corner of her eye. "I didn't fight through almost an hour of traffic on the freeway just to observe. I have a finite number of visits scheduled for this practicum and I need to make the most of every one. I want to start interviewing patients today."

Gentry looked at Hosta, who shrugged as if to say, "Your call." Jessie was surprised for a second before realizing that in this place, the security officer in charge must be authorized to overrule any decision made by medical personnel.

"Ms. Hunt," Gentry said, her voice low and calm. "You may notice that in here, we call the residents inmates rather than patients, the term used on the outside. Do you know why that is?"

"I'm guessing it's to remind everyone how dangerous these guys are."

"That's correct. Once we start using the term 'patient,' sympathy inevitably creeps in. And with that comes vulnerability. Do you know why we have visitors change into scrubs and women remove makeup before entering the unit?"

"No. Why?"

"Because," Gentry said, "in addition to being incredibly dangerous, these inmates are often frighteningly intelligent. They're not the garden-variety criminals you're used to. If they're here, they're a special kind of evil. Some of them will use any personal detail they uncover to manipulate you. They use the clothes you wear, your jewelry, your fragrance, your makeup to discern your weaknesses. The less they know about you the better."

"Why are you telling me all this?"

"Because I want you to appreciate that going into an interview with one of them cold, without having had the opportunity to observe beforehand, puts you at risk. It's not called the Non-Rehabilitative Division for nothing."

"I get that," Jessie said. "But you need to appreciate something about me. In order to really understand these people, I need to engage with them without any preconceptions. I want to interact with them for the first time without a filter, so that I can get a genuine sense of them as they react to me. I can better get in their heads when I'm in the room."

"Have you ever interviewed a resident of a non-rehabilitative facility before?" Gentry asked. "Have you ever interrogated a serial killer on your own, with only a glass window separating you from him?"

"No."

"Then what makes you think you could possibly be ready for what they're capable of in person?"

"I said I'd never interviewed one of them in a facility," Jessie said coolly. "That doesn't mean I haven't interacted with a serial killer up close. Let me assure you, Officer Gentry, I've been face to face with evil. I know what it looks like. I know how it moves and twists and writhes around inside a person. But I can only see that when I can get up close and personal. I'm not going to understand how these guys think, how to stop others like them, from behind some hidden observation mirror. I want to be in the room."

Gentry stared at her for a long time before speaking. Jessie could feel her evaluating, calculating, appraising. Finally, she seemed to make some kind of internal decision.

"Get changed," she said. "We don't have all day."

## CHAPTER TWELVE

Ten minutes later, after Jessie had changed into scrubs and signed a non-disclosure agreement so detailed that she worried that even mentioning the hospital to Kyle might get her arrested, they left the transitional prep area. The three of them passed through another security door and walked down a long, dimly lit corridor as Gentry talked them through the particulars of the unit.

She explained the procedure for interaction with inmates: never touch the glass, never reveal personal details about yourself, never make promises, never interact without a security officer in the room, and about a half dozen other "nevers" Jessie couldn't remember.

She noted that sessions were limited to fifteen minutes, unless otherwise specifically authorized. If instructed to leave the room, she was to do so without argument or delay. Refusal to adhere to any procedure could result in a permanent ban from the premises.

They reached the end of the hall, where another door buzzed open. Jessie glanced up to see a camera staring back down at her, one of dozens she'd noted throughout the complex. They entered a security station that reminded her of a nurses' station in a hospital.

Three men and one woman, all armed, looked up briefly before resuming their duties. Two of them were studying security monitors. One was inputting information into a terminal. The fourth, a large Hispanic man, scribbled something on a paper attached to a clipboard before standing up and approaching them. At full height, he was even more imposing. At about six foot six and around 250 pounds, he looked like a pro football linebacker.

"How goes it, Kat?" he asked Officer Gentry in a cheerful voice.

"Just bringing in some fresh meat, Cortez," she replied. "How are things with the Fab Five?"

"Same old, same old, I guess. Gimbel, Stokes, and De la Rosa are napping. Jackson is in restraints, on account of trying to bite through his wrists again. Crutchfield is working on the lyrics to one of his little ditties."

"So NRD only currently houses five inmates?" Jessie asked before being formally introduced.

"We have ten rooms," Cortez answered, eyeing her with curiosity. "But I'm perfectly happy staying half full. Fewer residents means fewer psychos."

"Not necessarily," Jessie argued. "It just means fewer *caught* psychos."

Cortez snorted and turned back to Gentry.

"Who's the Vogue chick slumming it with us today?" he asked.

"This is Jessie Hunt. She's doing her practicum through UC-Irvine. Assuming good behavior, she'll be visiting us multiple times throughout the rest of the year. But I wouldn't count on her lasting. It's doubtful that she'll be able to stick to procedure. She's a little on the impulsive side."

"Mouthy too," Cortez said. "Usually I like mouthy, but not in here. In here, mouthy can get you killed."

"Thanks for the pro tip, Cortez," Jessie said, deciding that being pegged as just another academic wasn't going to win her any friends in here. And if things went bad, she'd need friends. Might as well ingratiate herself right of the bat.

"See," Cortez said, smiling. "Mouthy. Maybe I buy you a drink after, Vogue chick. Whaddaya say?"

"I say that you're a real pleasure, Cortez. But I don't think my husband would be too pleased."

"Married," he replied shaking his head. "What a waste."

"Enough flirting," Gentry interrupted curtly. "Let's wake up De la Rosa so Ms. Hunt can meet him. He's a real charmer—a good introduction to the joys of NRD."

"No," Jessie said flatly. "I want Crutchfield."

The place went silent. The other three guards looked up from their tasks, their mouths open.

"That," Professor Hosta said, speaking for the first time since entering the room, "would be a mistake."

"Bolton Crutchfield is our most...challenging inmate," Gentry said. "He'd bat you around like a cat toying with a mouse. You might want to ease in a bit."

"I'm well versed in his history. I've studied his crimes in detail and know about his...proclivities." Jessie said. "I know what he's capable of."

"We're not talking about his crimes," Cortez interjected. "We're talking about the way he manipulates everyone he comes into contact with, even behind inch-thick glass in a secure room. He seems like a polite, unassuming country boy. But don't be fooled. He gets into your head. It's kind of his thing. Internationally renowned psychiatric professionals have come out of interviews with him shaken up."

"I understand," Jessie said, matter-of-factly. "I want to see him."

She watched as Hosta and Gentry exchanged a look she couldn't decipher. As she waited for a reply, she felt a tingling down her spine, the kind she often got when she sensed something was off. She couldn't pinpoint it, but all this sound and fury about her seeing Crutchfield seemed…manufactured.

"You'll need to sign a release," Gentry finally said, "indemnifying the hospital in case anything goes wrong. As professionals, we're here to keep you safe physically. We can't protect you from what he might do to you psychologically."

"That seems fair," Jessie replied. "Where do I sign?"

Five minutes later, after a final body search, she was led to the door of Crutchfield's room.

"This is where I get off," Hosta said. "I'll be observing from behind that two-way mirror you have such disdain for. Please remember, Ms. Hunt, you are here as a student. This is part of your assignment in your pursuit of a graduate degree. It is not an opportunity to turn into some kind of detective or FBI agent. You're not there yet. Understood?"

"Yes, Professor," she said.

He nodded skeptically and left for the observation room. She was now alone with Officer Gentry, who pushed a small contraption into her hand. It looked like car key fob remote.

"What's this?" Jessie asked.

"It's your security blanket," Gentry said. "See the red button in the middle? If things ever get too intense and you need to bail, push the button. It's discreet enough that he shouldn't notice. I'll be in the room with you and it will alert me silently that you want out. That way, I can pull you from the room without him realizing that it's at your request. I can say the session time limit has ended or come up with some other excuse. Anything to get you out without Crutchfield knowing he's gotten under your skin. You don't want that."

"Okay. Are you sure it's necessary?"

"In the history of my time here, only two people have ever managed to get through a session without pushing it, so yeah, I think it's necessary."

"I assume it's a waste of time for me to ask who didn't need it?"

"You assume right," Gentry said. "If you start to get rattled, just push the button and stay calm. Try not to let it show. He gets bored easily and messing people up gets him off. If you can get out of there without that happening, consider it a successful visit. You ready?"

"As ready as I'm going to be," Jessie said.

"Okay then. It's showtime."

Gentry nodded at the camera above them. There was a buzz, after which she swiped her card and a second, different buzz sounded through the hall. Jessie heard a click. Gentry opened the door and stepped inside. Jessie followed.

The room was softly lit, like a fancy restaurant in late evening, and it took a few moments for her eyes to adjust. Gentry must have known she'd have that issue because she guided her to a chair behind a small desk equipped with a dull pencil and legal pad. As Jessie's eyes settled, she saw that she was facing a thick glass partition that divided the room.

Gentry walked over to a panel on the wall next to the door and pushed a button. Slowly, the light in the room increased to the point that Jessie didn't have to squint. She took in her surroundings. Beyond the partition was what essentially amounted to a prison cell.

Attached to the back wall was a narrow bed frame suspended about three feet off the floor. It looked like the thin mattress on top was actually built into the bed and not removable. There was a small pillow made of what looked like a rubbery material.

To Jessie's right, there was a small desk and chair contraption, also built into the wall. It looked like the all-in-one desk and chair combinations she used in high school. In the left section of the cell, there was nothing but a small open space. Jessie suspected this was Crutchfield's "exercise" area, where he could move about without fear of slamming into anything.

The room was empty. Jessie was about to ask Gentry where the resident was when she heard a flush, followed by a male voice.

"Door, please," someone said in an unhurried drawl.

In the back right corner of the cell, a small curved door that Jessie hadn't previously noticed began to mechanically unfurl. A man stepped out and moved to the tiny metal sink, also built into the wall, where he washed his hands.

His back was to Jessie so she took the opportunity to study him as much as possible without him doing the same to her. He was smaller in real life than she'd expected, probably five foot eight and maybe 150 pounds. The news footage didn't give a sense of scale.

He wore what amounted to hospital scrubs, not unlike what she had on, only hers were gray and his were a bright aqua color. His shoes looked like some kind of Crocs. His hair, which had been shaved tightly against his skull, was something approximating blond.

He took his time washing his hands; so long, in fact, that Jessie began to suspect he knew she was there and was keeping her in suspense. Finally he turned off the water and dried his hands on his scrubs. Without turning around, he spoke.

"What you expected, ma'am?"

The drawl was even more pronounced now and Jessie remembered that Bolton Crutchfield was from the swampy bayous of southern Louisiana. He'd spoken so infrequently at his trial that it was easy to forget.

"I thought you'd be bigger," she admitted.

He turned around, a crooked smile on his face. He was in serious need of some dental work as several teeth pointed in odd directions.

"I get that a lot," he said.

Jessie got her first good look at him. What struck her most was just how unimpressive he appeared. His face was pleasantly bland, not quite handsome but not objectionable either. He was thirty-five but looked a good five years younger. His soft chin and borderline chubby cheeks made him appear harmless enough. Only the unblinking sharpness of his brown eyes gave any hint that there was something more under the surface.

"Is that how you got your victims off guard?" Jessie asked. "They underestimated you?"

"We're divin' right in then?" Crutchfield asked, feigning mild offense. "No introductions? No agreeable small talk?"

"I was led to believe I had limited time with you, Mr. Crutchfield. I didn't want to waste it on chitchat."

"But I don't even know your name, ma'am," Crutchfield insisted as he moved over to his bed and sat down facing her. "How can we get down to conversing if I don't know what to call you? It seems awful impolite."

"It's Ms. Hunt," Jessie told him, "although I'm fine with ma'am."

"Well, now we're finally getting somewhere," he said, flashing his toothy grin again. "Now that I know who you are, it's nice to meet you. You can call me Bolton. Some folks shorten it to Bolt, but I'm not a fan. Too familiar, you know?"

"Good to meet you as well, Mr. Crutchfield," Jessie replied, ignoring his commentary. "I was hoping to ask you a few questions."

"It seems like you already started in on that with your 'underestimating' talk."

"Well, is that how you lulled your victims into complacency? With the southern drawl and the unimposing build?"

"Are you taking a shot at my diminutive size, ma'am? Because that's mighty hurtful. I'll tell you what—I'll trade you an answer for an answer. I'll tell you something you want to know. Then you grace me with some information about yourself. I saw it done that way once in a movie. Does that seem like a fair trade?"

"I was expressly advised not to share any personal details with you." Jessie told him.

"I have no doubt," Crutchfield replied. "But you don't strike me as exactly the rule-following sort. And it seems like a waste for you to come through all those doors, wipe off your pretty makeup, take off that fancy wedding ring, and not even get more than a howdy-do from me."

Jessie heard Gentry shift uneasily behind her and sensed it was a silent warning not to comply with the request. But Crutchfield was right. She wasn't one to let rules get in her way. And there were questions she needed answered. After all, the practicum wasn't the only reason she was here.

"All right," she said. "Answer my question honestly and I'll answer one of yours."

She heard a soft sigh of frustration from Gentry and waited to be removed from the room. But nothing happened. She was surprised and thought she saw a monetary glimpse of something similar from Crutchfield too before he responded.

"Here's the thing, ma'am. If you're planning to kill someone and they're not expecting it, you don't really need them underestimating you or getting lulled into false comfort. You could pull out a carving knife right in front of them and, if they don't suspect that you've got ill intent, they ain't gonna blink an eye. It's only after you've done the deed, or at least started in on it, that they begin to realize that you meant them harm. But what can they do then? They've been—what's the word—incapacitated. Even good old Cortez out there could be butchered if he wasn't always on alert, you know? And he's a big boy. Does that answer your question?"

Jessie nodded and scribbled down a few notes on her pad, more to avoid making eye contact than to get it down on paper. Despite her best efforts, she was unsettled by his casual demeanor while describing his technique.

"Now I believe it's my turn, ma'am. May I ask my question?"

"A deal's a deal," Jessie said.

"I do appreciate your principled nature, ma'am. It's rare these days. So why are you really here? I mean, I know you're some kind of student, doing your field work study so you can get your diploma and then be a professional killer whisperer, telling cops what's in the heads of fellas like me. But we both know that ain't the real reason. You're after something more than that. Otherwise you could go to any loony lockup. But you came here specifically to see me. And while I'm flattered as all get out, I can't help but wonder: why are you here?"

Jessie tried to think fast. If Hosta or the folks here thought she had some ulterior motive for wanting to interview Crutchfield beyond academic research, they might shut her down. But if she lied, or even shaded the truth, she got the sense that Crutchfield would know and end the interview based on bad faith on her part. She also got the odd feeling that he'd rambled through his question specifically to give her time to come up with an answer, knowing that providing the right one would be crucial.

"Mr. Crutchfield," she said, debating how far to go even as she began, "my authorized reason for being here is to, as you say, complete my work study so I can get my diploma. But it's also true that I think you might have some particular insights into…unresolved matters that are of great interest to me."

She worried that her vagueness might make him feel he'd been short-changed. But Crutchfield simply gave a little half-smile and leaned back on his bed.

"Your turn," he said.

Jessie sat silent for a moment, deciding how best to ask the next question. Phrasing it the wrong way could have major consequences. Finally she hit on something she thought would work.

"Have you ever gotten any assistance? Or given any?"

"That's two questions," Crutchfield noted.

Jessie didn't respond. This was what she wanted to ask and she wasn't going to give him a chance to weasel out of it. She stared at him, waiting. He looked back at her, seemingly amused at her impudence.

"Oh, all right," he finally said. "I'll give you two, just this once, because I like your spunk. The answers would be 'yes' and 'yes.' But that's all I can say on those matters."

For now, it was all she needed. Before she could fully process his response, he had started speaking again.

"My turn. And I'll keep this brief since I can see from Officer Gentry's restlessness that we're about to close up shop here. You ready to be straight with me, ma'am?"

"Yes," Jessie replied, not sure where this was headed.

Crutchfield sat up straight and then leaned in toward the glass partition, as if he was going to whisper. The lopsided smile was gone. His expression was sober as his eyes locked on hers.

"Does he know you're here, Jessie?"

As she stared back at Crutchfield's gray eyes, the room began to swirl slightly. He knew her first name. And he knew much more than that.

She was vaguely aware that she was pressing the red button hidden in her hand but couldn't actually feel it. Her whole body felt weak and limp. She seemed unable to move.

"We're done here," she heard Gentry say from what sounded like far away as the officer grabbed her by the shoulders and began to pull her from the room. Crutchfield's eyes never left hers and his expression remained expectant. He was still waiting for an answer.

Just before she was dragged from the room, Jessie managed to yank herself free and turn back to face him. With an unexpected sturdiness in her voice, she responded loudly and clearly.

"No," she said and then she was hauled from the room.

*

"You weren't honest with me!" Hosta hissed angrily as they walked through the hospital parking lot back to their cars. "This is obviously more than just an academic exercise for you. What aren't you telling me, Ms. Hunt?"

"Nothing," she lied. "I just said what I thought he wanted to hear. He obviously thought I had some ulterior motive, so I let him think he was right."

"I don't believe that for a second. You clearly *do* have an ulterior motive; and the man knew your name!"

Jessie felt the conversation slipping out of control and decided she had to redirect it.

"I don't think you're in any position to call me out on honesty, Professor Hosta," she said indignantly.

"What are you talking about?" he demanded, taken aback.

"I mean, there's no way I could have gotten in there to interview to Bolton Crutchfield on my first visit. Not unless it was preapproved at the highest levels."

"I don't know what you mean," Hosta said defensively. But Jessie could tell she'd hit a nerve. She pressed it.

"You could have insisted I be prevented from talking to him. But you didn't. And Officer Gentry clearly had the authority to shut down the request. But she didn't. Both of you made a bit of a stink, but in the end you allowed an inexperienced master's candidate to question a calculating serial killer her first time there. Doesn't that strike you as peculiar?"

"What are you suggesting?" Hosta asked, notably not answering her question.

"I'm suggesting someone wanted me in that room and wanted to see how Crutchfield would react to me. Talk about ulterior motives!"

Professor Hosta continued walking, not saying anything else. It wasn't until they reached their cars that he finally turned back to her.

"It goes without saying that your time here is not to be disclosed," he said, apparently moving on from the prior discussion. "You signed waivers to that effect but I thought a reminder might be in order. You may not discuss it with anyone not already authorized. Is that clear?"

"Of course."

"And I'm not sure if I'll be able to get you back in here. You violated multiple protocols. It's possible we may have to reassign you to another hospital. You should be prepared for that."

"Noted," Jessie said, though she didn't believe it for a second. Someone wanted her in that hospital, in that room even. And she bet the chances were good she'd get back in eventually.

"Enjoy the rest of your day," Professor Hosta said frostily. "I'll see you in class."

Without waiting for a reply, he got in his car and peeled out, leaving her in a cloud of dust. Coughing, she hurried to her own car and got in. When the air cleared enough for her to see, she pulled out herself and headed back to Orange County.

The longer she sat in the car, the more excited she got. It was like the depression of the last few days had never existed. She thought back to the series of locked doors requiring buzzing in, to her interactions with guards, to all the tight lips and furrowed brows, and felt a thrill of adrenaline course through her body.

And then there was Crutchfield. True, her interview had ended badly, scarily even. But she'd been face to face with a serial killer and come out the other side. Part of it was thrilling. And productive.

73

She'd gotten part of an answer to a question that had been eating at her for a long time.

Admittedly, it had required opening up to man who had killed almost twenty people; a man who somehow knew her first name and seemingly much more than that about her.

But that seemed like a small price to pay.

# CHAPTER THIRTEEN

Eight weeks later, Jessie still hadn't been back to NRD.

Her confidence that being allowed to visit once would allow subsequent trips seemed to have been misplaced. As summer bled into fall and the weather turned crisp, she wondered if maybe she was genuinely being punished for violating protocol; or if whoever had let her in that room had changed their mind.

Whatever the reason, she'd had to go to other, sometimes far-flung state hospitals for her weekly practicum assignments. Most of her visits had been to Patton, a hospital in San Bernardino that housed mostly sexually violent patients. It was almost ninety minutes away. Every time she made the trip, she cursed herself for pushing so hard in Norwalk.

Still, the work was interesting and kept her busy, preventing her from obsessing over her increasingly insular life in Westport Beach. She and Kyle had settled into something resembling normalcy.

His work at the office was nonstop. According to Kyle, he was so busy that the firm having a location down here wasn't just opportunistic but essential. In addition to his bonuses and commissions, he was told he'd be given a second raise on top of the original one he got when they moved. But oddly, he was hazy about when that would kick in and how much it would be. Jessie didn't love that their financial state of affairs, which was always a shared responsibility in the past, was becoming increasingly one-sided. She felt a bit in the dark about where exactly they stood.

But she didn't push the issue for now. That was partly because she didn't want to encroach on the one area where Kyle truly felt like a master of the universe—his work. But it was also because she still felt guilty about the blowup with Kimberly, who hadn't spoken to her in two months.

As a result, Jessie had made an uneasy peace with her husband about the time he spent at Club Deseo. He seemed to have endless golf outings and Oath Minders get-togethers. And while she wouldn't describe him as distant, she couldn't help but notice that he didn't always seem totally…present.

For her part, despite not yet being a formal club member, Jessie went to the obligatory functions of the Hearthkeepers. And as long as she hung close to Melanie, who could always be counted on for an acerbic crack or two, she muddled through. There was still something unsettling about the club she couldn't quite nail down, a kind of groupthink when it came to propriety and social norms that she found off-putting.

But by mid-October, she gave up trying to name it and accepted that this just might be how things were done in a ritzy, beach-centric enclave. It was weird and a little stifling. But not so much that she couldn't lead her life.

It helped that Kyle, despite his constant absenteeism, did seem committed to their other major endeavor of the fall, making a baby. And on the Monday morning before Halloween weekend, after throwing up twice while getting ready for class, she took a test that proved it: she was pregnant.

She waited until she was in the car on the way to UC-Irvine to call him with the good news so she'd have uninterrupted time to talk.

"Guess what?" she asked when he picked up.

"What's that?" he asked, sounding mildly distracted. She'd have been annoyed if she didn't know that was about to change.

"You know that extra room, the one we left empty because we wanted to save it for any new potential housemates?"

"I do," he said, sounding more focused now.

"We're going to have to start buying some furniture—very small furniture."

"Are you serious?" he shouted, nearly blowing out her eardrum. "You're not messing around, are you?"

"Kyle Voss," she replied mock scoldingly, "do you think I would mess around about something like this? I am completely serious. We're going to have a baby!"

"Oh, Jess, that is so awesome! I can't tell you how excited I am. This is…life altering."

"You better believe it, mister," she agreed. "Our whole world is about to get turned upside down in the best way."

"Do you know how far along you are?"

"No, I just did the test this morning after throwing up a few times. I'll call my OB-GYN today to set up an appointment. But for now, we should celebrate. Maybe a fancy dinner, if I can keep it down? Want to go somewhere new?"

"Actually, this timing is perfect," he said. "I heard a rumor that the next time we go to the club, they're giving us our official membership invitation—no more provisional status. We should go tonight so they can do it and make it a double celebration. I'll call ahead so they can prep everything and I'll say we want to sit in the formal dining room."

"You're kidding, right?" she said, unable to hide the disappointment in her voice.

"What do you mean?"

"Kyle, we already visit that place two or three times a week. I don't consider going there a special celebration."

"But like I said, they'll pull out all the stops for us," he insisted. "And it will work out perfectly with the official invitation to join. It's karma!"

"That's not what karma means," she said, trying to contain the anger she felt rising inside of her. "And you're missing the point. I don't want to share it with anyone else. I don't care about the club tonight. I want this to be something special. Let this night just be about us."

He was quiet for a few seconds, which made her think he was chastened. She was mistaken.

"Jessica, we'll have all the time we need just for us. But I want to share our news with the people who care about us. They'll be excited for us. And the synergy with the invitation is just too perfect. Besides, it's much more convenient. Let's go there tonight and we can do something just for us this weekend, when it's not so hectic."

"Is this how it's going to be?" she asked, her heart sinking. "Everything's about convenience because things are so hectic? Are you even going to make it for my first doctor's appointment? Or do I have to schedule that at the club too?"

"I'll make it if I can," he said calmly, seemingly undeterred by her sarcasm. "But to be honest, if you continue to see the doctor in the city, it will be hard, especially in the middle of the work day."

"You're telling me you might miss the first medical appointment of my pregnancy because of work stuff?" she asked, incredulous.

"I'm just trying to be honest," he said. "It's really far. Maybe you could get a new doctor, somewhere closer. After all, you'll probably have the baby around here anyway, right? I can ask around at the club tonight. I'm sure we'll get lots of suggestions for good docs."

"I've got to go. I'm at school now," Jessie said, even though she still had fifteen minutes left to get there. "We can talk later."

She hung up without waiting for a reply, too upset to react. Instead, she kept her eyes on the road, focusing intently on every turn and lane change, refusing to think about anything other than the details of her route. Occasionally, she wiped a tear from her cheek.

*

She'd tried to call her college friend Lacey after class to decompress. Lacey knew Kyle from back in his hardscrabble undergrad days and might have some words of wisdom. But as she always seemed to these days, she got voicemail. So, needing someone to vent to and not up for a full therapy session with Dr. Lemmon, she took a chance and called Melanie Carlisle.

To her surprise, Mel offered to meet for coffee right away. A half hour later they were strolling through one of Westport's many shopping districts, beverages in hand.

Jessie was having second thoughts about reaching out because the second she'd mentioned the pregnancy, Mel began happily pummeling her with questions and suggestions about baby prep. It was more than she was up to at the moment so she steered to another topic.

"Do you know how this is going to go down tonight at the club, with this invitation?" she asked, not realizing until that moment that she'd acceded to Kyle's dinner preference.

"It's always different," Mel said. "Sometimes it's a big blowout. Sometimes it's low-key. I gather you're hoping for the latter?"

"Kind of," Jessie admitted. "I'm not really a big blowout kind of gal. So what happens after?"

"After what?" Mel asked.

"After we're officially in. When do I get a peek behind the curtain to see what the menfolk do at those Oath Minders gatherings? Kyle won't tell me anything about them and there are so many of them."

"To be honest, Jessie, I have no idea what they do there."

"How is that possible?" Jessie asked, stunned. "You've been members for years, right?"

"Three years," Mel told her. "Within days of moving here, Teddy seemed to know about the club and he just started fixating on getting in. I figured that once we settled in here, he'd be less secretive. But nope, he acts like it's a fraternity and he'd get blackballed if he revealed any of their precious secrets."

"No offense, but I didn't get the sense that you'd put up with such nonsense."

"Neither did I. Before we came here, I ruled the roost, made all the big family decisions, handled all the finances. But somehow, in recent years, the dynamic has shifted. I'm not even totally sure how. But he's much more hands on, much more…insistent that things be done his way. It just kind of happened."

"It sounds like you're not fully on board with the change," Jessie noted.

Mel looked at her and seemed about to say something before changing her mind at the last second. She glanced at her watch.

"I just remembered I have a thing," she said unconvincingly. "Mind if we cut this short?"

"No problem," Jessie replied even though she finally felt like she was getting closer to the bottom of what so unsettled her about this community.

After they parted ways, Jessie drove home. She kept thinking about how Mel, clearly a strong and capable woman, had somehow ceded so much of her authority and autonomy to her husband.

Maybe Teddy was a great guy behind closed doors. But everything Jessie had seen of him suggested he was a self-involved, feckless dullard. She didn't get why Mel was even with him and she certainly didn't love the influence he seemed to be having on Kyle. Every day, her husband seemed slightly less like the charming and thoughtful guy she'd fallen in love with.

Once home, despite feeling guilty about it, she found herself rifling through her husband's stuff, looking for something tangible to explain why he, like Teddy, had been drawn to Club Deseo like a moth to a flame the moment they'd arrived in town.

After fifteen minutes of frenzied searching, she gave up. She hadn't found anything suspicious or even mildly clarifying, other than a healthy portion of guilt, which nestled heavily in her gut.

Her cell phone rang. It was her doctor's office calling to set up an appointment. She scheduled one for a day she didn't have class. They asked if she wanted to make it early morning or late afternoon so her husband could come as well.

"Any time will do," she said, realizing that whenever it was, Kyle wouldn't be coming. She managed to wait until she'd hung up to start crying. Only this time, it wasn't just a few tears like in the car on the way to school that morning. This time she found herself sobbing. And she couldn't stop.

## CHAPTER FOURTEEN

Jessie felt nauseated. And tired. And out of sorts.

But she tried to ignore all that and make the best of the night. She told herself that Kyle wasn't being intentionally insensitive to her wishes. He was just so caught up in his own that he was oblivious to hers.

That's why she smiled her way through dinner at the club. They were seated in the formal dining room, as Kyle had requested. But it didn't make any difference. People came up to them all evening. Some offered congratulations on the impending club invitation, which was apparently an open secret. Others gave well wishes on the pregnancy, which was somehow also public information.

She would have preferred to keep that quiet until after her first appointment. But apparently Kyle was too excited to hold it in. Or to let her know that he'd spilled the beans. She told herself not to get upset with him, that his enthusiasm had just gotten the better of him.

Almost everyone was nice. Even Marguerite Brennan, her Hearthkeepers interrogator, was convincingly gracious. Their neighbor, Morgan Miner, stopped by as well. He seemed unaware of the accusation Jessie had made regarding him. But Kimberly, as usual, kept her distance.

The actual presentation of the invitation was underwhelming. The club president made brief comments, handed Kyle an embossed envelope, and everyone clapped. That was pretty much it.

When Kyle wandered to another table to talk to a golf buddy, Jessie snuck a glance at the invitation. She wasn't sure why she felt the need to be secretive. It was just as much hers as it was his. And yet, she still tried to be quick about it.

The formal invitation itself was pleasantly bland. Jessie was more interested in the accompanying receipt. Apparently the going rate for membership in Club Deseo these days was $100,000 a year.

*How can we afford this?*

Almost immediately that question was replaced in her head by another one:

*What the hell are we getting for a hundred grand a year? That's a lot of money for rubber chicken dinners, tea parties, and golf.*

Her curiosity was suddenly replaced by a sudden, strong urge to go to the bathroom, so she got up and excused herself. Even though she knew it might make things worse, she took a glass of water with her, as her mouth had gotten suddenly, unaccountably dry.

*Is this what pregnancy is going to be—endless, unpredictable body shifts that occur without any warning?*

She made her way to the ladies' room but immediately saw the line was way too long. She'd never make it. She tapped a passing server on the shoulder.

"Is there another restroom I can use? I'm pregnant and have to go bad."

The young woman seemed to waver for a moment before speaking.

"We're not supposed to do this," she said. "But there's a staff bathroom down at the end of the hall. When you see the swinging door, make a left."

"Thank you," Jessie said, deciding that maybe this pregnancy thing might have some unexpected perks.

She walked down the hall, which grew increasingly dark with each step. By the time she reached the swinging door, there was so little light that she had to squint to see. She was about push the door open when she saw a little dogleg in the hallway that headed left. It was easy to miss in the near-darkness. She was confused. Was she supposed to take that or go left after passing through the swinging door?

She continued down the hallway just to check. After rounding the corner, she determined that this wasn't the right route. The hallway extended for at least thirty yards and got so narrow that, at the end, only walking single file was possible. Clearly, that wasn't the way to the restroom or the server would have mentioned it.

But Jessie was intrigued. So, despite her unhappy bladder, she went in that direction. She moved quickly, intending only to see what was at the end of the hall. By the time she reached it, the walls were so tight that she felt an unexpected claustrophobia.

She rounded the corner and almost tripped over a flight of stairs leading to a second floor she hadn't known was there. At the bottom and top of the stairs were twin, red-hued, old-timey lanterns attached to the wall. They were the only source of light. Jessie was just putting her foot on the first step when she heard voices from above. One of them sounded familiar though the words were unintelligible.

For reasons she couldn't explain, she darted back around the corner, out of sight. Only then did she poke her head out slightly to see who was talking. She saw two people. The first was a gorgeous young woman in a tight black minidress and four-inch heels. Tall and tan, with thick black hair that cascaded over her shoulders, she looked vaguely familiar. It took a second for Jessie to identify her as one of the club's many hostesses.

The girl was adjusting her dress, which was a little disheveled. The bottom was riding up near her hips, revealing that she wasn't wearing underwear. After she managed to pull it down, she leaned back and groped the crotch of the man in the shadowy stairwell above her.

As she carefully stepped down, navigating the tricky steps, he followed her. When his face finally came into view, framed by the red lantern light, Jessie realized why the voice sounded familiar. It was Teddy Carlisle.

He zipped up his pants and tucked his shirt into them as he walked down the stairs. When he glanced up, Jessie dashed back out of sight. They were moving down the steps slowly but would reach the bottom soon.

Jessie turned and scurried down the narrow hallway, desperately trying to reach the dogleg bend at the end before they rounded the corner and saw her. She was just about to make the turn when she heard the girl's voice in the distance behind her, giggling as she said something about getting in her evening workout.

Suddenly her shoe snagged on the carpeting and she fell. She wasn't hurt but knew there was no way she'd be able to get up and round the corner out of sight before Teddy and the hostess saw her in the hallway. Already she saw their shadows bouncing off the wall at the far end. There was nowhere to hide.

Desperate, she glanced down at the half-full water glass she was still clutching in her right hand. Without even really thinking about it, she rolled over and flung it the length of the hallway toward them. It bounced on the carpet twice but still had enough force to shatter when it hit the far wall. The shadows froze.

"What the…" she heard the hostess say apprehensively.

Jessie popped up as quickly as she could and hurried to the bend in the hall.

"Stay back, Kelsey," she heard Teddy say.

She still needed more time.

"Whore!" she shouted in her loudest, grizzliest voice, hoping the screamed insult might give him a second's more pause.

"Teddy, wait," she heard the hostess whisper loudly and imagined her grabbing him by the arm.

Jessie gave one last glance back down the long hallway as she rounded the corner. There was no one in sight.

When she stepped out into the wider hallway again, she suddenly felt as if a weight had been lifted off her chest and placed back on her bladder, which was now screaming at her. She pushed through the swinging door and moved left, where the sign for the women's staff restroom was prominently displayed.

She opened the door and moved quickly to a stall, which she locked firmly before sitting down and taking what seemed like her first deep breath in minutes.

*

Jessie barely slept that night. Part of it was because of what she'd seen. It wasn't even that she was shocked to discover Teddy with another woman. It was more his brazenness, doing it essentially out in the open.

But what really ate at her, what kept her tossing and turning all night, was Kyle's reaction when she'd told him.

"She was literally pulling her dress back down when I saw them," Jessie had said indignantly.

"I'm not making excuses for him," Kyle had replied. "I'm just saying sticking our noses into their business seems like more trouble than it's worth."

"But he's cheating on Mel. I like Mel. I can't do nothing."

"After what happened with the Miners, you want to open that Pandora's box again?" he erupted.

"This isn't the same," she had insisted, equally agitated. "Melanie's not just a neighbor. She's a friend."

"Yeah, and so is Teddy," Kyle countered. "So why would you want to go and blow up the marriage of our friends?"

"I'm not trying to do that but she has a right to know."

"It's not our business, Jessie," he insisted. "Besides, how can you even be sure what you really saw?"

"What are you suggesting?"

"You said it was dark," he reminded her. "You had to go to the bathroom. Your hormones are all over the place because of the pregnancy. Maybe you misinterpreted things."

"Like you think I did with the Miners?"

"You have to admit it's possible," he said. "Did you ever change your medication like we talked about?"

"Yes, I did. And I'm fine. I'm not some crazy chick having hallucinations, Kyle!"

83

"I didn't say that," he said defensively.

"Not in so many words. Look, I'll talk to Mel and she can make up her own mind."

"No. I forbid it."

"You *forbid* it?" Jessie repeated incredulously. "Who do you think you are? I know things have changed since we moved here but not that much. You don't get to forbid me from having a frickin' turkey sandwich, tough guy, much less speak my mind. Have you forgotten who you're dealing with?"

They'd gone to bed without saying another word to each other.

*

Jessie replayed the conversation in her head as she showered the next morning. Neither of them had spoken as they got ready. When she got out of the shower, he had left for the day. It didn't really matter. Though she wasn't certain whether she was doing it out of concern for her new friend or spite for her husband, she'd made her decision. She was telling Mel the truth.

## CHAPTER FIFTEEN

Jessie showed up at the Carlisle house unannounced around mid-morning. Daughton, whom she hadn't considered, was napping. After a few minutes of chitchat that Jessie found ulcer-inducing, she decided to just dive in, regardless of the consequences.

"I saw something disturbing last night and I feel like I have to tell you about it, even though I'm worried you'll be upset with me," she said, abruptly interrupting Mel's dissertation on bottle nipple cleaning.

"Okay," Mel replied slowly, her brow already furrowed.

"I made a wrong turn down a hall at the club and stumbled across Teddy. He was with a woman, one of the hostesses. They were coming down some stairs. And it was pretty obvious that they'd just...been intimate."

Mel stared back for a few seconds without speaking. Jessie tried to place the expression on her face but couldn't identify it at first. It wasn't one she'd predicted, like shock, anger, or shame. And then it hit her. Mel's face displayed resignation.

"I'd hoped we wouldn't have to have this talk for a while," Mel said, sounding almost apologetic.

"This is not the reaction I was expecting," Jessie said.

"Yesterday, when you asked what went on in those Oath Minders meetings and I said I didn't know, I wasn't being completely honest."

"What do you mean?" Jessie asked.

"I mean, I didn't really want to know. But I could guess."

"You're going to have to help me out here, Mel," Jessie said, trying to rein in her frustration. "I'm a little lost."

"Club Deseo isn't just your standard issue country club," Mel explained. "Teddy told you the word 'deseo' means 'wish.' And that's true as far as the general public is concerned. But the word can also be translated as 'desire.' And behind closed doors, that's how members define it. Club Deseo is a safe space for couples who are into open marriages. Or more accurately, for *husbands* who are into them."

"Still lost," Jessie said.

Mel seemed to be having some internal struggle about how to proceed. But after a few seconds, her eyes took on a steely seriousness and the words spilled out.

"There are lots of members who are into open relationships. Or who just want to have affairs. But they're wealthy, powerful guys who don't want to risk their reputations by pursuing that stuff in public. So the club protects them. It creates a secure environment where members can have access to women without fearing exposure in the larger community."

She stopped talking and watched Jessie, seemingly waiting for the inevitable reply.

"This is a known thing?" Jessie asked, shaking her head, as if trying to wake herself up from a bad dream.

"In certain circles, yes," Mel replied. "It's all very organized. The club selects the 'hostesses.' It pays them so members are never at risk of being accused of solicitation. The girls are the most well-paid restaurant hostesses in the western world and that doesn't include their 'tips.' The club even has them tested weekly for drugs and STDs."

"And you're cool with this?" Jessie asked, disbelieving.

"Of course not," Mel snapped. "I mean, I wasn't. You have to understand—I didn't learn about all of this until we'd been members for a year. I still don't officially know. It's not like anyone ever sat me down for 'the talk' like I'm doing with you."

"The talk?" Jessie repeated.

"Yeah. I had to piece it together on my own over months. Teddy still hasn't come clean with me about what he does. It's just this unspoken thing that we both know is going on."

"But how can you put up with this? I would have thought you'd have kicked his ass and walked out the door the second you found out."

"There was a time when I would have," Mel said wistfully. "But by the time I found out, we were…entrenched. You have to understand, we lived a very middle-class life for a while. And then Teddy's favorite uncle died and left him a fortune in the will. Suddenly we were flush. Our lifestyle changed. I liked it. I never questioned the little club my husband wanted to join, or why. And then I had Daughton."

"So you felt trapped?" Jessie asked, trying to wrap her head around it.

"I wouldn't go that far," Mel countered. "But when I figured out what was going on, I was used to this new life. I was used to the money and the lifestyle, all of which was made possible by Teddy's money, not mine. And somehow, the club normalized everything, made it seem like it wasn't that big a deal. None of the other wives seemed all that perturbed. So why was I going to make such a big fuss? It felt like it would be almost…rude."

"They brainwashed you."

"No," Mel said. "I wish I could place the blame totally on them. But I'm responsible too. I made a choice. I gave up some of my freedom and a lot of my self-respect. But I got other things in return. As long as I don't rock the boat too much, I get this amazing life. I don't have to work. I can spend time with Daughton. I have financial security. And as long as Teddy doesn't rub my nose in what he's doing, I can pretend everything's copacetic. It was a trade-off I was surprised that I was willing to make."

"I don't think I could make that trade-off," Jessie said.

"You might surprise yourself. You've already started down that road and you didn't even realize it."

"Are you saying that Kyle is cheating on me?" Jessie demanded.

"No. But if he moved here based on Teddy's recommendation, then it's not a coincidence. And you're settling nicely into your big house, taking occasional classes at the local university, and having mid-morning coffee chats with other wives. You've already gotten used to it."

"But I would never get used to Kyle sleeping around."

"You never know what you're capable of until the moment comes," Mel said, her voice suddenly icy. "Please don't judge me for my choices."

"I didn't mean it that way—"

"Let's just move on. I don't want to talk about this anymore."

"I'm sorry."

"It's okay," Mel said. But it clearly wasn't.

# CHAPTER SIXTEEN

Jessie felt like she was going to explode.

It had been more than twenty-four hours since Mel had revealed the truth about Club Deseo. And in the time since, Jessie hadn't discussed it with anyone. Not that there were many choices. She couldn't just bring it up with Kyle, not until she'd fully processed it herself. She didn't feel ready to deal with it formally with Dr. Lemmon. That left one person.

She called Lacey Cartwright that morning, fully expecting to get her voicemail again. But this time, she actually picked up and she had a couple of free hours around lunchtime. That's all Jessie needed. She was in the car and headed for downtown LA within minutes of making plans.

"You need to be straight with Kyle," Lacey said at lunch after listening to the whole story. "Tell him where you stand before it's too late. If he doesn't get it, just move back here. I'll put you up for a while. Hell, I'll even help foot the bill for your divorce lawyer. I know a good one."

She fished a business card out of her purse and tossed it on the table. Jessie was about to reply when the waiter brought over another basket of chicharrones. Lacey had chosen B.S. Taqueria for lunch and Jessie approved, even though she couldn't have their signature drink. It was called a B.S. handshake—a Tecate beer in a can with hot sauce, lime, and salt piled around the mouth. Lacey was on her second and Jessie jealously salivated just looking at it.

While she waited for the server to leave, Jessie debated how to approach the topic with her longtime friend. With her tall, model-thin body, creamy auburn-colored skin, and traffic-stopping good looks, Lacey Cartwright wasn't well-acquainted with the concept of having to compromise. If she wanted something, it usually happened.

She'd known Lacey since college, even longer than Kyle, since they were freshman roommates. But they'd taken very different paths since leaving school. While Jessie had gotten married and had her academic fits and starts on the way to pursuing her master's, Lacey dived right into her passion a week after graduating from USC, working as a buyer in the fashion district for two years before locking in a position with a boutique fashion designer. She was well on her way to starting her own dress design firm before thirty, which had always been essential to her goal of becoming the most influential lesbian African-American fashion designer in America.

But because she was so singularly focused on her career goals (she hadn't been on a date in over a year), Lacey wasn't especially sympathetic to the concessions of a married, well-off white girl, especially one whose husband she had often described as "self-focused." Trying to explain why she didn't just come clean was going to be a challenge.

"It's more complicated than that, Lace," Jessie began. "We're entrenched down there now. We have a home. Kyle loves his job. And I'm having a baby."

"But if he's cheating…" Lacey started to say.

"I don't have any reason to suspect that. I don't even know for sure that he knows about how this club works. I don't want to make any assumptions. We moved there because of his work and conveniently, one of his friends lives nearby. It could be as simple as him wanting to hang out with his buddy and use the club for the connections. I know he's already signed up at least seven members as clients. He doesn't seem restless. If anything, I've never seen him happier, especially with the baby news. It's just that he's…changing."

"How so?" Lacey asked, surprising Jessie by not leaping in with another opinion.

"I don't know," Jessie said hesitantly. "He just seems a little emotionally absent sometimes. I don't know if it's all the work pressure or the new environment or what. He'd say I'm imagining it. He thinks I imagine a lot these days. And maybe he's right. Maybe I'm seeing things that aren't there. But I am seeing them."

"So what do you want to do?"

"He's the father of my unborn child," Jessie said. "He's the love of my life. What I want is to make this work. At one point I wanted us to move back here. But not now. Now I need to see if I can find the man I married in there somewhere. Otherwise it doesn't matter where we move. I need to see if he can be the old Kyle, even with all this new stuff in our lives. I believe that guy's still in there somewhere."

"And if you can't find him again?" Lacey asked.

"Then I guess I have to think about leaving."

The server returned with their entrees and Jessie was glad to stop talking because she was having trouble believing the words that had just come out of her mouth.

Jessie still didn't understand how she was here.

She'd pretty much given up hope of getting to return to DSH-Metro. So it was a surprise when Professor Hosta called her on her way back from lunch with Lacey to tell her she'd received authorization to meet with Bolton Crutchfield again the next day. Unexpectedly, he made no reference to their argument after her last visit.

Now, as she passed through the last exterior door and into the lobby of the NRD unit where Officer Gentry stood waiting for her, a belated thought occurred to her. She'd been so excited about the chance to return that she'd never asked Hosta why she had been granted permission.

She was certain that someone in a position of power was pulling the strings to let her make these visits. But for what purpose, she didn't know. Part of her desperately wanted to solve that mystery. But another, more ambitious part of her worried that asking questions might backfire and shut down the visits entirely. So for now, she resolved to keep her mouth shut.

Officer Gentry reminded her of the rules as they made the walk down the long hallway that led to the NRD unit. She repeated them with the same seriousness of purpose as before, as if it was for the first time.

Cortez was once again manning the security station, though some of the officers were different than the last time. He seemed focused on a task and merely nodded at her, skipping the flirtatious small talk. Maybe he'd been given a talking-to.

Just before they entered Crutchfield's cell, Gentry paused and turned to face Jessie. She was clearly debating whether to say what was on her mind. Finally, very quietly, she spoke.

"He's missed you. Use that to your advantage."

Then she pressed the emergency key fob remote into Jessie's hand and opened the door. They stepped inside. This time Crutchfield was visible right away. He was sitting crosswise on his bed, his back propped against the wall, reading a book.

It was too dark to see what it was and Jessie didn't want to seem overly interested anyway so she sat in the chair from her last visit and kept her head down until Gentry turned up the lights enough for her to actually see clearly. But Crutchfield didn't wait for that to engage her.

"I thought you'd done forgotten about me, Miss Jessie," he said with something bordering on amusement. Apparently he'd decided they were now familiar enough that "ma'am" was no longer necessary.

"I have other patients to visit, Mr. Crutchfield," she said, which was technically true.

She fought the urge to banter with him, even though she suspected it was what he wanted and that it might win her points. She doubted she could keep up. And she sensed, without being told, that keeping things professional, at least initially, would serve as potentially needed psychological armor against whatever he might throw at her.

"You here to answer some more of my questions?" he asked.

"I'm here to ask you some," Jessie said. "If you're forthright, maybe we can come to some accommodation."

"That's not going to be nearly good enough. You only get what you give, a great philosopher once said. I think I need one of those squid pro shows."

"A quid pro quo?" Jessie asked, certain he knew the proper term.

"One of those too," he said. "Question for a question—like last time. It's only fair."

"Can't happen—violation of protocol," Officer Gentry said from somewhere behind Jessie, speaking directly to Crutchfield for the first time during either of their visits. "Last time was a one-off."

Crutchfield glanced over at her and Jessie saw a nearly imperceptible hint of loathing in his eyes. It was gone almost immediately, though he made no effort to hide the nasty grin that came next.

"Then I guess we're plum out of luck," he said, shrugging. "Seems like a waste all around. But it ain't my call."

Jessie turned to Gentry, whose eyes were on Crutchfield.

"Can we please make an exception?" she asked, putting out her most ingénue-ish vibe. "After all, I'm not even a professional. I'm a student. The rules don't have to be so hardcore for me, do they?"

She got the impression that Gentry was playing a role too, helping her by pretending to play hardball.

"Yeah, Kitty Kat," Crutchfield chimed in. "Help a sister out, why don't you?"

Gentry stared hard at Crutchfield before turning her gaze toward Jessie.

"It's a violation of protocol," she repeated, before adding, "I might make an exception but not on those terms. Three questions of yours to every one of his. Take it or leave it."

Jessie turned back to the inmate.

"How about it, Mr. Crutchfield?" Jessie asked.

"A special dispensation!" Crutchfield cheered, his voice dripping with sarcasm and vitriol. "Courtesy of the heroic former Army Ranger. Miss Jessie, you may not be aware of this. But after her time abroad, she returned to protect people here at home, despite her personal scars, both internal and, you know, all over her face. How can I turn down such a generous offer from one who served and sacrificed in distant lands, all on our behalf? I'll take it!"

"Let's begin then," Jessie said quickly, not wanting to lose the momentum and hoping to move away from whatever personal animosity Crutchfield clearly had for Gentry. "Why don't we start with victim selection—what was your method?"

"You sure you want to make that one of your three questions, Miss Jessie?" he asked. "It seems kind of dry to me."

"I'm okay with dry," she replied, deciding to save the questions she really wanted answered for a moment when he was less agitated.

He shrugged and answered.

"I don't rightly know that I ever made a "selection.' I'd see someone and without saying a word, they just spoke to me in some way. It was like a little spotlight was shining on them and I had to follow the spotlight. I reckon that's part of why it took so long for the authorities to find me. I never really had a 'type.' White, black, man, woman, old, young. The light could shine on any of them equally."

As he spoke his voice was largely emotionless. He sounded more like he was reciting IKEA assembly instructions than his method for victim selection. It was as if he knew this wasn't Jessie true area of interest and was, therefore, uninterested himself.

When he was done, she moved immediately to a technical question about how he managed to avoid leaving any trace DNA or other incriminating personal details on the bodies. His answer was direct but equally uninspired and unenlightening.

She finished with a question about how he found and prepped the place where he tortured his victims. He treated it as more of a real estate inquiry than a forensic psychology one and answered it with as much enthusiasm as one would expect. She got the distinct impression that if he could be sure that she alone was hearing his answers, Crutchfield would be much more forthcoming.

As soon as he was done, she saw his eyes light up again. It was his turn. Of course, that was what she had hoped for—that once he got to ask his question, he'd more amenable to answering genuinely probing ones from her.

"Do I get to ask my first one now? Have I been forthcoming enough for you?"

"Go ahead," Jessie said, her voice calm but her spine rigid in anticipation of what was to come.

"All righty then. I was just wondering how the pregnancy's treating you?"

# CHAPTER SEVENTEEN

Jessie kept her expression stone-faced, even as she felt a chill run down her spine. He had asked the question almost giddily and couldn't help but continue without waiting for her response.

"I mean, I can tell you're having trouble keeping stuff down," he said. "I'm not asking about the physical stuff. I'm more curious about how you're handling the prospect of being a parent, because I get the feeling you didn't have much in the way of parental role models to fall back on."

Jessie relaxed her grip on the key fob for fear that her clenched fist might accidentally activate it. The she allowed herself a long, slow exhale before responding.

"How do you know I'm pregnant?" she asked, faking nonchalance at his seeming awareness of her personal family history.

"Now, now, Miss Jessie," he chided playfully. "It's my question time. Don't try to go sneaking in an extra one. So tell me, how are you handling being a future mama when you don't have anything positive to work with in the old memory toolbox?"

Jessie ignored her fast-beating heart as she pretended not to be shaken by his words.

"I'm reading a lot of books," she answered, "and watching *Family Ties* reruns. Those Keatons really knew what they were doing."

"That's not a real answer," Crutchfield said. "But I'm gonna let it slide because I can tell it's a painful subject. You go ahead and ask your next round of interrogatories. I'll just keep my fingers crossed that you'll put on your honesty cap next time it's my turn."

Jessie did just that, setting aside the odd hint of guilt she felt at shortchanging him. Still, she had a plan and she intended to stick with it. So she proceeded with three more procedural questions about the mechanics of his crimes. He responded to all of them fully but without any of his usual witticisms.

"My turn again," he said after finishing his third answer.

"I'm waiting," Jessie replied.

"What's got you so blue, Missy Miss—just the hormones acting up? Or is Mr. Jessie not living up to the image you had bouncing around in your head? Are you starting to doubt the constancy of

94

your other half? That's a dilly of a pickle, isn't it? Not knowing if your man is standing by you?"

"Is there a question in there, Mr. Crutchfield? I got a little lost in the roller coaster of words."

"My apologies, Miss Jessie," he said, all traces of playful sing-songiness gone from his voice. "Let me be more straightforward. You seem sad. Is it because you think your hubby might be stepping out on you?"

Jessie ignored the feeling that her chest was a bull's-eye and he'd just hit it. He seemed to know all her most vulnerable spots. She forced a tight smile and shook her head as if she was amused but disappointed in him.

"If you want me to actually answer your question, Mr. Crutchfield," she said, sounding more composed than she felt," you're going to have to spend less time going for shock value and more asking something I might actually dignify with a response. I'll give you a second swing, just to be polite."

"All righty. Since I think we both know I got my answer on that one, I'll ask you this: does he know how unhappy you are, how restless you feel? Do you think he's fearful he's losing you because of it? You can answer that simple question, can't you, Missy Miss?"

Jessie sized him up and decided to give him a taste. She needed some goodwill for her next question, the one she'd been waiting to ask.

"I've been instructed not to share anything personal with you, Mr. Crutchfield. But I will say this. Big life transitions are hard. Sometimes they make for difficult interpersonal stretches, even among loved ones. That doesn't mean things can't be fixed with open communication and mutual respect. I'm sure you had the same experience with your kinfolk before you moved in here."

She knew that last dig was risky, that taunting him might shut him down and put all her efforts to cultivate him at risk. But he seemed to enjoy her crack, smilingly impishly and revealing a set of crooked, yellowed teeth.

"You're just full of piss and vinegar, ain't you, Miss Jessie? Well, go on, it's your turn then."

"Tell me about your visitors," she said plainly.

His smile faded a fraction. His eyes bored into hers. She could tell he knew what she was after.

"My goodness," he replied, feigning a struggle to remember. "I've been locked up in here so long, I couldn't possibly recall all the doctors who done come in and out over the years."

"I think you know what I mean, Mr. Crutchfield. I'm not talking about psychologists or law enforcement. I'm asking about honest-to-goodness visitors—people here without a professional obligation."

"I don't believe I've ever had a regular visitor call on me just to chitchat, Miss Jessie."

Jessie stood up and started to gather her pen and notepad.

"I answered you honestly," she said. "I thought I could count on you to do the same. I thought you were a man of your word. But apparently you'd rather hide behind technicalities. So I guess we're done."

She started for the door and began to really believe she might have to leave when he finally called her back.

"Well, hold on there, darlin'. Give me a minute to review my recollections. I'm not as young as I used to be, after all."

Jessie turned and waited expectantly, still standing, making no effort to return to her seat.

"Don't play games. Either answer me or don't. But don't waste my time."

"Well, aren't you just a steel magnolia?" he marveled. "Like in that movie with the gal who was that New York City mermaid. Now that I'm refreshing myself, I can call to mind one guest stopping by under false pretenses."

"What do you mean?" Jessie demanded.

"A gentleman caller, if memory serves, who had the look of a medical professional, but as it turned out, was just pretending."

Officer Gentry stepped forward.

"Are you saying someone got in here and talked to you while pretending to be a doctor?" she asked, her voice filled with urgency.

"I only answer queries from Miss Jessie, G.I. Jane," he answered curtly.

Jessie looked back and forth between them, nearly choking on their shared animosity.

"Are you saying someone got in here and talked to you while pretending to be a doctor?" Jessie repeated, as much for herself as for Gentry.

"I am. A curious fellow, that one was."

"In what way?" Jessie asked.

"Well, we're way past your three questions, Miss Jessie. So I'm going to insist on asking one more of my own before I answer yours."

"Go ahead," Jessie said, just wanting to get it over with so she could get back to her question.

"No need to be rude, Miss Jessie. I was just wondering why you're asking me a question you already know the answer to."

Jessie had an answer for that one.

"Suspecting and knowing aren't the same thing, Mr. Crutchfield," she said. "I was hoping you could help me make the leap from one to the other."

"Indeed I might."

"So in what way was he curious, Mr. Crutchfield?"

"It's just that he made his visit a couple years ago, so his topic of discussion seems a little peculiar in retrospect."

"And what was that topic?"

"I expect you already know, Miss Jessie, that the topic under discussion was you."

# CHAPTER EIGHTEEN

Gentry waited until they had left Crutchfield's room, gone past the security station, and rushed down the long hallway and into her small office next to the changing room to speak.

"Do you want to tell me what the hell is going on?" she demanded as she shut the door.

"What do you mean?" Jessie asked, surprised by the intensity Gentry displayed.

"You're clearly not just here to do a master's practicum. What is this really about?"

Jessie felt a flush of angry resentment well up inside her and gulped hard to contain it.

"How about I answer that when *you* start being honest with me?" she said forcefully.

"Me? I've been trying to help you," Gentry said. "I'm not the one who has some secret conversation going on with a guy I've never met."

"No," Jessie spat back. "But you definitely have some secrets of your own. And maybe I'll start trusting you once you tell me why an inexperienced grad student like me is being allowed to interrogate a serial killer. Don't get me wrong. I'm glad to be here. But we both know that this is way outside of standard practice. And I can tell that you are seriously uncomfortable with it. But you keep letting me in there. Why?"

Gentry stared at her for several seconds, her eyes filled with a mix of surprise and frustration.

"That's something you'll have to address with your professor friend," she finally answered. "He's the one who ensured your authorization."

"But you're in charge of security for the unit," Jessie countered. "You could overrule him if you thought my visits were a security risk. And yet you haven't done that."

"Are you suggesting that your visits *are* a security risk, Ms. Hunt?" Gentry asked accusingly.

"I know that my visits rile him up and that you don't love that. But for some reason, you've decided that's a risk worth taking. What's the reason?"

Gentry stood there silently for a moment. She seemed to be weighing just how much she should, or even could, say. For a second, Jessie thought she was about to come clean. But then her expression changed and she knew that the security chief had decided to play it safe.

"Talk to Hosta," Gentry said reluctantly.

Jessie tried to keep her irritation in check, but couldn't help tossing out one last barb as she barreled out of the office.

"Way to follow orders, Kitty Kat."

\*

The next day, Professor Hosta asked her to stay after class.

"I understand your interview subject was especially chatty yesterday," he said, looking excited as they walked down the hallway toward his office.

Jessie had spent most of a sleepless night and all of her drive to school today debating how best to challenge Hosta about what was going on. But something about his tone made her stop.

She couldn't place exactly why, but she suddenly felt that calling him out would be a mistake. Revealing that she knew her permission to visit Crutchfield was part of some grand plan— possibly set in motion by The Panel—would put her at a disadvantage in whatever larger game was being played. So she bit her tongue.

"Yeah," she said as mildly as she could. "He seems to be warming up to me, which is both rewarding and terrifying."

"Well, good for you, Ms. Hunt," he replied. "You're well on your way in terms of your practicum. Barring anything unforeseen, I'd say your degree is almost a formality at this point."

Jessie let the "barring anything unforeseen" comment go, unsure whether it was innocuous or a subtle warning to stay in line. Clearly he still had a bit of residual resentment from their argument in the hospital parking lot all those weeks ago.

"Then I guess I can bail on classroom work for the rest of the semester?" she asked jokingly.

"That would hurt my feelings immensely," he said, playing along. "Besides, I think you'll definitely want to attend next session. I'll share a little secret I kept from the rest of the class."

"What's that?"

"We're having a guest speaker. He's actually from your neck of the woods; Detective Ryan Hernandez of LAPD, downtown bureau."

"Oh cool," Jessie said. "What will he be discussing?"

"I don't want to spoil too much. But I will say that he's in their Robbery Homicide Division. I think you'll find his perspective very illuminating. He was actually a patrol officer when your friend Crutchfield was apprehended. He played an instrumental role, although I'll let him share the details. Suffice to say, I wouldn't skip out."

Jessie nodded pleasantly and left. The whole walk to her car, she fought the urge to turn around, go back, and confront Hosta about whatever secrets he was keeping.

It was only when she pulled into her driveway that the feeling subsided. And that was because Kyle's car was in the driveway. He was home early.

She parked on the street and entered quietly though the front door. She slid off her shoes before going up the stairs. As she approached their bedroom, she thought she heard a distant squeaking coming from the direction of the future nursery. Part of her desperately wanted to go check it out. But reassuring herself that it was just typical house settling, she forced the urge from her mind and continued down the hall.

Opening the bedroom door, she could hear the shower running. Thankfully, the sound blocked out the now-distant squeak. She walked over silently to the half-closed bathroom door, listening for any unusual sound. Hearing none, she called in.

"Home early?"

She heard a gasp and a thump.

"Jeez, Jess, you scared the hell out of me."

"Sorry about that," she said. "Everything okay? I heard a noise."

"I dropped the soap."

"Don't slip on it," she said. "To what do I owe the honor of your early arrival?"

"The club is sponsoring an event at a Westport wine bar," he shouted over the water. "I thought it might be fun to go. You up for it?"

"It's not at the actual club?" Jessie asked, unable to contain her surprise.

"No, Jess," he answered, sounding slightly annoyed. "It's at another location entirely. I thought a change of pace might be nice."

"Sounds lovely," she replied, "even if I can't partake of the beverages. Should I dress up?"

"Sure. Maybe wear that red cocktail dress you look so great in. I'll be out in a few."

Jessie retreated to the closet to look for the dress. It was only as she was sliding hangers to the side that the realization hit her— she'd been snooping. Why else would she skulk up the stairs?

*Was I hoping to catch Kyle in the shower with some bimbo?*

Somehow she'd let Crutchfield's dig get in her head. But her husband wasn't cheating. He'd come home early so he could take her out for a fun night. And now she was consumed by guilt. She yanked the dress off the rod angrily, fuming at herself for not seeing how she'd been manipulated by a drawling hick stuck in an enclosed glass cell.

*

On the drive to the wine bar, Jessie wondered whether she should come clean with Kyle about the whole situation with Teddy and Mel Carlisle. He still didn't know she's told Mel about seeing Teddy with the hostess. Or that Mel had revealed the true nature of Club Deseo. She didn't love keeping secrets from him.

Besides, part of her wanted to ask if he was aware of what was really going on there. But she wasn't sure she wanted the answer. What would it mean if he did know? Was that what he wanted—to have an open marriage? Or did he not care about that stuff and just liked going because of the connections and the golfing?

By the time they got to the wine bar, she still hadn't decided, which she interpreted as a sign that she was better off keeping her own counsel for now. This was a discussion to have in the privacy of their home, not as they were pulling up to an event sponsored by the very club she was suspicious of.

The place was less of a classy wine bar and more of a music-thumping nightclub with a small private room that had a bar in the back corner. This seemed to be a different crowd from the folks Kyle usually hung out with at the club. She recognized faces but didn't know many names.

Kyle grabbed a huge glass of Cabernet and introduced her around. Pretty soon, he'd headed off in search of another drink and she was engaged in an agreeable chat with a woman named Gina.

"Are you guys going to the Bringing the Boats in Party tomorrow night?" she asked.

"I heard about that when we first moved here," Jessie said. "But I don't really know what it is."

"It's an East Coast tradition," Gina explained. "One last boat-centric hurrah before the weather gets too cold to go out on the water. Of course, in Southern California it never gets too cold to take a boat out so it's essentially just another excuse for a big bash. You should go. It's a great chance to see people embarrass themselves, maybe even me. Last year I woke up on a boat in the middle of the night wearing nothing but a life preserver. Still don't know how that happened."

After what had to be a half hour of listening to Gina's war stories without Kyle anywhere in sight, Jessie excused herself to go look for him. She was unexpectedly, voraciously itching to find some real food. There were only hors d'oeuvres here, all of which made her feel mildly nauseated.

She searched the main nightclub area and then the bathrooms but he was nowhere to be found. She grabbed a security guard, described her husband, and asked if he'd seen him. He nodded and pointed in the direction of a dark hallway toward the back of the club. She wandered back but only found one door with a "staff only" sign on it.

Reluctantly, she opened the door and peeked in. It looked like an employee break room, with a couple of vending machines and two circular tables littered with dirty plates. She heard voices from somewhere further back and headed in that direction until she came to a door marked "Manager's Office. It was slightly ajar.

Glancing through the opening, she saw a guy who looked vaguely familiar sitting behind a desk. She was pretty sure he was a Club Deseo member. He was giggling uncontrollably at something a person out of view had just said. She recognized the other voice immediately and pushed the door open all the way.

Standing with his back to her was Kyle. He was leaning over a corner of the manager's desk and snorting a line of white powder through a rolled up bill. Lying on the table nearby was his ludicrous gold "$" money clip. He did a second line, oblivious to the fact that his buddy, having seen Jessie, had suddenly stopped laughing.

"That works!" Kyle bellowed as he stood up and exhaled happily.

He glanced at his buddy and seemed to get that something was off even before turning around. When he did, there was still coke residue around his nostrils and his eyes were glistening in the fluorescent lights.

"Hey, Jess," he said, his voice an unsettling mix of giddiness and shame.

Without a word, she turned and stormed out.

# CHAPTER NINETEEN

Jessie took a Lyft home. By the time Kyle got there, she had a bag packed for him.

"This is for the hotel you'll be staying at tonight," she said, dropping it at his feet.

"Jessie, I'm sorry. I made a poor choice. But don't you think you're overreacting a little bit?"

"To what?" she demanded. "My husband abandoning his pregnant wife for half an hour at some strange, cheesy nightclub? Or finding him snorting cocaine in a back room like he's an extra in a Martin Scorsese movie? There are so many choices."

"Look," Kyle began, "Coy was doing it and he offered me a hit. I was super close to signing him as a client and I thought saying no would scuttle the deal. It was a dumb move, I admit. But it was a one-time thing."

"First of all, 'Coy was doing it'? I don't even know what to do with that sentence. And also, really? Because you weren't acting like it was a one-time thing. According to you, that was 'the stuff!' I barely recognize you these days, Kyle. Where's the guy who gets sleepy after two beers? Where's the guy who said every competitor who gets high just makes it easier for you to swoop in and steal his clients while he's not paying attention?"

"I'm right here," he insisted. "I made one bad choice."

"Well, it's a choice that's going to have you looking for a place to sleep tonight. Maybe the country club has special rooms for husbands who have been kicked out, not that any wives around here would have the courage to do something like that."

"I really think you're making a mountain out of a mole hill," he said calmly, though his eyes were still glassy.

"A mole hill? How am I supposed to trust you after this? What else are you doing behind my back?"

His face twitched slightly at the accusation and Jessie could tell his guilt had given way to something else. Anger maybe?

"What else am I doing?" he asked. "How about providing for our family!"

Jessie realized she'd judged wrong. He wasn't channeling anger but rather self-righteousness. That only infuriated her more.

"I'm not sure we have a family anymore," she replied, her voice steady and icier than she expected. "If this doesn't change, I'm leaving you."

He stared at her in disbelief. For several seconds he didn't speak. When he finally opened his mouth, she was sure it was to beg forgiveness.

"No, Jessica, you're not," he said, equally cold. "We are a family. This is just a hiccup. Besides, that is my baby you're carrying. So you won't be going anywhere."

"Is that a threat?" she demanded incredulously.

"It's a prediction."

"Get out," she said, pointing to the door. "Call yourself a rideshare and get out now or I'm calling the cops. You're still high and I don't think a drug bust will look too great down at the firm. They don't even approve of unmarried employees. How do you think they'll feel about a cokehead?"

He looked like he wanted to say something else but thought better of it. Instead he picked up the bag and left. It was only when she heard the car pull out and speed off down the road that Jessie felt everything give way.

She slumped to the floor, pressing her back against the wall for support. Heaving sobs wracked her entire body. It was ten minutes before she had the strength to stand again. When she rose, she slowly went to the kitchen table, where she'd tossed her purse, and fished around for the business card Lacey had jokingly given her at lunch the other day. It took a moment but she found it: Craig Plessey, Divorce Attorney.

She moved into the front room, slumped down on the couch, and dialed the number, which went straight to voicemail. After the beep she spoke, listening to her own disconnected voice as if she were a spirit, watching events from a distant remove.

"My name is Jessie Hunt. I'd like to make an appointment."

Overwhelmed by anguish and exhaustion, she dropped the phone on the coffee table and closed her eyes. She was asleep within seconds.

\*

The woods were thick and it was brutally cold. Jessie's small, bare feet, half-numb, were bloody from trampling on rocks and twigs. But she thought she saw a clearing in the distance so she ignored the pain she felt and kept moving. A branch tore at her "Sabrina, the Teenage Witch" nightgown but she didn't stop.

Finally there was a break in the trees. She started to sprint. Only at the last moment did she realize that the open space before her was actually the edge of a cliff. She pulled up hard, digging her toes into the dirt and teetering dangerously over the edge. She managed to halt her momentum and drop to the ground.

She clutched at the frost-covered weeds at the rim of the precipice and looked over. At least fifty feet below was a raging river with churning white rapids. The rumble of the water smashing into the ravine walls sounded like thunder. But even over that, she could hear another sound. Behind her were his heavy footsteps, moving steadily but unhurried, crunching the twigs under his boots.

She didn't look back. Instead she stood up, her toes poking out into nothingness, trying to muster the strength to jump. And every second, the boots behind her got closer.

\*

She woke up in a pool of sweat. It wasn't yet light out, but Jessie, breathing heavily and worried her heart might beat out of her chest, got off the couch and went upstairs to shower. After that, she went back down for some decaf coffee and whatever food she could manage to keep down.

It was hard to find something to take her mind off recent events. She couldn't concentrate enough to study or even read a book. She didn't feel up to going through the remaining unopened packing boxes. She turned on the television and flipped around.

But even mindless TV didn't do the trick. Food shows made her sick to her stomach. Home renovation programs only reminded her of her own depressing home life. Even her "go-to" fantasy series, *Supernatural*, was showing an episode involving a demon invading people's dreams. That hit way too close to home. So she spent most of the morning watching reruns of *The Office*.

When she heard the knock on the door, she glanced at the clock and saw that she'd somehow zoned out for close to two hours. She muted the TV and walked to the front door. Peeking through the dining room curtains, she saw that it was Kimberly Miner, who was carrying a box. Despite every fiber of her being shouting not to, Jessie opened the door.

"Hi," Kimberly said. "I brought you a peace offering."

She held out her arms to reveal that she was holding a box of doughnuts from the same place Jessie had gotten hers all those months ago. She looked from the box back to Kimberly's face to find an unexpected expression there: sympathy.

"Hi," she said, taking the box. "Thank you. Do you want to come in?"

"I'm sorry. I can't. I have to take my daughter to a swimming lesson. But I just wanted to give you these and say I'm sorry things got so... sideways between us."

"I'm sorry too," Jessie said, still confused. "I should have minded my own business."

"It's hard, when you want to do the right thing, when you want to help someone you don't know that well but you're not sure how."

"It is," Jessie agreed, not sure what else to say.

There was a long, awkward pause. Kimberly finally broke it.

"Will I see you tonight at the Bringing the Boats in Party? It's always a pretty good time."

"Oh jeez," Jessie said, her heart sinking. "I completely forgot about that. I'm not sure what's going to happen with it."

"Okay, well if you do go and you're looking for a friendly face, find me, okay?"

"Sure," Jessie promised. "Thanks, Kimberly."

Her neighbor reached out and gave her arm a friendly squeeze. Then she turned and headed back across the street. Jessie took the box of doughnuts into the kitchen and dropped them on the counter. Only then did she notice that the kitchen window, one that faced the Miners' house, was open, just like it had been last night when she kicked Kyle out.

Her stomach did a little, anxious somersault. How much of their fight last night had Kimberly heard? Clearly enough to feel she had to bring over compassion doughnuts. Suddenly Jessie knew what it felt like to have the secret doors of her private life pried open. She felt ill.

*

Jessie sat in the waiting room several hours later, trying to catch her breath without looking too frazzled to the women around her.

In addition to the Bringing the Boats in Party, she'd also forgotten about her first OB-GYN appointment. When her phone reminder went off an hour before she was supposed to be there, she had to scramble to throw on decent clothes and get out the door.

Traffic was bad and she was running late. But when she called to tell them, the receptionist said not to worry as they were backed up too. Still, she didn't arrive at the Beverly Hills office until fifteen minutes after her scheduled time.

When she was finally called back for her first ultrasound nearly a half hour later, she calmed down enough that she didn't fear having her blood pressure taken. The nurse ran through her history, took her pressure (*117/76—yay!*) and temperature and asked an endless series of questions.

Finally she had Jessie lie back so she could apply the gel for the ultrasound. She settled in and took deep breaths. Within moments, she heard the rat-a-tat drumbeat of a tiny heart. She looked over anxiously at the nurse.

"Sounds healthy," the woman said without even looking over. She must have been used to Jessie's reaction.

She moved the transducer around for several more minutes, doing a variety of calculations. Eventually she turned off the machine and wiped the goop off Jessie's skin.

"Can you tell the gender of the baby?" Jessie asked, both excited and apprehensive.

"Not yet, at least not using the ultrasound. We'll probably be able to tell between sixteen and twenty weeks. And you're only at about nine. There is a blood test you can take if you're really dying to know. Are you interested?"

Jessie nodded enthusiastically. She knew some people liked the mystery of it all but not her. She was a woman who liked getting answers. And if there was a way to get this one, she was going to use it.

"Oh," the nurse said as she reviewed Jessie's chart. "I realized I missed a section on your paperwork. Is there a spouse or significant other we should mark down with contact information for emergencies?"

Jessie looked at her and started to answer, then closed her mouth. She glanced away as tears welled up in her eyes. She realized she didn't truly know the answer to the question. Had her life partner just temporarily lost his way? Was he a cokehead now? Or worse? The possibility depressed her. But more than that, it scared her. She'd never felt more alone.

## CHAPTER TWENTY

Jessie was startled out of her afternoon nap by the sound of the garage door opening. She rolled over and glanced at the clock—3:45 p.m. That was way too early for Kyle to get home, even if he thought he was welcome. Nervous, she pulled on some sweatpants and a T-shirt and started down the stairs. She was tempted to grab the baseball bat from the closet but told herself not to jump to conclusions.

As she reached the bottom of the stairs, she heard the familiar sound of Kyle dropping his keys in the basket by the garage door. A wave of resentment overtook her and she stomped in that direction.

*He's just going to show up like everything's normal after last night?*

When she rounded the corner, she saw her husband on his knees on the kitchen floor. She stopped in her tracks, dumbfounded.

"What the…" she began.

"Jessie," he said, his voice quieter than she was used to, "please hear me out."

Something about his tone stopped her from ripping into him. She nodded and he continued.

"I'm sorry…for everything. I did go to a hotel last night where I got almost no sleep. Not because of anything wrong with the place but because of something wrong with me. I just lay in bed all night staring up at the ceiling, thinking about how I got in this situation. And I realized—I didn't just *get* in this situation. I put myself in it."

He shifted his weight and winced slightly. His knees were probably killing him on the stone kitchen floor. Jessie was tempted to tell him to get up but she didn't want to interrupt. And truthfully, she kind of liked seeing him uncomfortable.

"I couldn't concentrate all day," he continued. "My boss actually reamed me out at one point because I was so out of it. But all I kept thinking about was all the ways I've messed things up. I pushed you to move here, even though you loved living downtown. I insisted on joining Club Deseo because of the contacts I could make. I've been such a workaholic that I jumped at every golf outing on the outside chance that it might land me a client. I've been so focused on moving up that I didn't give enough thought to how you were adjusting."

"Get up," Jessie said, after he grimaced a second time. As he pulled himself upright, she added, "I know your work is important to you, Kyle. That's not the issue."

"I know. But still, sometimes I have to remind myself that not every human interaction is about work. I didn't have to make every visit to the club be about snagging another account. We could have simply enjoyed a night out there without making it a business opportunity. And I know last night was beyond. Obviously if I'm using the possibility of securing a possible client as an excuse to snort cocaine, I've crossed a line. I'm embarrassed that I didn't see it in the moment. Looking back now, I can't believe that was me."

"I couldn't either," Jessie agreed quietly. "I didn't recognize you."

"Neither did I, Jess," he said with an urgency that sounded almost anguished. "But all that stops now. I want to get back to the old me, the guy you recognize. The guy you love. So I have a proposal."

Jessie, despite being intrigued, felt a little lightheaded, as she often did these days, so she moved to one of the kitchen barstools and sat down.

"I'm listening," she said.

"Tonight is the Bringing the Boats in Party. I think it's the perfect chance to let folks at the club know that we—I—will be scaling back time spent there: far fewer golf outings, not going to as many Oath Minder meetings, that sort of thing. The pregnancy is a perfect excuse. I'll just let them know that for the foreseeable future, they'll be seeing less of me."

Jessie allowed herself to imagine a world where the two of them could just curl up on the couch to spend an evening binge-watching something.

"I have to admit, that sounds nice," she said.

"It does to me too. And this way, I can tell everyone on the same night, when they're all in a good mood because of the party. I don't have to sit people down for 'serious' conversations. I can just mention it casually in passing and move on to the next person. It'll be more natural that way. Plus we can just have fun, sort of a last big blowout before we go into nesting mode. What do you think?"

*I think I'd rather not go at all. But this seems like a reasonable compromise.*

"I think it makes sense," she said, keeping her thoughts to herself. "Although I'm not sure how much energy I have to go hopping from boat to boat all night."

"Then we'll cut out early if we have to," he said. "Or you can just crash in the cabin of someone's boat if you get that tired. I hear that happens all the time at this thing. Everyone's very accommodating, from what I've been told."

"I guess," Jessie said, not overly enthused at the idea of sleeping in some stranger's bed on an unfamiliar boat.

Kyle seemed to sense her hesitation.

"I'll follow your lead on that, babe," he promised. "Which is something I should have done this whole time. That's the other thing I wanted to say. If you really hate it here, we can move back. It's true I wanted our kids to have an actual house with an actual yard. But none of that matters if you're unhappy. It's not about *where* we live. It's about *how* we live. And I want to live with you, wherever we hang our hats at the end of the day."

"You'd just willingly move?" she asked, stunned. "After only being here a few months?"

"It's not ideal. And I'll admit it's not my preference. But I care about us more than any job or town. So if that's what you decide you need to be happy, then of course I'd do it."

Jessie, suddenly emotional but still too wiped out to get up at that moment, motioned for Kyle to come over to her. As he did she held out her arms. He leaned in and wrapped his own arms around her, enveloping her in the warmth and security she hadn't realized how much she needed.

"I missed you," she said quietly.

"Me too," he whispered back, his breath hot on her ear. "But we're going to get back to a good place. And if you're not up for it, we don't even have to go tonight. I just thought it made sense."

"It does. We'll go. Knowing that it's kind of a last hurrah will give me that extra boost of energy."

"Thanks, babe," he said, squeezing her tight. They stayed like that for a long time.

"Oh, I forgot to tell you," she said, when they finally separated, "I saw the doctor today. I heard the heartbeat!"

He looked excited and sad at once.

"I'm so sorry I missed that. Next time for sure."

"You want to see the first baby picture?" she asked, moving quickly past the still painful fact that he hadn't been there.

"Of course," he said, a goofy grin on his face.

"Now don't get too excited. It's kind of hard to discern too much. And we don't know the gender yet, although I'm getting that info expedited. But still…"

She showed him the ultrasound image. He stared at it, his eyes welling up. A tear trickled down his cheek but he made no attempt to wipe it away.

They moved over to the couch, where they spent the next couple of hours looking online at different crib options and searching baby name meanings. Kyle's phone rang once but he gave it only a passing glance before putting it on silent and settling in with her.

By the time they had to get changed for the party, Jessie felt like their blowup from the night before was ancient history. She tossed Kimberly's doughnuts in the trash, grateful for the sentiment but not wanting any reminders of the unpleasantness she hoped was now just a memory.

## CHAPTER TWENTY ONE

Jessie was worried the boat she was on was going to tip over.

She'd never seen so many people at the club at one time. And it seemed like all of them were crowded on the boat she was on. She pushed her way through the crowd and stepped out onto the dock, where she needed several deep breaths to calm down.

It had been like this since they arrived two hours earlier.

Members, some dressed in tuxes and evening gowns, swarmed the club and the adjoining section of the marina dedicated to it. Jessie felt underdressed in her top, slacks, and jacket. She'd heard they would be moving from boat to boat and assumed people would want to dress comfortably and warm, considering the chill in the air. Kyle must have assumed the same because he hadn't gone the tuxedo route either, opting for his standard suit and tie option.

They were on their third boat of the evening when Jessie bumped into Kimberly. The crowd was so thick that she hadn't seen her until they were face to face. Her neighbor, dressed in a slinky, cream-colored, beaded, flapper-style get-up, looked around and saw that Kyle was separated from them by a wall of people.

"How are you doing?" she asked quietly.

"I'm good," Jessie said, believing her words for the first time in a long while. "I'm actually doing really well."

"Remember what I said about friendly faces. If you feel like you need to get out of this madhouse and talk, I'm available."

"I appreciate that, Kimberly. But I think I'm okay."

Just then, Kyle arrived. Kimberly gave him a polite nod before moving on.

"Are things better between you two?" he asked, surprised.

"We made up," Jessie said, leaving it at that.

They walked down the dock to a section less choked with humanity and leaned against the railing, taking it all in. From here, they could see the array of twinkling lights that lit up the outside of the club. It was like Christmas had come two months early.

Staffers were everywhere. It seemed like the club had hired dozens more, just to handle the demand for drinks and appetizers. Every few seconds, a man in a trim suit or one of those hostesses in a tight black miniskirt would come by, offering something to eat or drink. Jessie marveled at the girls' ability to navigate the wooden dock in their high heels, even as she resented them for their true reason for being there.

"Do you want a bite to eat?" Kyle asked her. "You must be starving."

"I could nosh," Jessie admitted, suddenly aware of the gnawing pit in her stomach.

"And what about a drink? I know it's supposed to be verboten. But are you allowed to have a tiny bit? Maybe a few sips of celebratory champagne?"

"I think a few sips are okay," Jessie said. "But not more than that."

"Okay, I'll be back in a few minutes."

He headed off into the throng and within seconds, was lost in a sea of formal wear. While she waited, Jessie saw Melanie, wearing a simple black gown, one dock over and called out to her. They carefully made their way to each other and met on the bridge connecting the docks.

"Where's Teddy?" Jessie asked. He was nowhere in sight.

"Officially, he's checking in with some of the Oath Minder guys. Unofficially, I would guess he's checking in with someone else."

The acid in her voice betrayed the resentment she felt at the arrangement she claimed to have made her peace with. Apparently, Jessie wasn't such an outlier in thinking the "pact" so many of these couples had made was crazy. She realized they hadn't talked since Mel had revealed the truth about the club and wondered if the conversation had reopened some wounds.

"Are you okay?" she asked.

"I will be," Mel replied. "It just backs up on me sometimes. But it's the deal I made so I have to push through, you know?"

Jessie nodded, though she didn't know at all. Mel shook her head as if trying to shake the thought from her brain.

"And how are you handling your recent…awakening?"

"Muddling through," Jessie said, not wanting to rub her new friend's nose in her recently revitalized marriage. "But I'll get there."

"I have no doubt. You're a tough cookie, Jessie. I knew that within minutes of meeting you."

"What do you mean?" Jessie asked.

"Nothing. There's just something about you, something in your eyes. They're steely. I can tell that you've dealt with far more trying times than this. And clearly you found a way through them because here you are, standing tall and unbowed."

"Thank you, Mel," Jessie said, feeling an unexpected and unwanted rush of emotion hit her. "I really appreciate that."

"Of course. We have to stick together, right?"

Jessie nodded and was about to respond when she saw Teddy, wearing a loud blue tux, at the far end of the dock. Mel saw him too.

"I better get over there," she sighed. "He's had quite a few already. I'm a little worried he might fall in the water."

She squeezed Jessie's hand before disappearing in the crowd. Jessie turned her attention back to Teddy and saw that he was talking to one of the hostesses and another man, who was blocked from her sight by a crowd of partiers. But when one of them shifted positions, she realized the third person was Kyle.

He was holding two glasses of champagne and listening to some animated story Teddy was sharing and the hostess was giggling at. The girl, blonde and gorgeous, wore a tiny black number that barely covered her golden tan skin.

Every few seconds, she would look over at Kyle and touch his forearm or hand in a far too familiar way. Jessie noticed that he shifted slightly away from her each time she did it. But inevitably, she'd sidle up close to him again. Eventually, he said something to Teddy and turned back in Jessie's direction.

He deftly navigated the mass of people between them and when he finally reached her, extended one of the champagne glasses to her.

"Sip it stealthily," he said. "I don't want any moral finger-waggers giving us a hard time."

"I see you made a new friend," Jessie noted, nodding across the dock at the scantily clad bimbette, who was still talking to Teddy but kept glancing over at Kyle. Melanie arrived at her husband's side at that moment, looking none too happy.

Kyle looked confused at first but then followed Jessie's gaze and saw who she was referencing.

"Oh, yeah," he said in a tone of weary resignation. "That's Natalia. She's from Ukraine and she's been living here for three months. She's super-friendly, as you might have noticed; very touchy-feely. I think she's looking for a sugar daddy to pay for her English language lessons and her suntan lotion."

"You don't sound smitten," Jessie said as she surreptitiously took a sip of the bubbly.

"Is that jealousy I hear in your voice, Jessica Madeline? I wouldn't worry too much. She's a little transparent."

114

"I'm surprised the club would hire someone like that," Jessie probed, trying to determine how much her husband really knew about how this place operated.

"I think they scraped the bottom of the Westport Beach barrel for tonight because the event is so massive. My guess is they'd rather have a pretty girl who can't hold a tray properly than a legitimate server who weighs more than a hundred fifteen pounds."

"That's very evolved of you to say," Jessie replied.

"Don't give me too much credit," he said. "Part of what irks me is that this is supposed to be a classy place. And she is definitely *not* classy. She told me she works most nights at some strip club I can't remember the name of; offered me a discount on private dances."

Jessie let that comment settle into her skull, then forced herself to inhale and exhale deeply before replying.

"For the amount of money we shelled out for the membership here, you'd think they could have gone with lingerie models," she said after taking another quick sip.

She tried to sound as nonchalant as possible but could hear the bitter edge in her own voice. He didn't seem to catch it, chuckling appreciatively at her snark.

She tried to smile back but suddenly the weight of the evening hit her. She was already tired from the pregnancy. And that, coupled with having to dress up, play nice all night, *and* navigate rickety docks and unstable boats, had taken its toll. She felt a fog of exhaustion settle in on her.

"Are you okay, babe?" Kyle asked, apparently noticing her full body slump.

"I'm just really tired," she admitted. "Two hours of this is about my max. I'm on the verge of getting grumpy. Can we please wrap it up so I can go home and sleep for twelve hours?"

"Absolutely," he promised. "Just give me ten minutes to say my last round of goodbyes since I'll be scarce around here after tonight. Why don't you sit on that bench over there? I'll come and get you as soon as I'm done."

"Fine, but please hurry," Jessie said, finishing the last of her champagne. "Otherwise you'll be carrying me out of here."

Kyle nodded and hurried off. Jessie glanced at her watch—10:01 p.m.

*So late. So tired.*

She sat down heavily on the bench and watched him fade into the crowd. She breathed deeply, trying to regain her equilibrium. The sparkly lights of the club against the night sky, combined with the shiny clothes and jewelry of the women nearby, were giving her a headache.

She closed her eyes and pictured herself elsewhere. An image immediately popped into her head. She and Kyle were back downtown, in a huge new condo in their old neighborhood, unpacking all the boxes from their move back to the city. Then she pictured her master's diploma on the wall of her little nook of an office, where she'd set up shop during her maternity leave.

She imagined herself going into the baby's room to change a diaper and then rocking the little one back to sleep as she got up to speed on her new position at some impressive law enforcement agency. LAPD? FBI? Maybe on staff at NRD? The options were seemingly limitless.

Her daydream was interrupted by the sound of a brittle foreign voice. She opened her eyes and looked up to see the stripper/hostess Natalia standing in front of her, speaking in broken, nearly unintelligible English.

"What?" she asked.

"I say, you vant 'nother bubble dreenk?"

The girl was unsteadily balancing a tray of champagne glasses, despite using both hands.

"No, thanks," Jessie said.

"Okay, sure," Natalia said with way more enthusiasm than the situation required. "You vant food maybe? I see you here lonely looking. Maybe eat help?"

"No, I'm good," Jessie said, trying to keep the frustration bubbling up inside her from spilling over. The gall of this woman, flirting with her husband and then acting as if everything was cool, had her feeling testy. "I'm just waiting for my husband."

"Oh yes, Kyle. Very nice man. Very funny. You very lucky lady."

"You think?" Jessie said, pushing off from the bench to stand up. She towered over Natalia by at least six inches. Looking down at the woman, she noticed that she wasn't as pretty up close. Her foundation was caked on to hide her acne and her mascara was heavy and clumping in places.

"Yes," Natalia repeated. "Kyle is nice husband, for sure."

"Yeah, and he's *my* husband," Jessie said, unable to contain her vitriol. She knew her voice was louder than she intended but she was beyond caring.

Natalia looked startled and stumbled back. She lost her balance and several of the champagne glasses teetered dangerously.

"Yes, good husband," she said, apparently unable to think of anything else to add.

"Yeah, *husband*," Jessie repeated furiously, taking a step toward the smaller woman. "That means not available for you to get your claws into. So you can stop touching him and giggling every time he coughs, got it, Natalia?"

The girl took another step back and snagged her heel in a divot in the dock. She crumpled to the ground and the tray of glasses went with her, shattering on the wood. Jessie stood over her, glaring down, full of rage and a little bit of satisfaction.

Suddenly Kyle was at her side.

"What is going on?" he demanded, looking back and forth between them.

"Just getting a few things straight with your little friend," Jessie said, feeling self-satisfied.

"Jeez, Jess. Don't you think you're going a little overboard?"

"Are you defending her?" Jessie shot back.

"No," he insisted. "It's just...you're yelling at the staff. She doesn't deserve this."

"She's a gold-digging skank, Kyle. I'm just calling her out on it."

The people nearby, already talking in hushed voices, fell completely silent. The only sounds were waves sloshing against boat hulls and Natalia's quiet whimpering. Some random guy rushed over to help her to her feet. As he did, Jessie noticed the girl wasn't wearing any panties.

She was about to comment on that when she suddenly felt lightheaded. She reached out for the back of the bench but it was too far away and she felt herself falling backward as her legs gave out. She raised her arms instinctively around her abdomen to protect that area from the impact of the imminent fall.

But before she hit the ground, Kyle was there, his arms underneath her, easing her descent and resting her on the ground gently.

"Jessie, what's wrong?" he asked, his voice anxious and tight.

"I feel out of it—dizzy," she said, noticing that she was slurring her words slightly. "All the walking, the champagne, the slutty hostess—I'm really struggling here."

Kyle kept his hand under her head so that it wouldn't lie on the hard wood dock. She watched him look around desperately before his eyes fell on something that calmed him.

"What is it?" she asked.

"We're pretty close to Teddy's boat. I'm going to carry you over there and you can rest on a bed in the cabin until you feel better. He won't care. Hell, you can spend the night there if you don't feel up to going home."

"You sure?" she asked, still dizzy but relieved at the idea of being able to lie down somewhere quieter and more secluded.

"Of course," he assured her. "It's the perfect spot. We're lucky it's right there."

Jessie felt Kyle scoop her up in his arms. She tried to keep her eyes open so she could get a better sense of where they were going. But it was useless. She felt weak and disoriented and within moments, gave up. She sank into the warmth of her husband's comforting embrace and allowed her eyes to close.

## CHAPTER TWENTY TWO

Jessie was awakened by a piercing pain in her skull. She opened her eyes slightly so that only a slit of light could get in. But somehow the sun's rays found her and bored into her. She closed them again and only dared reopen them when her hand was there to serve as protection.

She lay quietly on her back, trying to get her bearings. She didn't recognize her surroundings, though she could tell she was in a bed. Her limbs felt heavy and her mouth was dry and puffy. She opened her eyes a little more. Her environment became clearer. She felt a slight rocking motion and noticed that the room she was in was tiny, with all the walls extremely close to the bed. The mostly porthole windows were the final indicator. She was on a boat.

And then the memories flooded back. The party, the champagne, the argument with the floozy hostess, the sudden pregnancy-induced exhaustion and dizziness, nearly falling before Kyle carried her away to a boat, this boat.

After that, everything went blank. She didn't remember getting on the vessel or being placed in the bed or anything up until this moment. Glancing out the window, she knew she hadn't slept a full twelve hours, as she'd told Kyle she wanted to. The sun, with its unforgiving rays, was just barely peeking out above the hills in the distance. It was still pre-dawn.

"Kyle?" she muttered, the word coming out garbled, even to her.

She tried to prop herself up on her elbows but the attempt made her dizzy and nauseous and she immediately slumped back down and closed her eyes.

"Kyle, are you in here?" she asked slightly louder.

There was no response.

She took several deep breaths before rolling to her side and pushing herself up to a seated position on the edge of the bed. She waited for the nausea to return but it held back, apparently taking pity on her.

She sat there for several minutes in just panties and a bra, slumped over, her elbows on her knees, her face in her hands, gathering the strength to move again. When she finally felt able, she turned around to face the bed again.

119

To her surprise, she saw someone else lying there next to the indentation from where she had slept. There was a sheet over the head and most of the person's torso, but one tan leg poked out.

"Kyle?" she said warily even though she knew it couldn't be him. It was a woman's leg.

She leaned over and pulled the sheet away to reveal Natalia, lying on her side away from her. Despite her diminished state, Jessie felt a modified version of her anger from last night and gave the woman a rough shove.

"Wake up," she hissed. "What the hell are you doing in here?"

Natalia continued to lie on her side, oblivious to the world.

"Hey," Jessie said again, this time louder and more forcefully, "I said, what are you doing in here?"

She grabbed Natalia's shoulder and yanked her onto her back. The girl, still wearing her black minidress, offered no resistance and lolled over lazily, her left arm splaying out across the bed. Her eyes were open.

Jessie blinked several times, trying to process what she saw. She felt as if she was disconnected from her own body, hovering over the scene, detached from emotion, methodically taking it all in.

Natalia was staring emptily up at the ceiling, her unseeing eyes dotted with red splotches. Her skin was a light blue. Her neck was an ugly rainbow of red, purple, blue, and black and it had deep indentations and puncture marks.

Jessie blankly glanced down at her own hands and saw that her nails were rimmed with dried blood. She held them up close to her and saw what looked to be skin underneath the nails. She reached out and touched the girl's arm closest to her. It was cold.

Something about that snapped her out of her nightmare reverie and back into the reality of the moment. The horror of what lay in front of her suddenly swallowed her up and she opened her mouth to scream.

"Kyle!"

A second later, she heard a banging on the door, which startled her into silence.

"Jessie? What is it?" she heard her husband call out as she heard him shake the door handle. "Why is the door locked? Are you okay?"

Jessie leapt up and moved to the door, unlocked the chain latch and the doorknob, and swung it open. Kyle stood before her in a T-shirt and boxers, sleepy-eyed and bed-headed.

"I don't know what happened," she said, pointing at the bed.

Kyle glanced around her. His eyes fell on the bed and his mouth dropped open.

"What the…? Is that Natalia?"

"I don't how she got here or what happened," Jessie pleaded, her voice rising. "I just woke up and found her there."

Kyle looked at her, stunned, then back at the dead body on the bed. He seemed at a loss.

"What is going on?" Jessie wailed.

That seemed to drag him out of his state of shock.

"Shh," he whispered, glancing back over his shoulder. "Get back inside the room."

He guided her in and closed the door behind her, locking it after them. He looked around the room for few seconds, his mind clearly racing.

"You don't remember her coming in here?" he asked.

"No. I don't remember *me* coming in here. The last thing I can remember is you carrying me from the dock, saying that Teddy had a boat I could sleep on."

"You don't remember me undressing you or saying I was going to go find a water bottle and some ibuprofen in the club?"

Jessie shook her head.

"And you don't remember her coming on board the boat at all?" he asked.

"No, Kyle. You say that like I should."

"It's just that I ran into her on my way up there. She asked if she could go on the boat and smooth things over with you. I said she'd be better off not, that you weren't feeling so well. But when I looked back I saw that she was heading this way so I assumed she was going to try anyway. When I got back a few minutes later the bedroom door was locked and you weren't answering. I just assumed you locked the door so she couldn't get in, that she left and you passed out."

"I don't remember any of this," Jessie said. "Are you sure?"

"I'm not sure of anything now," he said, glancing back at Natalia's body. "I just figured I'd let you sleep and check on you in the morning. So I crashed on the couch out there. I didn't hear anything until you started calling for me."

Jessie felt slightly dizzy again and sat back down on the bed, as far from Natalia as she could get. After a long silence, she spoke.

"Well, I guess we better call the cops," she said, not sure what else to do.

"Yeah, of course," he agreed, kneeling down in front of her and taking her hands in his. "I'm sure they can help sort all this out."

He glanced down and then back up at her. His eyes were questioning.

"What?" she asked.

He looked over at Natalia and then back at Jessie's hands.

"It looks like she was choked," he said quietly.

"Yeah," Jessie agreed, shivering slightly. "I saw that too."

"And your fingernails are bloody," he said, again very quietly. "Is it possible that…"

He didn't finish the sentence but she knew what he was thinking. She glanced down at her hands again. It was like she had forcibly forgotten the state they were in until now.

"You don't think I…?" she began.

"I don't know, Jessica," he said reluctantly. "Could she maybe have startled you when she came in and you thought she was an intruder or something and fought back; maybe you didn't realize who it was because you were so out of it?"

"No! I don't know. I really don't remember anything."

"That's what I'm worried about," he said. "That girl is dead. It appears like someone choked her and your fingernails are all bloody. It doesn't look good, especially with your memory so hazy. Plus…"

"Plus what?" Jessie asked, her stomach doing a somersault.

"You were arguing with her last night. You were pretty aggressive. Lots of people saw it."

"What are you saying, Kyle?"

"I'm saying whatever happened, it looks bad."

"Then we'll just have to explain it so that everyone understands," she said firmly.

"Yeah, you're right," he said, getting off his knees and sitting on the bed beside her. He was noticeably looking away from Natalia.

"I *am* right," Jessie said, choosing to believe it.

"You're the law enforcement type so you'd know better," he said, then reluctantly added, "but how likely are they to believe you? I mean, with her neck and your hands and the argument and all?"

Jessie didn't reply, though an answer popped up her brain.
*Not very.*

"Can I offer an alternative proposal?" he asked hesitantly.

"What?"

"Maybe we could just make this all go away," he suggested.

"What do you mean?"

"I haven't totally thought this out," he admitted. "But no one but me knows she was going to see you. There were so many people milling about that I doubt anyone even noticed her. And the last anybody saw of you, I was carrying you, half-conscious, to this boat."

"What are you getting at?"

"I'm saying that no one has to know she died on this boat or anywhere near you. She was drinking, just like everyone else. Who's to say she didn't just stumble on the dock, hit her head, roll in the water, and drown? It's not inconceivable."

"You're saying we should just take her up on deck and toss her overboard?" Jessie asked incredulously.

"No. We couldn't do it here. Someone might see. And her body would be found right away. The cops would see the marks on her neck and know she didn't just drown. We'd have to take her further out in the bay, so she wouldn't be discovered for a while."

He got up and carefully avoided Natalia's body as he moved over to the largest window and stared out.

"It's barely dawn," he said. "We could go out, dump her, and be back before anyone woke up. No one would miss us. Or her."

"Kyle, her family would miss her," she said, shocked at the suggestion. "They'd demand a search."

"What family?" he asked. "She told me she just moved here from Ukraine a few months ago. She's new to the area. She's a stripper. It's not like that's a nine-to-five job. If she's gone, they'll probably just assume she flaked out. It could be months before anyone asks about her."

"I don't like it. I didn't do anything wrong. If I turn myself in, the authorities might understand."

"They might," he acknowledged, glancing over at Natalia. "But they might not. The doors and windows are all locked from the inside, so there's no way to deny it was you. And her neck looks really bad. It might be hard for them to buy that you did this in some daze or in self-defense."

"I don't know. That's a decision you can't come back from."

"So is turning yourself in for murder, babe," he pressed. "You're carrying our child. You're about to finish graduate school. Do you really want to risk all that on the chance that some prosecutor will be super understanding?"

Suddenly the nausea that she'd been able to subdue resurfaced. Jessie stumbled to the head, barely making it in time. She stayed hunched over the toilet for a while, throwing up until only bile came out. When she was done, Kyle flushed the toilet, helped her to her feet, and led her to the room where told her he'd slept.

123

"Let's do this," he said firmly. "I'll take care of it, okay. I can't lose you."

He eased her down on the couch he'd slept on and stroked her hair. Within seconds, she had drifted off.

*

When she came to, Jessie could tell they were no longer in the marina. The boat was rolling vigorously over what felt like much bigger waves.

She sat up and found that she felt somewhat better. Glancing through the doorway toward the bedroom where she'd spent the night, she saw that the door was closed. She gingerly got to her feet, wrapped a blanket around herself, and walked to the stairwell, where she grabbed the railing. Holding tight, she took each step carefully until she was topside.

The sun was brighter now and she had to squint. They were somewhere out in the bay. The air had a frosty bite and goose bumps magically appeared all over her body. Kyle was at the bow with his back to her. He seemed to be pushing something heavy.

A second later she heard a loud plop and knew what had happened. He turned around and looked so surprised to see her that he nearly toppled back in the water himself. He steadied himself and came over.

"It's done," he said. "Let's get back quick, before anyone notices the boat was missing."

Suddenly Jessie felt the urge to vomit and it had nothing to do with morning sickness. She leaned over the side and gagged on the bile in her throat. She couldn't get the thought of Natalia's body hitting the water out of her head.

Kyle held her shoulders until she stopped. Then, without a word, he went to the helm and turned the boat back to the marina. As they headed back to shore, Jessie leaned against the gunwale and stared back in the direction they'd come from.

A prominent rock outcropping jutted up near where Kyle had dumped Natalia, surrounded by lighted buoys to warn sailors away. Jessie suspected he'd dumped the body there so boats would be less likely to find it.

"Jessie," he called out, "I need to you take the helm so I can hose down the deck. I don't want to leave any skin residue or anything, just in case."

Jessie moved absentmindedly in his direction, still in a half-haze, only barely beginning to accept that they'd just covered up a murder—one that she'd apparently committed.

Ten minutes later they were back at the dock. Kyle tied the boat off while Jessie went down below and got dressed in the main cabin. He joined her below, going to the bedroom to replace the bed sheets and stuff the used ones a duffel bag he found in the closet. Then he took her hand and led her off the boat, down the dock, and back to the club. The sun was completely out now but there still wasn't a soul in sight.

Kyle opened the door to the club and they walked through the darkened, silent dining room. It was barely 7:30 a.m. and the sun had been up less than an hour but they could hear activity in the kitchen. Pots and pans were being moved and distant voices could be heard. Soon members on boats would start to stir and come inside, ready for a hot breakfast.

Kyle led Jessie up the stairs and through the door to the lobby, which was also empty, and out the front door of the club. They were in their car five minutes later and home ten minutes after that. Jessie went straight upstairs to shower. She stayed under the water for twenty minutes, scrubbing at her nails nearly the whole time.

# CHAPTER TWENTY THREE

When she woke up, her vision was fuzzy. She glanced down and could tell that she was seated in a wooden chair with her wrists tied to the arms with coarse rope. Her head was strapped against the chair back so that she couldn't move it from side to side. Her feet dangled loosely. She was too small for them to touch the ground.

As she blinked to clear her sight, she felt rough fingers on her face, pulling the skin just below and above her eyes so they were wide open, then placing something like tape on the skin so she couldn't close them. Her eyes began to water but her vision, now almost normal, allowed her to take in the scene in front of her.

She was in a dark cabin and there was a woman standing in front of a lit fireplace. She was naked. Her arms were above her head, attached to manacles suspended from ceiling beams. Her eyes were wide with fear but she couldn't yell because her mouth was stuffed with some kind of cloth.

Jessie opened her mouth to scream but found that she too, had something in her mouth, preventing her from doing anything more than grunt. A male voice spoke softly in an oddly soothing tone from somewhere behind her.

"You have to see, little junebug. You have to know the truth," the voice said.

Then he stepped forward and she saw that he had a long knife in his right hand.

Again she tried to scream, without success. As he approached the woman, Jessie used all her might to try squeeze her eyelids shut. But it was no use. They stayed open, forcing her to watch through watery, tear-stained eyes.

*

Jessie woke up screaming, her heart pounding. Kyle, seated at the edge of the bed, asked if she was okay but she didn't answer. She just rolled over and pulled the covers over her head, trying to block the world out.

She spent the rest of the morning in bed, and the afternoon too. It was only around dinnertime that Kyle was able to coax her downstairs to sip some chicken noodle soup while bundled up on the couch.

He gave her some hot tea and she retreated to the bedroom again. This time, she was able to sleep for a full twelve hours. She considered it a blessing that she didn't have any nightmares. Or if she did, that she couldn't remember them.

They sat on the couch that Sunday morning with the TV on but muted. Jessie sipped decaf coffee and Kyle nursed what looked like a scotch. No one spoke for several minutes. Finally Kyle cleared his throat and began the conversation she knew was inevitable but dreaded all the same.

"It's going to be okay, Jess," he said, trying to sound reassuring. "I've been checking the news. She's been gone for almost thirty-six hours and I haven't read a word about her. Like I suspected, she's not going to be missed."

"I don't know if I should be comforted or horrified by that," Jessie said.

"Maybe both. But for our purposes, I'll take comforted. And as long as we're smart, I think we can stay that way."

"It sounds like you were thinking about this while I slept, so I'll bite: what constitutes 'smart'?"

"I *have* been thinking about it," he conceded. "And I've come to a few conclusions, some of which I doubt you'll love. Are you ready for them?"

"No time like the present," Jessie said bitterly, half-pleased that she was capable of any reaction other than depression.

He ignored her tone and dived in.

"I don't think we should make any big, dramatic moves for the next little while. And that includes moving. I know I said I'd be willing to do it for you. And I am. But if we up and sold the house and moved away right now, only months after arriving, it would definitely draw unwanted attention, don't you think?"

Jessie wanted to argue with him but his logic was sound. It would look strange. She nodded.

"Same goes for the club," he continued. "I did tell some folks that they'd be seeing less of me. But if I suddenly dropped out of sight after being there so often, right at the time this girl goes missing, people might make a connection."

"I thought you said she wouldn't be missed," Jessie protested.

"I doubt she will," Kyle reiterated. "But I can't be sure. And if someone does take notice and the authorities start asking questions, the focus might fall on the person she was arguing with the night she was last seen."

"But that was me, not you."

"And that's exactly why I think *you* need to come back and go to events too. We can justify you being gone for a few days, what with morning sickness and all. But anything more than that and those gossips are going to start asking questions. You need to be seen there, looking normal. Maybe even happy."

Jessie looked at him like he was crazy. Forcing herself to keep her tone level, she responded.

"I don't know if that's possible, Kyle. I am *not* happy. I wasn't before this happened and I'm definitely not now. I want out of here!"

"I get that," he said patiently. "But for our own safety, we need to reboot the time table for any possible move. Let's just stick with the current program for a while."

"How long?" Jessie demanded. "How long before we can reasonably bail on this place without drawing suspicion? I need a date."

"I can't say exactly. Maybe a year?"

"A year?" she repeated, dumbfounded. "In a year we'll have a kid. You'll be settled in at the office. We'll be entrenched. You'll never want to leave."

"It was just an estimate, Jess. Maybe we can go earlier, if things seem quiet and the Natalia situation isn't a problem. But we need to be careful. Better safe than sorry."

"I'm already sorry," she muttered, looking down to study the coffee table.

"Listen," he replied, with more of an edge in his voice than before. "I meant what I said. I think this will all blow over. You're lucky this happened when it did, with no witnesses, to a girl no one cared about. No one besides me will ever know and I'll keep your secret."

Jessie looked up at that comment, startled by it. He had started for the kitchen to refill his drink. She opened her mouth and was about to call him back, to point out that he must have misspoken.

*Your secret? Doesn't he mean our secret?*

But something stopped her. She wasn't quite sure what. Instead she took a deep breath, blew it out, and closed her mouth.

Kyle kept talking as he poured himself another glass.

"I'm going to go into the office today. I hadn't planned to. But after getting that dressing down on Friday and…everything else, I think it would be wise to show my face. I want to appear as the bright-eyed and bushy-tailed new guy in the office, especially now.

The more normal my behavior is in the days right after the party, the better for both of us."

"So you're just going to leave me here alone?" she asked.

"Sure. I typically go in for a few hours on Sundays and this is just a regular Sunday, babe, right?" he said, then continued without waiting for a response. "I'll only be gone for a few hours and I'll call you when I'm headed back."

*

Kyle had been gone for about ninety minutes when the pain started. It began deep in her abdomen and radiated outward from there. Jessie stood up to get some medication but quickly sat back down, overwhelmed by the sudden, piercing agony she felt.

She tried to stand again but couldn't find the strength. Her back was screaming and she felt weak and nauseous. Just as she processed that, she began to vomit uncontrollably on the living room carpet.

She glanced over at her cell phone, resting on the coffee table three feet away. It seemed like a mile. She reached out, trying to ignore the cramps that came out of nowhere and began wracking her body.

As her hand clasped the phone, she realized she might pass out at any second. She only had time to make one call, if that, before she'd be completely useless. She dialed 911 and rolled herself off the couch as the phone rang on the other end.

With the phone in one hand, she crawled across the floor, through her own sick, to the front door. It seemed to mock her from across an ocean of carpet. She put her head down and focused on moving one hand forward, then the other, then a knee, then the other.

She had just reached the door, when a voice came on the line.

"Nine-one-one. What is your emergency?" a female asked calmly.

The front door was locked and she had to put the phone down on the floor to grab the handle. She fumbled with it for a few seconds before getting a good grip.

"This is nine-one-one. What is your emergency?" the voice repeated.

Jessie wanted to talk but she didn't think she could do that and turn the doorknob. So she focused on the latter. She used both hands to twist the knob, then flung herself at the door, knocking it

129

open as she collapsed with her top half on the stoop and her bottom half still in the foyer.

Her thoughts were getting cloudy as she heard the voice on the phone for a third time.

"This is nine-one-one. Are you having an emergency? Can you speak?"

Jessie tried to focus her thoughts on that last question and opened her mouth, forcing herself to say something, anything. And just before she collapsed into unconsciousness she was able to groan a single word through her grimacing lips.

"Help!"

## CHAPTER TWENTY FOUR

The hospital room was cool and quiet. Jessie knew that was where she was, even before she could open her eyes. The regular beeping of the heart monitor was an all too familiar sound to her.

She lay there for a minute with her eyes closed, giving herself a moment to adjust. She could feel slight pressure in the crook of her left elbow and knew that likely meant she had an IV taped there. The cold, whooshing air blowing in her mouth combined with her badly chapped lips suggested she was wearing an oxygen mask. She could feel the flimsy material of a hospital gown pressing against her skin, offering little protection against the chilliness of the room.

Finally, reluctantly, she opened her eyes. The lights had been dimmed and it took her a few seconds to adjust. She was in a private room. There was a small, square glass window in the door, through which she could see nurses milling about in the hall.

Kimberly Miner was seated in a chair by the door, asleep, with her head slumped to the side in what looked like an extremely uncomfortable position. Jessie glanced up but the heart monitor was facing away from her so she couldn't see the numbers.

She looked down at her body, covered by the thin hospital sheet, and tried to make sense of her situation. She didn't remember how she got here but she knew why. The memory of the throbbing anguish she'd felt at home was still fresh, even if it was gone now. She refused to allow herself to speculate as to what that might mean.

She sensed movement at the window of her door and looked up to see Melanie Carlisle right outside, talking animatedly to someone out of her line of sight. They were speaking in loud whispers.

Seeing her friend filled Jessie with a feeling of enormous relief. But that quickly faded as it became clear that Mel was agitated about something. Jessie tried to make out her words but couldn't, no matter how hard she focused. That realization made her consider, for the first time, that she might be on some kind of pain medication that was dulling her perceptions.

Mel stepped through the door and plastered a smile on her face where a frown had been only moments earlier. The sound made Kimberly stir in her chair and she opened her eyes.

"You're awake," she said, sounding relieved. "I didn't know what to think when I found you on your front stoop."

Jessie wanted to reply but couldn't with the oxygen mask on her face. She pointed lazily to it.

"Hold on, sweetie," Mel said, then opened the door and called out loudly to someone in the hall. "She's awake and she's trying to talk. Can someone come in here and get that mask off her face please?"

A few seconds later a nurse came in. She checked vitals and then began removing the mask. As she did, Mel took Jessie's hand and spoke.

"I've left multiple messages for Kyle. They've all gone to voicemail, which makes me think he turned his phone off. But I'm sure he'll get them soon and be here right away."

Jessie tried to reply but her throat was dry and she only coughed.

"Can you get her some water please?" Mel asked the nurse, who nodded and began to fill a cup with a straw in it.

Just then the doctor came in. He was young and his eyes were focused on the chart in his hands, which were shaking slightly. Jessie could tell he didn't want to look at her.

"Hello, Mrs. Hunt," he said, finally looking up at her when he had no choice. "I'm Dr. Farah. I know you must be disoriented and frightened. First, let me tell you that you suffered no permanent harm. We're going to keep you overnight for observation. But you'll be able to go home tomorrow."

He'd been talking quickly, as if hoping that the speed of his words would distract her from the obvious question, the one she suspected she already knew the answer to.

"The baby?" she managed to croak.

The doctor looked at Mel, who stepped over and grabbed her hand. Dr. Farah's eyes fell to the chart again before he apparently reminded himself to make eye contact.

"I'm sorry to tell you this but I'm afraid you had a miscarriage, Mrs. Hunt."

Mel squeezed her hand. She barely felt it.

"I'm so sorry, sweetie," she whispered quietly.

"It's a good thing you called nine-one-one," Dr. Farah said. "You were hemorrhaging and if it had gone untreated, you might have been at risk as well. I know that's not much comfort. But you should be commended for your quick thinking. I know it must have been hard to think at all with the pain you must have been in."

"Permanent damage?" she asked hoarsely, trying to get answers before she shut down completely, which she could tell was imminent.

He seemed to get what she was asking.

"In terms of future pregnancies, it's a little early to be certain. But I'm optimistic that you will be able to try again."

"Reason?" she muttered, feeling the anguish starting to close in on her and trying desperately to keep it at bay for just a little longer.

Dr. Farah sighed, clearly reluctant to go there.

"Reason?" she demanded louder, her dry voice bouncing off the walls.

"It's hard to know that sort of thing for certain," he said. "Your initial lab work was inconclusive, although it's clear that your stress hormone levels were elevated. But we can't draw too many conclusions from that. We'll be getting back more results in the coming days. But you should prepare yourself for the possibility that we may never know definitively why this happened."

"Thank you, Doctor," Jessie whispered before the dam broke. Her eyes welled up so much that she couldn't see anything but blurry colors. She heard a loud wailing and though she couldn't be sure, she supposed it was her. Her body began to rebel, convulsing involuntarily in spasms of grief.

"Sedate her!" she heard Dr. Farah say from somewhere far away. She wanted to tell him not to, to let her feel this, to let her suffer. It was part of her penance for what she'd done. But before she could get any words out, the colors turned to black and so did her world.

*

When she woke up on Tuesday morning, Jessie decided she would get out of bed. Except for bathroom breaks, she hadn't left it since Kyle brought her home from the hospital the previous morning.

She'd been ordered to stay on bed rest for twenty-four hours. And while she was slightly shy of that, she couldn't stand to stay holed up in the bedroom with her thoughts and little else for one second longer.

Kyle had been supportive but subdued. He was always there with Jell-O, soup, tea, or medication. And he offered the standard platitudes one might expect from someone in this situation. But she could tell he was disappointed. His eyes, usually bright and focused, were dull and withdrawn. He seemed to be struggling to muster the energy to console her. She didn't blame him. He'd lost something too.

Jessie waited until Kyle had left for work before getting dressed. He'd already skipped Monday to stay home with her and it was obvious that he was worried about what was happening at the office in his absence. But she knew that if she'd told him she planned to go to class today, he would have balked and insisted on staying home with her.

So she said nothing. When he was gone, she slowly went through her routine. She could move around but everything took longer than usual. By the time she was ready to walk out the door, she was running late for class.

As she drove over she tried to keep her thoughts on academics. She told herself that it was actually the perfect day for her to return to school. This class session was supposed to have the detective from downtown division. She was relieved to have something new and intriguing to focus her brain on rather than the dark thoughts that bounced around her head when she had quiet, solo time. And at least at school, no one knew what had happened to her so she wouldn't have to deal with any more pitying faces from well-wishers.

By the time she got to the classroom, she was a good five minutes late. She took a seat in the corner as Professor Hosta gave her a frustrated scowl. Luckily, he was going over thesis requirements again, something she'd already done, so she hadn't missed anything exciting.

He went on for another couple of minutes before introducing the man who had been sitting quietly in the chair behind him. Jessie couldn't really see the guy because the professor was blocking her view, but she listened with interest to his introduction.

"Class, now that we've gotten the obligatory stuff out of the way, I'd like to introduce the man I know you're all here for today. This is Detective Ryan Hernandez of the downtown bureau of the Los Angeles Police Department. He works in their Robbery-Homicide Division, in a special unit called the HSS. You should ask him what that means. So without further ado, please welcome Detective Hernandez."

The class applauded as the detective stood up, giving Jessie her first look at him. Her first reaction was that he was young for a detective in what sounded like such a prestigious unit. She doubted he was much older than her, maybe thirty at the most.

He wasn't hugely imposing at first glance, maybe six feet tall and 190 pounds. His jet black hair was cut short, not military short, but close. His brown eyes were alert, surveying the students as he walked up to the podium.

When he got there, he placed his hands on the sides of it. Jessie saw his muscled forearms flex from his elbows all the way down to his wrists. Even his fingers, including the one with the gold wedding band, looked strong.

Jessie also couldn't help but notice that under his torso-hugging uniform, there didn't seem to be an ounce of fat. Before he opened his mouth to speak, he flashed a friendly smile and Jessie could feel the entire room relax. She wondered if he'd given acting or modeling a chance before settling on law enforcement.

"Hey gang," he said in an authoritative, charming tone. "My name's Ryan. But you can call me Detective Hernandez."

Professor Hosta hooted with laughter but the rest of the class remained silent.

"So much for starting with a joke," Detective Hernandez said. "As your professor indicated, I work Robbery-Homicide for LAPD. I've been on the force for eight years, five as a detective and two with HSS. To save you the trouble, I'll tell you what that means. HSS stands for Hollywood Security Squad. Our job is to go around the city and eliminate, permanently if necessary, overly enthusiastic fans of celebrities. It's a fairly secretive new unit, so please keep it on the down low."

This time it was Jessie who snickered, despite her best efforts to control herself. The other students all glared at her as if she'd spit on a priest.

"Man," Detective Hernandez said, shaking his head in disappointment. "I count fifteen people in this room and my first two jokes have landed with two of you. I'm thinking I may need to get my money back from that improv class."

"You should sue them," Jessie said.

Hernandez looked at her appreciatively.

"I will take that under advisement, ma'am," he said before addressing the entire class. "Seriously though, HSS stands for Homicide Special Section. That means we investigate cases that have high profiles or intense media scrutiny. We also investigate arsons, homicides involving multiple victims, and serial killer cases."

There was a collective murmur among the class but no one spoke up so he continued.

"Before I blather on, I thought it might be interesting to do a little case study. This is an academic environment after all. Once we're done and you all are a little less star-struck, we can have the

135

Q&A you're all dying for. Professor Hosta, can you dim the lights please?"

While Hosta did as requested, Detective Hernandez opened his laptop and hit a key. A blank screen popped up on the whiteboard at the front of the room.

"What I'm about to present to you is a real case, although actual names have been left off for the privacy of those involved. This is the 'Smith' family."

On the screen appeared a young boy of about five and then a girl who looked to be seven. Both were light-haired with blue eyes. After that an image of an attractive woman with flowing dirty-blonde hair and blue eyes in her mid-thirties popped up. And finally a man in his early forties appeared. He was bald, with a long scar running down the left side of his well-shaven face from his ear to his jaw. He had some kind of tattoo on his neck but it wasn't clearly visible in the photo.

"This family unit is fairly recent. One parent was widowed several years ago, then remarried recently. Unfortunately, there was a lapse in judgment as it turned out the new spouse had a history of insinuating into the lives of families who had just lost someone and sweeping everyone off their feet.

"Then, when everything seemed like it was headed for happily ever after, the new spouse would murder the rest of the family, clean out bank accounts, steal any valuables, and disappear into the ether. That's what happened in this case, about four years ago. It was the third incident we're aware of. Luckily, the perpetrator was caught and is currently serving a life sentence so you can sleep easy tonight."

No one in the class felt especially comfortable at that news. Other than some awkward shifting in their seats, everyone remained silent. Hernandez continued.

"I'm going to pass out a fact sheet with basic information about those involved. Then I'll give you five minutes to see if anyone can guess how the perpetrator was caught. Sound fun?"

As Jessie waited to get her fact sheet, she studied the faces on the screen. She felt an unexplainable itch in her brain, as if she should be picking up something that was hovering just at the edges of her consciousness. And yet, she couldn't quite identify what it was.

Someone handed her a fact sheet. There weren't many facts. She'd been slightly off on the ages of the kids. The boy was four and the girl was six. The wife, thirty-eight, worked in child care and the husband, forty-two, was retired military who now worked security. At the time of the murders, they'd been married for about seven months after a year of dating.

The parent had been killed first, throat slit and then stabbed multiple times in the chest. The children only had their throats slit. The bodies were discovered the next day when neither the children nor the deceased parent showed up for school and work. By then, the killer was long gone. That was all the information available.

Jessie reread the notes and looked up at the family faces again. There was so little information to work with that she knew the solution had to be fairly straightforward, something that didn't require poring over case files for hours. It was something that, once she figured it out, would make everything else obvious.

She could hear other students whispering among themselves. The phrase "PTSD" was used more than once. Some guy in front of her mused that maybe the dad felt emasculated by going from G.I. Joe to Paul Blart, Mall Cop.

"Two minutes," Detective Hernandez called out.

He was smiling broadly, looking like the cat that ate an entire family of canaries. It only reinforced her suspicion that the whole case was a trick.

Jessie closed her eyes and took a deep breath, trying to push all of her assumptions out of her head. She returned to basics, but not the basics of the case—the basics of Detective Hernandez. He was the one trying to trick them and he was one the one who had total control over how the information had been presented to them. He was not, for the purposes of this case study, to be trusted. She doubted he would give them outright false information. That wouldn't be playing fair. But he could shade the facts however he wanted.

*How might he do that?*

And then it hit her—what the detective had done—a move so casually sneaky as to be almost imperceptible. She glanced up at the screen again, reprocessing the information she'd been given in the light of her realization, and a theory began to percolate.

"Time's up," Detective Hernandez said as Professor Hosta turned the lights back on. The faces on the whiteboard were harder to see now but Jessie could still make out their outlines. Looking at them from that new perspective only reinforced her quickly evolving hypothesis. She glanced back down at the fact sheet to check one more thing. It fit. She was almost certain she knew now what had happened, or at least how the class had been played.

"No more discussion," Professor Hosta instructed, chastising two chatty young women in the front corner of the room.

"Any ideas on what happened?" Detective Hernandez asked. "Feel free to shout them out. We work collaboratively at HSS. Brainstorming is a big part of what we do. No reason it can't be here either."

"The dad snapped," the guy in front of Jessie said eagerly. "You didn't say how long ago he left the military on the fact sheet. I'm guessing he was unemployed for a while after he left, and had to get what he considered demeaning security work to help support the family. It was too much for his ego to bear and one day he just lost it. Maybe the wife said something to set him off. That's why he stabbed her a lot. He didn't have the same anger toward the kids so he just slit their throats."

"That doesn't explain the serial nature of the crime," one of the chatty girls up front pointed out. "Detective Hernandez said this was at least the third time this had happened. So I doubt he just snapped. The fact sheet didn't say *how* he left the military. I bet he was dishonorably discharged, bouncing from town to town, puffing up his soldier bona fides. That would be very comforting to a widowed single mom. She might dismiss the scar on his face, an obvious sign that he was troubled and probably got in lots of altercations, if it meant she had someone to lean on. Unfortunately, it looks like at least three women put their trust in the wrong guy."

It went on like this for quite a while longer—people throwing out theories and Detective Hernandez writing abbreviated versions of them on the whiteboard. Jessie noticed that he made sure not to write on the faces of the family members. Some might have thought it was out of respect but she suspected there was another reason.

"We're almost out of room on the board," he said. "Anyone want to throw out a last-minute theory before I say if someone got it right?"

Jessie looked around the room. Everyone seemed either stumped or satisfied that they'd already given the proper answer.

She raised her hand.

# CHAPTER TWENTY FIVE

Hernandez was about to speak, but seeing Jessie's arm in the air, stopped himself.

"Yes?" he said, nodding at her.

"I think they caught the killer by sending out digitally altered photos of the suspect to potential places of business in other cities."

"What, to the security offices of other malls?" the guy in front her asked derisively. "Or do you think FBI agents went from town to town posting 'wanted' posters in local food courts?"

Jessie smiled sweetly at him, convinced that his overabundance of cockiness was about to be deflated. Up until then, she'd been hesitant to say too much, for fear of being shot down. But now that someone had tried, she felt even more sure of herself and decided there was no reason to hide it.

"I doubt it was the FBI," she said, "more likely Interpol. And I don't see the point of going to malls. A better bet would be preschools, daycares, and even better, private nanny referral services."

"You think it was the wife?" the girl up front with the dishonorable discharge theory demanded, incredulous. "You think that little thing overpowered that big guy?"

She actually snorted at the prospect. Jessie glanced down at Detective Hernandez, who had conspicuously not snorted, and who was looking up at her expectantly with the hint of smile on his lips. That was all she needed.

"I don't think she had to overpower him, because she'd slit his throat already. But she wasn't prepared for how much of a fighter he was. She probably should have been. After all, he had that tattoo right there on his neck, which looks like it might be some kind of Special Forces insignia. That, along with the scar on his face, suggests he'd been through at least one serious scrape. That's likely why she had to stab him multiple times in the chest, because the throat slash alone didn't put him down right away."

The classroom was silent. Jessie, emboldened, went on.

"Of course, that wasn't necessary with the kids. They trusted her implicitly. After all, she'd been their nanny for almost two years. That's probably how she wormed her way into the heart of the grieving widower father. He saw how good she was with the kids and for the first time imagined himself with someone new."

"How could a mall cop afford a private nanny?" the jerk in front of her wanted to know.

Jessie tried to keep herself from letting her disdain for this punk slip into her tone.

"You assumed he worked in a mall," she noted calmly. "That wasn't in the fact sheet or anything Detective Hernandez said. And there's no reason to think he was. He was former military, likely in a highly trained unit. He's clean cut and professional looking in the photo. My guess is he worked private security, maybe corporate. And I'm guessing he had some life insurance money after the death of his wife. It's not crazy to think he could afford a nanny."

"Why did you say Interpol would be doing the investigation?" another student asked.

Jessie had forgotten to explain that earlier but was happy to now.

"If there was a serial family murderer, especially a woman, who had been caught and given life in prison, I think someone in here might have heard about it. It would have been all over the news. That is, unless it happened overseas. And Detective Hernandez said she got a life sentence. If it had happened here, she'd likely be on death row. But most European countries don't have the death penalty."

"Anything else?" the jerk asked, obviously irked that his theory hadn't panned out.

"Yeah, her hair is clearly dyed blonde. And it looks pretty thin and wiry. Like she's dyed it often and amateurishly, almost like she had to do it quickly for disguise purposes. That's why authorities would send out various pictures, to take into account a likely change in appearance."

Everyone turned to the front of the room.

"Is she right?" the jerk asked.

"About the hair dye?" Detective Hernandez mused. "I don't know. But in general, yes. This woman was captured in Belgium after committing one family murder in Switzerland and two in France. Most of the other details were correct, although the husband was not Special Forces. That tattoo was for his bomb squad unit, which is how he got the scar. He was given a medal for bravery after he lost his left hand defusing one. That's why he left the service. Pretty good work there."

"Thank you," Jessie said, her face turning red.

"May I ask what tipped you off?"

"Sure. I wish I could say it was facts from the case but it was actually more you. I did notice that both kids had the father's nose and mouth but that was only after I had started to think he was the victim. One hint was that you put up the kids' pictures first, then the stepmom and finally the dad, which gave the impression that he was newest member of the family, even though you never said that."

"Oh yeah," the jerk said, as if it was his discovery.

Jessie ignored him and continued.

"Then I started to think back to how you described them. You never said the gender of the victim or perpetrator. Initially, I thought you were just being formal. But in retrospect, that struck me as so odd that it had to be intentional. The fact sheet was equally non-specific. And then I remembered that you said the killer had been caught and convicted. So it didn't make sense that you couldn't use their names. There was no need to protect anyone's privacy. The case was in the public record. So there had to be another reason you were being so cagey about it. After I made the leap that she was the killer, everything else started to fall into place."

"Well, I have to say, ma'am…"

"Jessie," she corrected.

"I have to say, Jessie, that in the three years I've been presenting this case study, you are only the second student ever to arrive at the correct conclusion. Kudos."

"Thanks," she said, blushing a second time.

"It also goes without saying," he said, now addressing the whole class, "that this case is instructive in regard to something that we as law enforcement officers always have to stay on guard against—making assumptions. We all enter these situations with preconceptions about the people involved. But it's our job, and it will be your job, to set those aside so you can focus more clearly and see what's going on. Thanks for your time."

The class applauded as he turned to Professor Hosta and gave him the floor.

"Thank you, Detective. And well done, Ms. Hunt," Professor Hosta added. "I'd like to use what time we have left to let you all ask Detective Hernandez all the questions you've been holding in until now. Would that be all right, Ryan?"

Hernandez nodded and was almost immediately pummeled with a series of questions, which he answered in rapid succession. He'd grown up in East LA and had actually been in a gang through much of his teen years. He had joined the police academy after his younger brother was murdered on a street corner and the killer was

141

never found. Apparently the investigation was perfunctory at best, which motivated him to pursue justice for his community.

He'd been a beat cop for three years when he was working the scene of a murder and discovered some clues detectives had missed. Those clues helped tie the murder to a serial killer who had been operating in the city for years. He was assigned to the team investigating the case and played a role in apprehending the killer, a man named Bolton Crutchfield, who was currently being held in a psychiatric hospital.

He was promoted to detective and then assigned to HSS, where he'd served ever since. In answer to one of the chatty girls up front, he revealed that he was married but had no children, although he hoped that would change someday.

"That's all the time we have today," Hosta said stepping forward.

Jessie looked at the clock. The class was over. It had flown by. Students started filing out, though many stopped to talk to Hernandez. Part of Jessie wanted to stick around too. She had lots of questions about his work.

But she also remembered that only four days ago, she had killed an innocent woman in a drunken incident she couldn't even recall. Maybe chatting up a homicide detective wasn't the best move at this moment.

So, sore from sitting so long after what she'd been through, she gingerly made her way down the steps and started for the door. She was almost there when Professor Hosta stopped her.

"Well done, Ms. Hunt. I have to admit that I would have been quite disappointed if you hadn't solved that mystery. For a while there I had my doubts."

"So did I, Professor," she admitted, hoping to short-circuit the conversation and exit quickly.

"Are you excited for your final meeting with our friend in Norwalk?" he asked. "I understand he's been surprisingly responsive when conversing with you."

Jessie bit her lip. She didn't know why she'd been allowed to interview Crutchfield. But it was clearly a decision of The Panel. And despite his pretensions of obliviousness, Jessie was increasingly suspicious that Hosta might himself be a member. Whatever was going on, she didn't want to reveal just how much she suspected. So she played up the image of the enthused, but naïve, grad student.

"I am looking forward to it, Professor. I've learned a lot so far. Thank you for going out on a limb for me."

"It was my distinct pleasure," he said, clearly flattered.

Jessie felt a gentle tap on her shoulder and turned to face Detective Hernandez, who was beaming at her.

"I just wanted to say well done. It was nice to listen to how you slid all the puzzle pieces into place. I think you may have picked the right line of work."

"Thank you," she replied, half-thrilled, even as her stomach lurched nervously, recognizing that she was staring into the eyes of a man whose job was to catch people involved in crimes—people like her. She wondered how much her body language was giving away at that very moment. Luckily, there were several students, including the chatty gals, waiting impatiently to speak with him.

"It looks like you're heading out and I think I'm stuck here for a while," he said. "But here's my card. Please keep in touch. The department can always use good profilers, even raw ones. I'm sure we could find some way to put your talents to use."

"Thanks very much. I'll do that," she said, feeling beads of sweat suddenly drip down her back. "But you're right. I do have to be somewhere. Thanks again for coming. It was really...instructive."

He opened his mouth to respond but she was out the door before he could get in another word. She waited until she was halfway across campus before entering a bathroom and wiping herself down. Even with deep breaths, it took another ten minutes for her shoulders to unclench and her heart rate to return to normal.

\*

Jessie was halfway home when the divorce lawyer called her back. She let it go to voicemail and listened to the message asking her to call back at her convenience. When it was done, she deleted it and the record of the call. She wasn't sure she wanted that anymore. And it didn't really matter anyway.

There was no way she could pursue a divorce now. Kyle had been supportive of her in recent days. But she didn't imagine that would continue if she served him with papers. What might he do in that situation? Could he conceivably reveal what she'd done? It didn't seem like the ideal time to alienate him.

Shaking the thought from her head, she veered off in the direction of Balboa Harbor. She couldn't say why but she felt the strong urge to see the water. She parked at the top of the hill and walked down the same steep steps she'd taken on that first visit to the club with the Carlisles as Daughton yelled "boom!" every few steps.

The weather had turned since that morning and what had been chilly was now downright cold. The ocean winds ripped through her and she zipped her coat up to the neck. When she reached the bottom, she stared out at the waves, as they slowly rolled in and lapped up against the dock.

The sight sent her thoughts back to another time when she stood over a body of water. She had been tempted to jump in that day too. But back then it had been to save herself. Today it might be to end herself.

How had this happened so quickly? Less than hour ago, she had been on top of the world, solving a mystery that left the rest of her class stumped. Now she was staring at her reflection in the water, contemplating a bruised marriage, the loss of her unborn child, and the fact that she had killed someone, a girl whose last name she didn't even know.

Jessie knew it was her depression taking hold and that she needed to fight it off with reason and very soon, medication. But in this moment all she could do was stare into the blue and contemplate how freeing it would be to end all the anguish she felt.

"There a mermaid down there?" a familiar voice asked.

"What?" Jessie said, looking up to find Melanie Carlisle, in workout gear, staring curiously at her.

"You just seemed to be studying that water so closely. I thought maybe there was a magical creature just under the surface."

"Nope," Jessie said, trying to shake off the shroud of despair that had enveloped her. "Just seaweed. But you know, sometimes that can be cool too."

"Uh-huh," Mel said, unconvinced. "How are you doing, sweetie?"

Jessie knew she was talking about the miscarriage and decided it couldn't hurt to allow herself to reveal a fraction of what she was feeling.

"I'm kind of struggling a bit," she admitted, unwanted tears coming to her eyes.

"Of course you are," Mel said, walking over. "I'm a little sweaty but you mind if I give you a hug?"

Jessie shook her head and wrapped her own arms around Mel first, squeezing her tight. They stayed like for that for a while and it was Jessie who released her grip first, feeling slightly embarrassed. Mel looked at her, smiled, and brushed a stray hair out of her eyes. Then she looked out at the water.

"Looks like they finally cleaned the place up," she said, somehow sensing that Jessie wanted to change the subject.

"What do you mean?"

"You know, after the Bringing the Boats in Party, there was a huge mess on the docks and in the water. You wouldn't believe some of the shocking stuff that washed up in the last day or so."

Jessie's whole body went cold and rigid. It took all of her self-control to not scream out the question in her head. Instead, she glanced out at the water with an expression of mild interest, then turned back and asked as casually as she could, "What kind of stuff?"

"Well, for one thing, a full-sized sex doll! The first person who saw it, some retired biddy, thought it was a human body and freaked out, started screaming, almost had a heart attack. I'd love to know the back story on how that got in there."

"Yeah, me too," Jessie agreed, relieved.

"All right, sweetie," Mel said in a voice that suggested she was done talking. "If you think you're okay, I'm going to continue my walk. It's my workout for the day and I can already feel the sweat starting to dry in this cold. That's not a good sign. Besides, I want to get back home. Teddy's been a jangle of nerves lately and I'm worried he might accidentally burn the house down. Do you mind?"

"Of course not. Go," Jessie insisted. "And Mel, thanks."

Mel blew her a quick kiss and was off, walking briskly along the harbor path in the direction of the marina. Jessie ambled slowly after her until she found a spot where she could clearly see the rock outcropping where Kyle had dumped Natalia's body. From this distance, it looked like an innocuous little bump in the ocean, not the final resting place for a girl who deserved better.

She could feel herself slipping again and tried to shake it off. Her phone rang and she answered it immediately, happy for the distraction. It was the nurse from her OB-GYN's office. Her voice was peppy and it took Jessie a second to realize why. She didn't know about the miscarriage. Apparently the Westport Beach ER doctor hadn't yet reached out to hers and they had no idea what had happened.

"We got the blood work back for the gender test you asked for," the nurse said. "You're having a boy!"

"Thank you," Jessie said, hanging up without another word.

## CHAPTER TWENTY SIX

Jessie sensed herself sliding back into the dark place. Desperately trying to cling to the lip of the emotional chasm, she searched her mind for anything to shift her focus, to distract her from the awful knowledge that she would never get to meet the little man who could have been her pride and joy. Her knees buckled and she grabbed onto the dock railing for support.

She stood there, trying to fight off the hyperventilating she felt overtaking her, when she heard her phone ping. She grabbed for it, happy to have anything but herself to focus on.

It was a short text from Professor Hosta: "Reminder-last Crutchfield interview."

That was enough to calm her down. She had her final meeting with Bolton Crutchfield tomorrow.

"You need to prepare," she said out loud.

So for the rest of the walk back to the car, the drive to the house, and the remainder of the afternoon until Kyle got home, she maintained her equilibrium by focusing on Crutchfield and the lingering question she still had for him, the one she had to find some way to ask. At one point, she even half-chuckled at the notion that she was being saved from misery by thoughts of an upcoming meeting with a serial killer.

When Kyle arrived, she felt half-normal again. She had made dinner and even baked a pie. Kyle thanked her but barely seemed to notice. He still asked her all the standard questions—how did she feel? Did she need anything?

But he seemed distracted, like his focus was elsewhere. He absentmindedly played with the "$" money clip Teddy had given him, turning it over repeatedly with his fingers. Apparently one day back at work was all it took for him to return to his old workaholic self. It was almost as if the whole thing—killing Natalia, the miscarriage—had never happened.

*

The next day Jessie sat in the viewing section of Bolton Crutchfield's cell, nervously waiting for him to return. He'd been taken for his obligatory weekly shower. With all the required security precautions, the process took an hour. Officer Gentry had offered to let her wait in her office until he returned but Jessie thought it might give her an advantage to already be waiting in his space when he returned.

When Crutchfield walked in, he didn't seem surprised to find her there even though Gentry had told her the visit would be unannounced. He ambled over to the bed as if he didn't have a care in the world and casually sat down.

"So nice to see you again, Miss Jessie," he drawled, lingering on the "ee" in her name. "Where were we?"

"Unfortunately, this will be our last visit, Mr. Crutchfield. My practicum is nearly complete and I don't think I'm authorized to come beyond today. So we'll have to make the most of our remaining time."

"What a shame," he replied. "And just when we were finally getting to know each other."

"You feel you know me?" she asked, sensing a chance to get in a question before the whole "three for one" procedure had been reestablished. She sensed Gentry, standing near the door, stir and knew she had picked up on the attempt as well.

"Why certainly," Crutchfield said. "For example, I can tell that right now, you're carrying a mighty burden, though not a physical one anymore."

He chuckled to himself at the line. Jessie, realizing what he was referencing, stared coldly back at him, refusing to let him see the shock and hurt he'd ignited. He continued, either unaware or unconcerned.

"At first I surmised that it was losing the little one growing in your belly that had you low," he said, looking up at Officer Gentry and clearly taking pleasure in the reaction he was able to get from her, if not from Jessie. "But then I realized it was something else eating at you."

"Pray tell," Jessie said without emotion.

"Don't mind if I do," he replied, his piercing brown eyes boring into her mercilessly. "You're carrying a weight, some sort of guilt at something you've done, or at least think you've done."

"How can you be so sure?" she asked.

"Not feeling much in the way of guilt myself, I have a gift for seeing it plain in others. It kind of pulsates, you know? It's like, if you don't have an itch yourself, it's real easy to see everyone else scratching. And you're scratching somethin' fierce, Miss Jessie."

"Why is that?" she asked, ignoring the creeping fear that he was going to accuse her of killing someone right in that room based simply on her body language.

"Your head's telling you that you've done something abominable. But your gut is screaming something else. And you don't know which to trust. It's got you all twisted up inside. Well, here's my advice. And you know that I'm not in the advising business, so this must be good. Trust your gut, Miss Jessie. Trust your instincts. Maybe you ain't the one who should be twistin'."

Jessie stared at him, trying to determine if what he was saying was genuinely intended to help her or just another perverse game. He was a serial killer, after all, she reminded herself, not a therapist. He simply stared back, lips pursed slightly in amusement, offering nothing.

Before she could draw any conclusions, a deafening siren went off, the room darkened, and a red light began flashing. Jessie, who half-jumped out of her seat, couldn't help but notice that Crutchfield didn't react at all to the chaos. He gave her a quick wink, but otherwise remained still. She turned to look back at Officer Gentry, who was already on her radio.

"Sitrep!" she demanded.

"Jackson's going crazy," Cortez shouted back urgently. "He's slamming his head against his bed frame and chomping at his wrists with his teeth. Blood is spurting everywhere."

"I'll be right there," Gentry said, then pointed at Jessie. "You come with me!"

Jessie glanced back at Crutchfield, whose face was still impassive. But he seemed to be willing her to understand something with his eyes. In that moment, she made a choice. She grabbed her notepad and stood up. As she turned for the door, she feigned tripping and fell to the ground, ripping a sheet of paper as she dropped.

"Move now!" Gentry ordered, pulling her to her feet. Jessie let herself be yanked up, quickly crumpling the paper into a tight ball as the officer pulled her from the room. As they got to the door, Jessie stumbled again and "accidentally" slammed into the doorjamb. As she used her left hand to brace herself, she shoved the paper wad into the lock jamb. Once in the hall, Jessie forced herself to focus her attention on Gentry and not the door closing behind her.

"Go to the security station," Gentry ordered. "Stay there until this is resolved. Got it?"

"Got it," Jessie said, nodding.

She started in that direction as Gentry rushed off the opposite way. Only when she was sure the other woman was out of sight did she turn back around and return to Crutchfield's door. Without pausing to think, she grabbed the handle and tugged. It opened without a fight.

To her surprise, Crutchfield was no longer sitting at the edge of his bed but standing close to the glass partition with an expectant look on his face. He didn't speak, rather motioning with a single finger for her to approach him. Pretending like getting within inches of a serial killer was no big deal, she hurried over to the glass, gulping despite her best efforts.

"We don't have long," Crutchfield said in a hushed voice, still twangy but without any of the deliberately lazy drawl from before. "Jackson can only keep them busy for so long. My instructions were for him to delay them for at least two minutes but there are no guarantees. So ask me the question you've been gathering the courage to pose for weeks now."

Jessie didn't need any further prodding.

"All your kills are copycats," she said in hurried whisper. "But the man you're copying covered up his murders by burning the bodies afterward. The authorities never revealed the methods he used—they weren't even aware of all of them. Yet you are. How is that possible?"

"I think you already know the answer to that question, Miss Jessie. That visitor I had a while back wasn't just someone looking for a friendly chat. He was—what's the word folks use these days—my mentor. And he wanted to check up on me."

"But how did you find each other?" she demanded. "How did you first meet up?"

"I was an admirer of his work," Crutchfield said.

"I get that. But how did you first learn how he committed his crimes? You didn't bump into each other in a coffee shop."

"I think you know the answer to that too, Miss Jessie. But I'll humor you. I got my hands on the statement from the only surviving witness to his crimes, a little girl named Jessica Thurman. She was only a wee thing at the time, about six years old. And the things she described were so awful that the cops thought she was spinning nightmares because of what she'd been through. They thought she'd gone and created a boogeyman to explain away what she couldn't rightly understand. They wrote it all down but they didn't really believe her. It was too crazy. But *I* believed her. And I went looking for the artist whose work she'd illustrated with so much vivid clarity. And I found him, Miss Jessie. I found your boogeyman and he taught me his craft. Maybe not all his tricks, but most of them—the real good ones at least."

"So he's alive?" Jessie said, more to herself than Crutchfield. "After all these years, he's still alive?"

"Alive and kicking, as the song says."

"And he knew I'd come to see you eventually?" she pressed. "That I'd see the similarities between your crimes and his?"

"That he did, Miss Jessie. He knew that someday you'd recognize his handiwork. He knew you'd find a way to reach out to me. He left me a message for you. You want it?"

Jessica nodded. But just then, the door burst open behind her. She turned to see Gentry and Cortez barreling toward her. Quickly she turned back to Crutchfield.

"Tell me," she demanded.

But before he could respond she felt herself being slammed hard from behind. Her face smushed up against the glass as she felt her hands being cuffed behind her back. Crutchfield bent down and, for a brief moment, she thought he might whisper the message. But instead, he leaned over and kissed the glass where her cheek was pressed against it, then stepped back.

"Tell me!" she screamed as she was pulled back forcibly. But all he did was watch solemnly as she was dragged from the room.

## CHAPTER TWENTY SEVEN

"I could have you arrested!"

Jessie was sitting in a chair in Gentry's office, her left hand handcuffed to a pipe near the wall. The officer had reviewed the video of Jessie's exchange with Crutchfield multiple times. But because of the sirens and how close they were to each other, the audio was useless. Clearly frustrated, she was now resorting to threats.

Jessie understood her frustration and tried not to exacerbate it. Instead, for what had to be the fourth time, she apologized.

"I'm sorry. I didn't realize it was a violation to go back in there. The door was unlocked and I thought I heard him calling for help."

"Just stop!" Gentry yelled. "You're just making things worse for yourself. You were explicitly told the rules about interaction with inmates each and every time you went in there. The door wasn't open. We found the wad of paper in the doorjamb lock. You put it there. He never called for help. He knew you'd be coming back in. He was waiting for you. And you talked calmly for nearly a full minute before I came back in. Why shouldn't I bust you for aiding and abetting a prisoner? How do I know you weren't trying to help him escape?"

Jessie looked at the woman in front of her, who was so obviously furious. And yet, Gentry hadn't actually called the cops. She hadn't done anything other than read her the riot act. And this was hardly the first time Jessie had broken protocol. It was a regular occurrence. So why was Gentry holding back? Why was she giving her a chance to explain, even at this late date?

"Officer Gentry, can I ask you a question?"

"What?" Gentry shouted, then repeated more quietly, "What?"

"Why am I not in a black-and-white right now on my way to being processed at the local police station?"

Gentry looked like she was going to yell again but managed to stop herself. She sat down and heaved a long, deep sigh.

"Ms. Hunt," she finally said, her tone mostly level now, "I will be honest with you if you will do the same for me. Why don't we make an arrangement like the one you had with Crutchfield? Only let's make it a little more even. Say you ask me one question and then I get to ask you one. Does that seem fair?"

"It does."

"Okay, the reason I'm reluctant to bust you is this: Crutchfield almost never consents to interviews. And when he does, the person usually leaves crying or twisted in knots. For whatever reason, he doesn't seem interested in messing you up as much as those others. My hope is that his willingness to talk to you might lead to an eventual willingness to reveal details he's kept to himself. Of the nineteen victims we know of, only fifteen bodies were ever found. And folks smarter than me think he had way more than nineteen victims. Maybe he'll tell you where the other bodies are buried. Maybe he'll admit to other killings. Some experts think he had an accomplice. Maybe he'd talk about that. Anything he shares with you is more than he's shared with anyone else in years. So I'd rather not shut out the one person he's willing to talk to. But you make it damn hard not to. Does that answer your question?"

"Yes," Jessie conceded. "It does."

"My turn now. And remember, you promised to be honest. What did you two discuss in there?"

Jessie looked at Gentry for a long time, studying the scar under her eye and the tiny burn marks on her face. She sensed that Gentry had likely seen things in war almost as bad as Jessie had seen herself here at home. And in that moment, she decided to trust her.

"Can we go outside?" she asked quietly.

Gentry immediately stood up, uncuffed her, and led her quickly through the multiple security checkpoints until they were standing out in the parking lot. The air was cold but the sun was shining brightly and Jessie had to squint to see.

"So?" Gentry prompted.

Jessie dove in, knowing that she had to just start and keep going if she was going to get it all out. She decided to be honest about everything she said, even though she planned to exclude a few details.

"When I was a little girl, I grew up in Southeast Missouri, at the edge of the Ozarks. My parents were divorced and I was raised by my mom. One day, I was abducted by a man who took me to an isolated cabin deep in the woods. He had several imprisoned people there. He would show me videos of how he'd captured them. Then he would kill them in the cellar, in unspeakable ways. He made me watch."

"Oh, Jesus," Gentry muttered but Jessie kept going.

"When he'd killed everyone he had, he'd go away for a few days to collect more victims. He left me manacled to a post, with some food, a bucket for a toilet, and a dirty mattress to sleep on.

When he came back, he'd have three or four more people and he'd work his way through them, always making me watch."

Gentry reached out for the wall behind her for support, then bent down on her knees, looking at the ground.

"One of his victims, a woman, had a bobby pin that fell out of her hair. I snapped it up. When he was sleeping I managed to jimmy the manacles and escape into the woods. I was barefoot and it was winter. There was snow on the ground. I didn't know where I was going but I kept running. Eventually I could hear footsteps behind me and knew he was chasing me. I got to a cliff overlooking a river. I looked down. It was easily fifty feet down and portions of the river were frozen over. He caught up but I was far enough away that I could have jumped before he got to me. But I couldn't do it. I just stood there.

"He grabbed me and carried me back to the cabin and said I had to watch one more time; that he had something special for me to see. He taped my eyes open and said, 'You have to see, little junebug. You have to know the truth.' He used to call me junebug all the time.

"Anyway, he had a woman manacled to the ceiling beams. Only this time it wasn't in the cellar. It was right there in the living room so I knew this one was different. I can still remember the sound the wooden ceiling beams made as those manacles weighed on them. They creaked and groaned, almost like they were in pain themselves. Sometimes I can still hear it."

In that moment, Jessie had a realization. The creaking and moaning she'd been hearing in the new house—that she'd spent so much time trying to find the source of—was always only in her memory. No wonder she'd never found it.

She looked down at Gentry, who was staring up at her expectantly. Jessie took a deep breath and continued.

"Then I saw who the woman was. It was my mother."

Gentry forced herself to stand upright. It was clear that she wanted to say something but couldn't find any words.

"It's okay," Jessie told her. "There's nothing you can say that will make it better. Trust me. So he killed her. I won't describe how. When he was done, he cut into me from my shoulder to my neck. He said it was a souvenir."

She pulled down the collar of her shirt to show the pink scar that jutted out from her skin.

"And then he left. He never came back. I was trapped in that cabin, bleeding, with the body of my dead mother feet away from me, for three days before some hunters came across me. By then, the fire had long gone out in the fireplace and I was starving and hypothermic. They got me to a hospital where I stayed for two weeks. I gave my statement to the police. But while they found some of the videos and some burned bodies, they never found everyone I told them about. I think they thought I made a lot of it up."

"Where did you go after that?" Gentry managed to ask. "Did your father take you in?"

"No. He wasn't the type. And the FBI was worried that even though there was no known suspect to prosecute, that this guy might come after me in case he was ever caught, so that I couldn't be a witness. So the US Marshals placed me in Witness Protection. I was adopted by a family in Las Cruces, New Mexico. The father was in the local FBI office and they had recently lost their toddler son to cancer. It made sense. They were looking for a child to love. I needed a secure environment far from Missouri. So my life as Jessica Thurman ended and I started a new one as Jessica Hunt. But they called me Jessie because my mom used to call me Jessica and it was too painful to hear."

"I'm so sorry," Gentry said. "I can't imagine what that was like."

"Thank you. But I haven't answered your question yet, about what we discussed."

Gentry nodded, apparently having forgotten that was what she originally wanted to know.

"Okay," she said. "Tell me."

"The abductions I saw in those videos and the murders I saw in that cabin were only known to me and the man who committed them. I described them in my statement, but only generally. Besides, no one believed me. Yet Bolton Crutchfield knew all about them."

"How do you know that?" Gentry asked.

"Because his murders were performed in the exact same way," Jessie said. "He was coached by the man who originally committed them."

"How can you be sure?"

"Because he admitted it to me. He referred to the man who killed my mother—the cops back then named him The Ozarks Executioner—his mentor. He told me that the man knew I would come calling one day. That's why he visited Crutchfield in this hospital. It's what he's wanted all along."

## CHAPTER TWENTY EIGHT

Jessie made the long drive back to Westport Beach, barely aware of the traffic around her. As unsettling as they were, the revelations from Crutchfield about the origin of his crimes reconfirmed her suspicions more than upended them. She'd suspected as much for a long time and it was reassuring to know those suspicions were correct.

It was something else he'd said that was circling in her thoughts; that she couldn't let go. She could still hear his words echoing in her brain: "Trust your instincts. Maybe you ain't the one who should be twistin'."

Her instincts were screaming at her that if she couldn't recall killing Natalia, then she probably hadn't. Jessie had many memories she'd like to block out forever. But they were all right there, ready to reappear in her dreams if not when she was awake. She'd learned the hard way that banishing them wasn't really an option for her.

But if she accepted that she hadn't killed the girl, then that meant she had to consider the possibility that the person who told her she must have—her own husband—might have.

The idea seemed absurd. She'd known Kyle Voss for almost a decade and nothing about him had ever hinted that he was capable of such an act. Until they'd moved to Westport Beach, the worst things she could say about him was that he was a bit of a workaholic and tended to be on the possessive side. But considering all her psychological baggage, those things always seemed minor.

Since the move, things had gotten worse, for sure. Insisting on joining a country club that was a front for a secret sex club was not great, even if that wasn't his reason for joining.

And while he'd taken care of her after the miscarriage, he had become distant and withdrawn. Then again, everybody handled tragedy differently and she wasn't in a position to judge.

She had caught him snorting coke at a nightclub. And while troubling, she wasn't inclined to draw permanent conclusions about his character based on that. She'd done far more in her high school and college days and it hadn't turned her into a monster.

The one thing that had really stunned her was how willingly he'd covered up Natalia's death. True, it was a crisis moment and

155

anyone can panic in a situation like that. But he didn't seem panicked. He seemed... purposeful.

As she exited the freeway, something Detective Hernandez had said yesterday popped into her head. It was something about, when conducting an investigation, guarding against making assumptions and setting aside preconceptions about people.

It occurred to Jessie that her best bet might be to talk to someone who had a different perception of Kyle than she did. She could think of one person who knew him long before she'd ever met him. And he just so happened to live a few blocks from her.

*

Jessie rang the doorbell of the Carlisle house and waited, trying to keep her nervousness in check. Melanie opened the door, clearly both happy and surprised to see her.

"Twice in two days," she noted. "To what do I owe the honor?"

"I'm sorry to come by unannounced. I'm actually here to see Teddy. I called his office and they said he came home early. Is he here?"

"He is," Mel said, clearly taken aback. "Do you want to come in?"

"Actually I need to talk to him privately. I know that sounds weird. But it's kind of important. Do you mind?"

Mel obviously did. But she made an admirable effort to hide it.

"Of course not," she said. "Give me a second and I'll get him."

Jessie stood awkwardly at the front door while Mel retreated into the house. She could hear whispering but couldn't make out the words. However, from the tone it was clear that Mel was suspicious and Teddy was confused. A minute later he appeared.

"What's up?" he asked through narrowed eyes.

"I just wanted to talk to you about something. Can we go over near my car?" she asked and headed in that direction without waiting for a reply.

When they got to the driveway, she turned to see him with his arms crossed defensively.

"I can't take long," he said. "I promised Daughton I'd be right back."

Jessie doubted that was true but didn't say so.

"No problem. I actually feel kind of silly asking this," she said, slipping into the story she'd prepped in her head on the way over. "But Kyle's birthday is coming up in early December. It'll be about ten years since his high school graduation and I thought it might be fun to give him a few gifts that called back to that era. The problem is I don't really know much about those days beyond what he's told me. Then I realized I have a great resource from back then—you. I was hoping you could tell me a bit about what he was like in high school. Maybe some stuff he wouldn't be willing to share with me himself."

"What kind of stuff?" he asked, clearly intrigued even if he was still a little on guard.

"Nothing too revealing. I don't want to make him uncomfortable. Maybe something mildly embarrassing or silly? For example, was he popular? Did he date a lot?"

Teddy screwed up his face and Jessie could tell he had bought in and was genuinely trying to think back for some good stories. Then he looked back at her.

"He actually wasn't a ton different than he is now. He was a real go-getter even back then; always knew what he wanted and how make it happen."

"Okay. Can you think of any stories that show that in action?"

He seemed stumped for a second but then his face broke into a grin of recollection.

"I do remember one cool story that shows how persistent he was," he said, then seemed to reconsider. "But it involves a girl. Are you okay with that?"

"Of course. I never assumed I was the first girl he ever dated."

"Okay, he took the head cheerleader to the prom," Teddy said. "Pretty cool, huh?"

"That is cool, Teddy," Jessie agreed. "But it's not a story. It's a declarative statement. Can you give me some details?"

Teddy squirmed a little as he stood there, clearly still not sure what was out of bounds.

"Just tell me," Jessie cajoled him. "This stuff is a decade old. It's all water under the bridge. I'm just looking for colorful material."

She could see the furrow in his brow soften and knew he was convinced.

"All right then. There was this girl named Becky Patrone. He was seriously into her. I mean everybody was, but especially Kyle. She was the head cheerleader and super smart—she was almost class valedictorian. She had a scholarship to Harvard."

"Sounds like a real slacker," Jessie said, trying to keep the banter light.

"Yeah, right. Anyway, Kyle wanted to ask her to the prom. But she already had another date—her boyfriend. His name was Reese something. He was the quarterback of the football team and president of the student council. They were like this star couple. And even though Kyle was generally well-liked, there was no way Becky was going to dump her football star boyfriend to go to the prom with some guy she was just friends with."

"Sounds like a serious dilemma," Jessie said.

"It was. That is until Reese got busted," Teddy said mischievously.

"For what?"

He paused again, the furrowed brow returning. Apparently he had remembered something else about the story and was now having second thoughts about sharing it.

"Tell me, Teddy," she said in her most reassuring voice. "There's no point in stopping now."

That seemed to make sense to him and he continued.

"Actually, it was pretty awful," he said, suddenly serious. "He was charged with drugging and raping some girl at a party a few weeks before prom. He denied it and Becky stood by him for a while. But then the cops found some, um, physical evidence that he'd been with this other girl. So even if it was consensual, he'd cheated. Becky dumped him and was really devastated. But Kyle offered her a shoulder to cry on and convinced her that she shouldn't miss out on prom because of something another person had done. He offered to take her and she went."

"Good for Kyle, I guess," Jessie said, trying to keep the judgment out of her voice. "But not so great for Reese."

"No, it kind screwed up his life. And the thing is—I think the charges were eventually dropped for lack of evidence or something. But it was too late. His reputation was ruined."

"So did Kyle and Becky start dating?" Jessie asked.

"Not really. I think she always viewed him as more of a friend than a possible boyfriend. I know he hoped to join her at Harvard too—he applied. But he didn't get in, not that there was ever much of a chance of that."

"That's too bad," Jessie said. "So they drifted apart then?"

"Actually, it looked like he might have another shot for a while," Teddy suddenly remembered. "Becky got accused of cheating on some final exam late in the year. It was kind of crazy because she was already set for college and had a great GPA. Remember how I said she was almost valedictorian? Well, she would have been if not for cheating on that one test. And it cost her the scholarship to Harvard too. She couldn't afford to go without it and all her other schools bailed after that, including USC, where

Kyle was headed, as you know. So she ended up having to go to a community college."

"That really sucks," Jessie said. "Did she go somewhere nearby at least?"

"No. Kyle was hoping she would. He thought she'd stay close to home to save money after losing Harvard. But she surprised everyone. She went somewhere in Arizona. I think she wanted to get away from all the gossip at home."

"That is really sad. I hope things turned around for her."

"Oh, don't feel too bad," Teddy said. "I heard she still did fine. After all, she was super hot and super smart. I think I read in an alumni email that said she's a lawyer in Phoenix now."

"I'm glad to hear it worked out for her," Jessie said neutrally. "Otherwise I'd feel bad using any part of that story for his birthday gift. But since she's okay, maybe I can make some reference to him taking the head cheerleader to prom."

"He'd love that," Teddy agreed.

"I was thinking I might do it at the club. But now that he's scaling back going there, I may need to find a nice restaurant instead. Any recommendations?"

"Scaling back?" Teddy asked, perplexed. "What are you talking about?"

"Didn't Kyle tell you that he'd be cutting back how often he'd be visiting the club?"

"No," Teddy said. "I'd remember that, considering how much effort he put into getting in there."

"What do you mean?" Jessie asked, trying not to sound like she cared too much.

"It's just that, well, Kyle and I knew each other in high school but we weren't super tight. So I was actually a little surprised when he called me out of the blue one day."

"What did he want?" Jessie asked. She could feel her blood pumping faster but tried not to let her voice betray it.

"He said you two were moving down here and he'd heard great things about Club Deseo. He wanted to know how get in."

"He already knew about it when you first talked?" Jessie asked. "You didn't tell him about it?"

"No. He knew all about it and that I was a member. He had lots of specific questions."

Like what?"

Teddy looked suddenly uncomfortable again, as if he'd revealed something he shouldn't have.

"Just stuff," he said unconvincingly.

"What kind of stuff?" Jessie asked again, trying to be playful.

But it didn't work. She could see Teddy shutting down.

"Listen, I really should get back to Daughton," he said plaintively.

Jessie decided the time for a light touch was over. She needed to play hardball.

"Teddy, I know about the club. I know what really goes on there."

"I don't know what you're talking about," he said, looking over her shoulder in the direction of the front door.

Jessie glanced back as well. Melanie wasn't there but clearly he was worried that she would hear. Could he really think his wife was oblivious to the goings-on there? The things he'd been doing?

"You *do* know," Jessie said. "You know because you've been taking advantage of what they offer. I saw you with that brunette in the little upstairs nook off the dining room. What was her name again—Kelsey? I really liked her black minidress, even though she wasn't wearing anything under it."

Teddy's eyes went wide and Jessie realized he must have gotten so used to not being called on his behavior that it didn't occur to him that it wasn't a secret.

"Listen, you can't tell Mel about Kelsey," he said, his voice pleading.

"I don't want to," Jessie insisted. "And I won't if I don't have to. But I need you to tell me the truth about Kyle."

Teddy stared at her, trying to gauge just how serious she was. She decided to jumpstart things for him and turned toward the house.

"Let's see how Mel reacts to the minidress story," she said over her shoulder.

"Okay, wait, stop," he hissed.

"Spill it," Jessie said, turning around. "Last chance."

"Fine. Listen, your husband may be a successful businessman but he's also got some desires he'd rather keep under wraps. He told me a while back that he was bored with married life; that he wanted to spice things up. Someone had mentioned Deseo to him. He did all this research and knew everything about it when he called me. He had very specific questions about how he could partake of stuff they had there without risking his reputation."

"So you're saying our whole move down here was just so he could join that club?" Jessie asked skeptically.

"He's the one who suggested expanding that satellite office and offered to come down here. He knew you'd never go for the lifestyle he wanted to live. He said you were super straight—definitely no swinging or orgies. But he figured that once you were here, living in a fancy house, with a ton more disposable income, a baby on the way, away from anyone you knew but him, you'd feel like you had to stay. And if you discovered something fishy, by then you'd be so entrenched that you'd just have to put up with it. That's not unusual around here."

Jessie stared at him, wondering how he could be so dense as to not get that what he was describing was going on his very own house. But since he didn't get it, she wasn't going to say anything. His fear of his wife "finding out" what she already knew was really her only trump card.

"And the boat?" she prompted.

"How do you know about the boat?" he demanded.

Something told Jessie that they weren't discussing the same thing and she decided to let him take the lead, lest she say the wrong thing.

"You tell me," she said.

"You know, you act all holier than thou. But you and Kyle are more alike than you think. You threaten to tell my wife about Kelsey. He did the same thing when he heard I'd taken her out to the boat a few times."

"You had sex with Kelsey on your boat?" Jessie asked, equally shocked and disgusted.

"Mel gets seasick even when it's docked," Teddy said. "I knew she'd never go out there. I'm just glad he didn't know about the bonus feature or he'd probably have tried to blackmail me with that."

"Bonus feature?" Jessie asked.

Teddy looked panicked. It was clear that he'd said more than he intended.

"Um, yeah," he said, obviously coming up with a bogus answer as he spoke. "I bought an upgraded navigation system. It was really expensive. I didn't tell Mel. If Kyle knew, he'd have held it over me."

"Teddy," Jessie said, doing her best to sound comforting and forceful at the same time. "You're independently wealthy. You cheat on your wife with a club hostess. I just don't believe that you'd care what she thought about you buying a new navigation system. Tell me about the real bonus feature or Mel hears about Kelsey. I'm not going to give you another chance. And I'm getting pretty tired of your pathetic attempts to snow me. Spill it all *now*."

She stared at him, her eyes burrowing into him. For a long, ecstatic second, there was an electric silence between them, as she waited to see if he would break.

*Is this what all my interrogations will be like?*

The complicated cocktail of adrenaline, anticipation, and dread was more intoxicating than any drink she'd ever had.

"I have a camera," he muttered, finally caving.

"A camera?" Jessie repeated, suddenly breathless.

"Yeah. I have a security camera in the bedroom. It's motion activated and I sometimes like to...review the footage. If he knew about that, he'd absolutely hold it over my head."

Jessie said nothing.

Teddy seemed to belatedly realize the can of worms he'd opened and quickly asked, "You're not going to say anything about that, are you?"

"Of course not, Teddy," she said, trying to sound as reassuring as possible. "I promised that if you were honest with me about Kyle, I wouldn't tell Mel anything. You lived up to your end of the bargain. So will I."

Teddy glanced over her shoulder again and she knew Mel must be at the door. She turned around to see a scowl on her diminutive friend's face.

"Everything okay out here?" Mel asked.

"Everything's great," Jessie said. "Your husband was just giving me some good birthday ideas for Kyle. Sorry to be so cloak and dagger about it."

"You didn't think I could keep a secret?" Mel asked.

"You? Yes. But I wasn't sure how much little 'boom!' boy in there might pick up. I didn't want to risk it. Isn't that right, Teddy?"

Teddy nodded unconvincingly.

"And I can count on you not to spill the beans to Kyle, right?" she added with extra emphasis. "It would really be a bummer if someone revealed something they shouldn't, don't you agree?"

Teddy nodded more vigorously this time.

"All right. I've got to go. See you guys later," Jessie said as she got in her car.

As she pulled out, she waved to Mel, who didn't wave back but stared at her with a mix of doubt and disdain.

## CHAPTER TWENTY NINE

Jessie's mind was racing. With the new information about why they'd moved to Westport Beach, she began looking back at everything over the last decade through a new lens. She made two calls on her way to the marina where Teddy's boat was docked. The first was to Lacey. Amazingly, she picked up.

"Hey, lady," her friend said warmly.

Jessie was surprised at how normal Lacey's voice sounded until she remembered that they hadn't spoken in days. That was actually a good thing, as Jessie wanted to cut to the chase and that wouldn't be possible if Lacey knew everything that was going on.

"Hey to you," she replied, putting on her happiest voice as they engaged in a few minutes of catch-up conversation.

Only when she was sure that it wouldn't seem out of left field did she pose the question she'd been meaning to ask all along.

"Hey, can I ask you a random question?"

"They're my favorite kind," Lacey said.

"Kyle and I were telling a neighbor about how we met and he mentioned how we ended up going out the first time. He reminded me that I was supposed go out on a date that night with some guy who stood me up. Do you remember that?"

"Of course."

"What was that guy's name again?" Jessie tried to recall.

"Khalid. He was a sophomore."

"Right, Khalid. Didn't he end up getting kicked out of school or something crazy like that?"

"Um , yeah. But not just that. Maybe you don't remember because Kyle was busy sweeping you off your feet. But the guy got deported."

"What?" Jessie asked, incredulous. "How did I not hear about that?"

"The school tried to keep it quiet. I only found out all the details months later. He got busted for selling drugs. They found a huge stash in his dorm room. He was here on a student visa from Jordan. It got revoked and he was deported less than a week later."

"How did they find out about his stash?" Jessie asked. "I mean, half the kids in school, including me, could have been busted for what we had stashed in our sock drawers."

"It's been a while so I don't remember all the details but I think it was an anonymous call."

"That's weird," Jessie said. "Who would even know to call that in?"

"You think that's weird?" Lacey countered. "How about this? Khalid was a devout Muslim. From what I heard, he'd never even had a sip of alcohol, much less taken drugs. His friends said the idea that he was a dealer was beyond ridiculous. But he was gone so fast that there was never even a chance to mount a defense."

"I had no idea."

"Well, you were off falling in love around that time. I don't remember you paying attention to much of anything other than Kyle in those days."

"Yeah, I guess not," Jessie agreed, wondering how much else she hadn't paid attention to.

"Hey, are you okay, sweetie?" Lacey asked. "You sound troubled."

"No, I'm good," Jessie quickly assured her. "I guess I just feel bad that I was so unaware of what was going on back then."

"Don't feel too bad. I know he came from a well-connected family. I think he ended up transferring to a school in England."

"That's good to hear," Jessie said, glad she'd thrown her friend off the scent. "Listen, I've got to run. But let's get together soon, okay. I miss hanging out."

"You got it," she heard Lacey say just as she disconnected the call.

At the next stop light, she pulled the business card for Detective Ryan Hernandez from her purse and dialed the number. It went to voicemail.

"Hi, Detective," she said. "It's Jessie Hunt, the student from Professor Hosta's class who figured out your case study. I'm sorry to bother you but I had a…law enforcement question I was hoping to ask you. Can you please give me a call back when you get a chance? Thanks."

She considered calling back with more specifics but by then she was pulling into the marina parking lot and decided vague was safer for now.

*

It wasn't hard to get on Teddy's boat. A leathery-looking older guy held the security gate to the dock open for her without asking any questions and the guard who wandered the dock never gave her a second look as she walked purposefully past him.

When she got on board she headed straight for the bedroom, making sure not to look at the bed itself. It took only seconds to find the hidden camera, which wasn't actually hidden so much as out of the way, nestled on a tiny bookshelf between two books.

From what she could tell, it had a clear view of the whole bed and most of the room. Now all she had to do was find a way to access the footage on it. Thinking about what she knew about Teddy, it wasn't hard to guess where he'd left the instructions for the camera. He wouldn't have wanted Mel asking questions about why he had the thing so he would have kept the information here on the boat, where she was unlikely to visit and find it.

Within minutes, she found a cabinet with a plastic bin marked "Paperwork." Inside were several manila folders. One was marked "boat docs." Another read "scuba docs." The one on the bottoms said simply "camera docs."

She flipped it open and found the page that listed information on the camera website and app. Just below that were spaces for the owner put in the username/email and password. Written in neat handwriting was the email address, TeddyCWestport@deseo.com, followed by the brilliant password, "TeddyCWestportboatcamera." Jessie gave quiet thanks that Teddy was such a simple guy.

Jessie punched them into the app on her phone and was heartened to see the login work. A video log popped up for the last six months. She scrolled chronologically until five days ago and found the timestamp for 10 p.m., the last time she remembered being conscious.

She decided to watch the footage somewhere more private. So she quickly put everything back where she found it and left the boat, trying to look as casual as possible. As she walked down the dock, she passed the spot where she and Natalia had argued and where she'd subsequently collapsed. Seeing it, a comment Kyle had made that night popped back into her head. As he'd scooped her up to take her to Teddy's boat, he'd said, "It's the perfect spot. We're lucky it's right there."

*How very convenient.*

When Jessie got back to her car, she opened the app again and watched the video. It picked up at 10:09 p.m. with Kyle carrying her into the bedroom, placing her on the bed, and pulling the sheets over her. He left the bedroom and after about thirty seconds with no movement, the video ended.

The next clip began eighteen minutes later, at 10:27 p.m. as Kyle carried a second woman into the room, her head lolling sloppily over his arm. It was clearly Natalia. Jessie couldn't help but notice how impassive Kyle's expression was, as if he was just taking the trash out to the curb.

He laid her down next to Jessie, who hadn't changed position from the previous video. Then he took each one of Jessie's individual fingers and scraped her nails along the skin on Natalia's neck.

Jessie paused the video briefly as the magnitude of that action threatened to overwhelm her. Her gut twisted into a knot of revulsion and she had to step out of the car for a minute to regroup. When she was sure she could handle it, she hit "play" again.

The video resumed with Kyle concluding the fingernail scraping. When that was done, he rolled Natalia on her side and pulled the sheets over her as well. He then locked the bedroom door and pulled the chain latch across. After that, he opened the large portal window, climbed out, and closed the window behind him. Seconds later, the video cut out.

A new clip picked up the next morning as Jessie stirred into wakefulness. It was unsettling to watch an incident she'd personally experienced from such a distant remove, especially without any sound to give it context. But it was as she remembered it: the slow creep into consciousness followed by the awareness of the woman next to her and finally the realization that the woman, whom she recognized, was dead.

She watched herself unlock the chain latch and the doorknob, Kyle come in looking confused, then shocked. She watched him close the door, talk to her, help her to sit on the bed and talk to her some more. Jessie remembered that was around the point he proposed dumping Natalia's body.

She watched him maneuver around the body to look out the large portal window. But this time, from the camera's angle, which was different from hers that awful morning, she noticed something new. As he looked out the window, he slid its locking latch closed.

Only moments later, as he talked to her some more, he would note that only she could have committed the murder because the door and windows were locked. But in front of her was clear evidence that he had left through the window, surreptitiously locked it later, and then tried to claim that she was responsible for the crime because everything had been locked.

She may not have had video of him actually strangling Natalia, but what she did have certainly suggested he—her own husband—

was trying to frame *her* for it. The video cut out again. It resumed again later as Kyle, and Kyle alone, returned to carry Natalia's body from the room.

The next clip was later that morning, as Kyle returned to the bedroom one last time to change the sheets. After that, the only remaining clip was of Jessie from this morning, entering the bedroom and discovering the camera.

She sat in her car for a long time, deciding how to proceed. Part of her, the desperate panicky part, wanted to just delete the whole thing. Until she'd watched the footage, it had been marked as "unviewed," so she knew she was the only one to see it so far.

But the longer she sat there, as the late afternoon sun began to dim over the horizon, the less inclined she was to dump the video. Instead, a plan began to percolate in her head. The more she thought about it, the more she liked it, despite the enormous risks.

As the last bits of sun dropped below the Pacific Ocean, she resolved to go for it. She'd been a patsy for too long. Now she was going to take charge of her own destiny, regardless of the consequences.

She started the car and peeled out of the parking lot.

# CHAPTER THIRTY

Jessie was so pumped up with nervous adrenaline that it wasn't until she was pulling into her neighborhood that she noticed the voicemail from Detective Hernandez. It looked like he'd called when she was on the boat, which had spotty cell service, so her phone had never even rung.

She was about to check it when a call came in. It was from Dr. Farah, the young OB-GYN who'd told her she lost the baby that day in the hospital. She sent that straight to voicemail too. Then she listened to both messages.

Hernandez's was brief and his voice sounded harried. "Sorry I missed you. Happy to answer any questions I can. Call me back when you get a chance."

Dr. Farah's was only slightly longer and also got straight to the point.

"Hello, Mrs. Hunt," he said, sounding more confident and professional than he had in person. "We got your blood work back today and there were some...unusual results. We found an unexpected medication in your system. I was hoping you could come in sometime tomorrow. I'd like to rerun the tests to make sure there wasn't an error. Please call me back at your earliest convenience."

*That was weird.*

What kind of medication could be that unexpected? Other than the prenatal vitamin she'd been taking at the time, Jessie hadn't had any change in medication since she got the revised antidepressant prescription from Dr. Lemmon two months ago.

She was tempted to call him right back but she was just pulling into the driveway. She opened the garage door and saw that Kyle's car was already there. Any calls would have to wait. This wasn't a time to be distracted. She needed to keep all her focus on what she was about to do.

She pulled in next to him, put her phone on silent, turned on the recorder, and walked inside. Kyle wasn't in the kitchen or breakfast room but she did see an open bottle of bourbon on the counter.

"Kyle, I'm home," she said in the most casual voice she could muster.

"In here," he called from the living room.

She walked in to find him sprawled casually on the couch, a near empty glass in his hand. On the coffee table in front of him were two plastic containers of supermarket sushi. One was mostly empty. The other was unopened. Behind him, a roaring fire, complete with crackling logs, was burning in the fireplace.

"First fire of the season," she noted, trying to sound playful. "These brutal Southern California winters require it, I guess. I think it might dip below fifty tonight."

"I got you dinner," he said, ignoring her attempt at a joke as he nodded at the table. "But you didn't show up."

She noticed he was slurring slightly and wondered how many of those bourbons he'd already had. She pretended not to notice.

"I see that. If I had known you were going to take the initiative, I would have tried to get back earlier."

"Where were you?" he demanded. "Why are you back so late?"

"I hit bad traffic on the way back from my practicum. And then I stopped by the school to check out something in the library. You didn't call or I would have skipped that last stop and come straight home. You know how I love sushi. And now I can eat it again."

There was a bite to that last line that she wished she had held back. But Dr. Farah's message was still swimming in her head and it had led to a thought.

*What if the unexpected drug in my system didn't get there accidentally?*

Kyle didn't seem to notice her tone. He took another swig before speaking again.

"You better get started. It's been sitting out a while."

"Sure, just let me get comfortable," she said, returning to the kitchen to put down her purse and take off her jacket. She made sure her phone, in her pants pocket, wasn't visible before she returned.

"I don't think you're being completely honest with me," Kyle said when she returned.

"What are you talking about?" she asked as innocently as she could, considering the sudden cold ripple that ran through her body.

"You almost never show up late. And when you do, you always call to let me know. The fact that you didn't makes me suspicious about your whereabouts. Should I be suspicious, Jessica?"

He sounded even more slurry than before. But the sharpness of his question made her wonder if he was drunk at all or just pretending in order to get her guard down. She wouldn't put anything past him at this point.

169

"I show up late once and I get the third degree?" she countered. "I can't count how many times you've stayed out late without letting me know. I get that you're bummed about the miscarriage, but please don't look for reasons to poke at me."

She paused for a moment, debating whether to continue. If she said the next line, there'd be no going back. Then again, she suspected her husband of killing a woman and framing her for it.

*At this point, what is there to go back to anyway?*

"And please," she continued before he could respond, "don't blame me for your whole plan falling apart."

His eyes narrowed and he sat up straighter.

"What plan?" he asked sharply.

She noticed he still had the slur, suggesting the drunkenness was legit. She wasn't sure if that was a good or bad thing but suspected she was about to find out.

"Your plan to frame me for killing Natalia," she said, letting it hang out there, watching his reaction.

His eyes widened but when he spoke, his voice was steady.

"What are you talking about?"

She pressed, knowing that she only had a brief window to get a true reaction before he regrouped and entered "cover mode."

"You know, how you killed that young waitress, and then tried to convince me that I did it, even though I was unconscious the whole time."

She could tell from his eyes that, despite the mild alcohol haze, he had already recovered and was thinking of his next move, now that his feigned ignorance had fallen flat. But what he said next genuinely surprised her.

"Teddy made me do it," he said, his voice thick with shame.

"What?" she asked, taken aback.

"I know this doesn't absolve me," he said, his head down, refusing to make eye contact. "But I wasn't sure what to do—I panicked."

"What are you saying?"

"Teddy was having an affair with Natalia," he said, his voice barely above a whisper. "When I got back to the boat that night after getting water and ibuprofen for you, I found him below deck with her lying at his feet. He'd strangled her. He said she was going to tell Mel about them and he just lost it. I told him that we had to go to the police. But he turned on me. He said we should pin it on you; that you wouldn't remember what happened that night after your argument with Natalia and that if I tried to persuade you that you'd done it, you'd believe me. He said to convince you that you were guilty and then dump the body. I refused. Then he got nasty and said that if I didn't do it, you and the baby would be in danger; that I'd never know when or how, but that you would pay for it if I didn't go along with his plan. It was like he was a different person."

Jessie tried to process whether this was even possible. She was unconscious at the time this was supposedly going on so there was no way to know if what Kyle described had happened. The camera on the boat didn't show the main cabin so there was no way to verify the story.

Kyle took her silence for skepticism and pressed on.

"Teddy said that if I came clean to you, you'd be in danger. That's why I was hesitant to say anything until now. And that's why I've been so out of it lately. First that happens, then you losing the baby? I was completely lost. And Teddy visited me while you were in the hospital just to tell me not to get any smart ideas; that even though you'd miscarried, he could still do something to you. He was so cold about it."

Jessie turned over his words in her head. Everything about his story was technically plausible but something just didn't sit right. First, she knew Teddy Carlisle. And unless he was the best actor in the world, he didn't strike her as the type who could come up with a plan like that. He was weak and craven. But he was also kind of thick-headed. She just didn't buy that he was capable of such Machiavellian maneuvers.

And while she had no reason to doubt her husband's honesty until recently, a decade of knowing him had proven one thing. He was a quick thinker. She'd seen it in his work life many times—his ability to massage supervisors or clients. It was a gift. But for some reason, it had never occurred to her that he might use that same gift on her. Not until now.

"I don't believe you, Kyle," she said matter-of-factly. "Teddy isn't exactly a criminal mastermind. And when I spoke to him this afternoon, he did not act like a man who had covered up the murder of his mistress and threatened my life. Try again, babe."

She saw a glint of anger pass across Kyle's eyes, followed by momentary frustration. That was quickly replaced by an expression she couldn't identify at first.

"Okay," he said in a resigned tone. "I'm going to come clean. Clearly I've lost your trust and I'm just going to lay it all out there and hope that you'll see things from my perspective."

"I'm all ears," she replied.

"It's pretty simple. *I* slept with Natalia," he said, refusing to look at her. "It was only one time but I did do it. It was on a night when someone at the club gave me Ecstasy. I don't know why I took it. I told myself it was to win over clients but I'm not really sure anymore. Regardless, the next thing I knew I was…with her. I regretted it immediately. I tried to forget about it. I avoided the club. That was one of the reasons I agreed to stop going. I let you think it was because you asked but this was as much the reason. And then the night of the party, she approached me. She said she was going to tell you about that night. I begged her not to and I thought I'd convinced her. But when I came back to the boat later with the water and medicine, she was there, about to open the bedroom door. I guess I just snapped."

"You strangled her?" Jessie asked.

"I was so angry. This woman was trying to destroy my family and I just…yeah, I just couldn't stop myself."

"And then you blamed me?" Jessie pressed.

Kyle nodded and as he was about to resume talking, she noticed the same expression on his face, the one she couldn't quite identify before. Only now she could. It was determination. That struck her as odd, considering his confession.

"I sat there next to her body for a while," he admitted. "I debated calling the police. And then I got this idea, like a thunderbolt, a way to get rid of the threat she posed and keep you from trying to leave. I was in a dark place, I'm ashamed to say. But once you woke up and saw her body, I was committed."

He hung his head and he slumped down in the easy chair across from the couch where she sat. He seemed completely deflated. And yet…

*I can't see his face. I don't know what he's thinking.*

"I can't help but think that the stress of all this is why you lost the baby," he muttered under his breath. "And I don't know how I'll ever live that down."

And that's when she finally knew. He almost had her for a second. But he pushed just a little too hard, tried to wring out one bit of pathos too many.

"Mentioning the miscarriage was a mistake, babe," she said, impressed by the lack of emotion in her own voice. "It reminded me of the real reason it happened: you drugged me. Whatever you put in that champagne made me pretty volatile. And then you placed me in a position where conflict with Natalia was almost inevitable. You set it up so that everyone would see me go off on her. And then, whatever that drug was knocked me out, conveniently right next to Teddy's boat. You drugged me. You planned my public outburst. You planned for me to end up on that boat. You probably lured

172

Natalia there while I was sleeping. Then you killed her and pinned it on me. But you didn't expect the drug you gave me to make me miscarry. And you couldn't have known the doctor from the hospital would call me to tell me about an unexpected medication in my blood work. *You* did all this, love. I'm just wondering why."

He sat across from her with his head down for several seconds before moving at all. Then he reached into his pocket and for a second, Jessie thought he was going to pull out a gun. But it was just that obnoxious money clip with the dollar sign on it. He tossed it on the coffee table and looked up. His eyes were glinting with something close to mischievousness.

"I know you hate that thing," he said mildly. "But I had to take it out. It was digging into my thigh and making it hard to concentrate."

"Concentrate on what?"

"On what to do next," he said. "After all, things can't continue this way, can they?"

Jessie felt the vitriol rise up in her throat and for the first time, decided not to even try to hold it back.

"You mean with me living with the man who murdered some girl, framed me for it, and gave me a drug that made me lose my unborn child? Yeah, I'd say this is breakup material."

"You asked me why," he reminded her, untroubled by her tone. "Do you really want to know the answer, Jessica?"

"I really do."

"Okay," he said. "But I'm not sure you're going to like it. Here goes. I'm tired of you. I'm tired of being married to you. I just wanted a little fun, to spice things up. I heard about this club that made that sort of thing possible. But I knew you'd never go for it."

"For an open marriage?" she asked. "Yeah, very perceptive on that one."

"You make things so hard, Jessie. You've got all these demons that haunt you. The job you want is in this dark world and it weighs you down. I just wanted to have a good time, mess around a bit. I thought maybe you'd embrace it. And then, when it became clear that you wouldn't, I decided to embrace it on my own. But you made even that effort miserable."

"Why didn't you just leave me if you were so unhappy?" she asked.

"I can't do that, Jessica. You know the firm doesn't look kindly on broken marriages. No one who's been divorced has ever made partner there. They all eventually get dumped. But happily married men, especially ones with little ones, seem to move up the ladder at lightning speed. I couldn't jeopardize that. So I came up with a plan."

"To force me to be the perfect little wife?" she volunteered.

"Exactly. It wasn't my first choice. But I figured that if you feared that leaving me or moving away might lead to prison time, you'd find a way to make do. And once the kid was born, you'd be so entangled in the community that you'd give up on the idea of moving back downtown."

"So you killed someone to keep me in line?" she asked, still barely able to process it.

"Desperate times, desperate measures," he said, shrugging. "Which is why the next little bit is going to get kind of ugly."

"What does that mean?" Jessie asked, as the hairs on the back of her neck stood up.

"What it means, my dear," he said, standing up, "is that things are going to end badly for you."

## CHAPTER THIRTY ONE

Jessie stood up too, trying to anticipate whatever might happen next. But she wasn't prepared when Kyle stepped quickly forward, reached across the coffee table, and punched her flush on the jaw.

Her legs wobbled and she crumpled back down on the couch as stars exploded in front of her eyes. Even as the pain radiated down her torso, she tried to push up from the couch. But before she made any progress, he was above her. He hit her twice more in the face and she slumped down, stunned and unable to move.

She couldn't see but over the rush of hot pain in her ears, she heard him moving around nearby. After a minute, he was above her again. She could feel him grab her wrists and hold them together as he wrapped them in duct tape. Then he did the same thing with her ankles.

She blinked away the tears in her eyes and saw him going through his phone.

"I guess you're wondering what the plan is now," he said in a more relaxed voice than she would have expected under the circumstances. "Unfortunately, it looks like I'm going to have move on to plan D. Or is it E?"

He looked over at her as if he expected her to reply, then must have realized she was incapable of speaking. He continued.

"Plan E is to make it look like one of the explanations I gave you earlier was legit. You see, for the purposes of this evening's alibi, it *was* Teddy who had the affair with Natalia. He *did* threaten your life when I found out he killed her. And after you went to talk to him, he realized he had to follow through. So he came over here and shot you with an untraceable gun I just happened to buy last week. I was upstairs and rushed down here. When I saw what happened, I went at him. He shot me but I kept coming. We struggled, fought over the gun. It went off and killed him. I called the police, devastated by the turn of events, the only survivor of my high school friend's descent into madness. It's very sad, really."

Jessie tried to tell him he'd never get away with it but it only came out as a mumble.

"That reminds me," he said as he cut off another piece of duct tape and put it over her mouth. "I can't have you warning him by calling out or something. I know it's uncomfortable and I'm sorry

175

for that. Under other circumstances, I'd just shoot you now and put you out of your misery. But for this to work, both of you have to die around the same time. I don't need a curious coroner noting times of death that don't fit my story. So you'll have to wait until he gets here for all this to end. Besides, who else can I tell about my grand plan? After tonight it'll have to be my little secret. So can you blame me for blathering on a bit to someone who won't be able to tattle? And if I don't brag on myself, no one will."

He had found Teddy's number and was about to call when the doorbell rang. As Jessie watched, he disappeared into the front room. A moment later, he came back.

"You're not going to believe this," he whispered. "But Mel is at our front door and she looks pissed. Think I should let her in?"

Jessie shook her head vigorously from side to side, sending flashes of pain shooting through her skull.

"I get it," he said sympathetically, as the doorbell rang again. "You don't want anything bad to happen to your friend. But this might actually work out. It will make more sense if Teddy gets a call to come over from his wife. And then, when they do the investigation later, it will look less suspicious than if I called him using my phone. Of course that means Mel has to die too. But I can come up with a cover story for that. I'm getting pretty good at it. Be right back."

He headed off toward the front door, ignoring Jessie's nearly inaudible grunts of protest. When he was gone, she looked around, desperate for anything to change the dynamic.

She cursed herself for the arrogance that made her think she could get a confession and somehow just waltz out of the house. Nearly ten years with him had made her complacent and overconfident. But he wasn't the same person she used to know.

She'd had visions of calling out Kyle for his crimes then storming out and going straight to the police station. Had she really thought he'd be so stunned that he'd just let her go? Did she imagine that as he curled up in a ball of guilt, she could just call 911? She could barely stomach her own idiocy.

*Stop it! This won't help you or Mel. Find a solution, fast!*

Jessie forced herself to look around the room again, this time focusing on anything that might help her get the duct tape off. The fireplace poker was too clumsy and too far away. She'd never get to it in time, much less be able to use it. There was a huge glass vase on the mantel. But reaching it, knocking it down, and finding an appropriate shard of glass with which to cut herself free seemed impossible, even if she had the time to try it.

Then her eyes fell on Kyle's money clip, the top of the "$" symbol glinting in the light of the fire. He'd taken it out of his pants because it was digging into him. The edges were too sharp.

As she heard Kyle open the front door, she leaned forward and scooped it up into her closed hands.

"Hi, Mel," Kyle said from the foyer. "You seem upset. Is everything okay?"

"Can I come in?" she asked, sounding borderline angry. "I need to discuss something with Jessie."

"Of course," he answered, without a care in the world. "Come on in. She's in the living room. Is there anything I can do to help?"

"No. This is a woman to woman thing."

Jessie could hear Mel walking in her direction, oblivious to Kyle quietly closing and locking the door behind her. As she waited for her friend to enter the room, Jessie glanced down to make sure the money clip wasn't visible.

Mel rounded the corner, saw Jessie sitting on the couch, tied up and bloody-faced, and opened her mouth to scream. But before she could, Kyle appeared behind her, grabbed the back of her head, and slammed it hard into the wall. She dropped to the ground with a thud.

Kyle leaned over and pressed his ear against her chest as he checked her pulse. After a moment he looked up.

"Still alive," he said cheerily. "Thank goodness. That would have complicated things."

Jessie watched as he felt around in Mel's pocket and pulled out her phone. He dialed a number and waited, smiling at Jessie pleasantly while it rang.

"Hey, buddy," he said when Teddy picked up. "Don't freak out but your wife asked me to call. She came over here to talk to Jessie but she tripped on the stoop and really sprained her ankle. I'd drive her back but Jessie is really upset about the miscarriage. She's super depressed. I'm actually afraid to leave her alone. Can you run over real quick and pick up your wife?"

He waited while Teddy replied, kneeling casually over the unconscious body of his friend's wife.

"No, I don't think you need to wake up Daughton. I know you don't want to leave him alone but we're talking ten minutes tops. He'll never know you were gone."

He listened again, then nodded.

"Okay, buddy. See you soon."

He hung up and exaggeratedly wiped pretend sweat from his brow.

"That was close. For a minute I thought he was going to bring the kid. That would have been a messy obstacle. Kid crying in his car seat while his parents are dead inside? Not a good look. Anyway, he'll be here soon so I better get that gun. Don't worry, babe. This will all be over soon."

He stood up and went upstairs, where he had apparently stashed his illegal weapon. When she was sure he was on the second floor, Jessie maneuvered the money clip so that she could scrape its sharp top edge against the duct tape holding her wrists together. It seemed pointed enough but because she had trouble getting any kind of grip, it was slow going. She'd barely made a small tear at one end when she heard Kyle stomping back down the stairs. She stopped cutting, hid the clip between her palms again, and looked up.

"She still out?" he asked, glancing briefly at Mel when he got down. "Good. We don't need any complications. I figure that I'll have to shoot Teddy first, seeing as he's the only real threat at this point. I think I'll have him come in here to get Mel. Then I'll get real close and shoot him in the gut. It has to look like we were struggling in close quarters. I don't know if it matters if I kill you or Mel next. I'm thinking I'll tell the cops that she somehow found out about his affair with Natalia and threatened to tell the cops so he had to off her too. Maybe we do her first because that's more of a crime of passion. He'll shoot her in the chest in a moment of crazy panic. Then he kills you next as he threatened me that he would. That's more methodical. He'll shoot you in the head as punishment for me not keeping his secret. Then I'll have to find some way to shoot myself without making it look obvious that I did it. I'll need to hold it far enough away so that it looks like *he* did it as I was running toward him. Or maybe I can attach the trigger to something. You know what—I'll figure that out afterward. I'll have a few minutes after you're all dead before I have to call nine-one-one. Sometimes you've got to improvise, right, babe?"

He looked at her as if he was actually expecting her to reply. When he got none, he shrugged, grabbed Mel under the arms, and dragged her over next to Jessie on the couch.

"Can't have her anywhere near the blood splatter from my 'confrontation' with Teddy. Someone might piece it together."

A light from the driveway suddenly shined through the dining room curtains.

"Oh, looks like he's here," Kyle said excitedly. "It's showtime!"

## CHAPTER THIRTY TWO

The second he disappeared from view, Jessie began cutting at the small incision she'd already made in the tape. Every few cuts, she tugged her wrists apart, trying to open the tear farther.

"He's coming up the drive, baby," Kyle called out in a loud whisper from the other room. "This is so intense, I feel like I might pee my pants. Maybe I do that after I get shot? That might look more realistic."

She was almost free but worried that the last yank on the duct tape might be loud enough for Kyle to notice. Then she heard Teddy's footsteps on the porch and had an idea. She waited. The doorbell rang and at that moment she ripped her wrists apart with all the strength she could muster. The tape split loudly, freeing her hands. She immediately went to work on the tape at her ankles.

"Hey, buddy," she heard Kyle say as he opened the door. "So sorry about this. I know you didn't want to leave Daughton home alone but you'll be back in a jiff."

She cut hard and fast at the tape. This time it was much easier as she could grip the money clip and put her full force behind it.

"I thought you might be waiting outside with her," Teddy said, "so she could just get in and we could bail."

The tape came loose and Jessie stood up, using the arm of the couch for balance. She looked around for anything she could use to defend herself.

"Oh no, man. Like I said, I didn't want to leave Jessie alone at all. Mel is on the couch in the living room with her. She's keeping an eye on her for me. You'll have to carry her out."

Jessie's eyes fell on the fireplace poker. It wasn't perfect but it was heavy and it was better than nothing at all. She scurried around the couch and gently removed it from its holster.

"Okay," Teddy said, his voice getting closer and echoing slightly as he stepped into the foyer. "Let's make this quick then."

Jessie shuffled across the living room and into the kitchen as quietly as she could. She knew Kyle would direct Teddy into the living room the same way he had with Mel, so that he could walk behind him and maintain the advantage.

"She's right in there," Kyle said. "Let me just close the door to keep the bugs out. I'll be right behind you."

Jessie rounded the corner of the kitchen and peeked out in time to see Teddy walking down the hall to the living room. Kyle was a few steps behind him, his right hand holding the gun behind his back.

Jessie glanced at the front door. For a second, she was tempted to make a run for it. Kimberly's house was right across the street. Or if Teddy had left the keys in his car, she could just jump in and peel out.

But that meant both Teddy and Mel would almost certainly die. And if they did, this time she would actually be partly responsible. Besides, she was tired of running away.

"Hey, Mel, how are you doing?" Teddy asked as he rounded the corner into the living room. "What the…"

Jessie knew he must have seen his wife slumped unconscious on the couch. Kyle rounded the corner right after him. Jessie quickly tiptoed after him, knowing that the second he saw she was gone, she'd lose the advantage.

"Sorry about this, buddy," she heard Kyle say and realized he hadn't yet looked at the couch. His attention was focused on his friend, the one he was about to shoot. "I'd like to explain, but it's complicated."

She knew he might fire at any second and broke into a run, raising the poker over her head. He must have known something was off because she heard something like a "wha?" right before his head appeared from behind the wall.

She was only a couple of feet away and brought the poker down hard as she ran at him. His eyes opened wide and he yanked the gun, which had been pointed at Teddy, in her direction. She made solid contact with the top of his skull just as she heard the gun go off.

As she slammed into her husband, she heard glass shattering behind her and knew he'd missed. They fell at the same time and she landed on top of him, breaking her fall. She rolled over onto her back and saw that he was woozy but not out.

Blood was running down his face from the wound on his head. Despite that, he got to his knees beside her and fumbled with the poker that had fallen from her hands. Grabbing it by the shaft, he lifted it high above his head and brought it down hard toward her face.

Jessie managed to throw her hands up and deflect the poker away from her head. A moment later she felt a searing burn on her left side. She gasped at the sudden pain. Before she could fully process it, she saw Kyle lift the poker a second time. She knew she didn't have the strength left to fight off another blow.

As she raised his arms again, she caught a blur of motion out of the corner of her eye before everything exploded into a mist of shiny glass. She felt Kyle's body land heavily on top of her chest. Glancing down, she saw that he was unconscious.

She looked up to find Teddy staring at her, his mouth agape. In his bloody hands were shards of the vase from the mantel, the one she'd briefly considered using to cut herself free earlier.

She tried to talk but realized the duct tape was still covering her mouth. She ripped it off, ignoring the raw skin below.

"He wanted to kill all of us," she rasped. "He killed that Natalia girl. And he was going kill us next."

Teddy seemed at a loss for words. Finally he managed to mutter just one.

"Why?"

"Not really the most important question right now, Teddy," she said, feeling suddenly lightheaded. "Just call the cops. And make sure he doesn't wake up before they get here. He was half a second from shooting you and he'll try again if he gets the chance."

"Okay," Teddy agreed, "but Jessie…"

"Yeah?"

"You're bleeding pretty bad."

"What?" she said, now more aware of the burning sensation on her left side. She glanced down to see blood seeping from her gut. She was just reaching her hands down to put pressure on it when she felt herself falling forward and everything went dark.

*

She was in the same hospital as before and wondered if it was the same room too. The paint and room setup were identical.

Jessie had been awake for about a half hour now and she still hadn't gotten any answers. The doctors and nurses wouldn't tell her anything other than that the poker had punctured her in the left abdomen, that it had missed all major organs, and that she would eventually make a full recovery.

"Can someone please tell me what's going on?" she demanded in a hoarse voice for what had to be the fourth or fifth time. "Is my husband in custody? Is Melanie Carlisle all right?"

"I told you," said the obviously annoyed nurse, "we're not allowed to share any additional information until the authorities have spoken to you. There are several detectives talking outside right now. I'm sure one of them will be in soon to discuss the situation with you."

She walked out, leaving Jessie alone with a muted television, a case of cottonmouth, a dull throb in her left side, and an IV in her right arm. She was pretty sure it was the reason she felt slightly drunk.

The door opened to reveal someone she was genuinely shocked to see. Looking down at her with a mix of sympathy and wonder was Detective Ryan Hernandez of LAPD, downtown bureau.

"What are you doing here?" Jessie croaked.

"Nice," he replied, shaking his head. "I come all the way from downtown Los Angeles to see you and this is the greeting I get?"

"I'm sorry. I'm just confused."

"Well, you were shivved with a fire poker," he acknowledged. "So I'll give you a pass this time. Your voice message to me sounded fairly urgent. I called you back and didn't hear anything. So I called again—still nothing. I called a third time and when I didn't hear back I got a little worried. So even though I felt a little weird about it, I took the extra step of having your phone GPS tracked and discovered that you were in this hospital. So I figured I'd stop by. Looks like I made the right call."

"Oh," Jessie said, getting most of that despite feeling a little loopy throughout. "Does this mean you can tell me what's going on?"

"I think so. But you should know that I'm not the only one here to talk to you. There are some local detectives out there who have quite a few questions. I managed to hold them off for a bit on the pretense that you'd want to see a semi-friendly face when you woke up."

"I appreciate that," Jessie said, trying to sit up to take a sip of water from a straw. "It's always nice to see a semi-friendly face. But can I ask you a question?"

"Sure," Detective Hernandez said as he moved to her side and helped prop her up so she could drink more easily.

"Why did you need a 'pretense' to talk to me?"

"Ah, that word jumped out at you, huh? Here's the thing. The detectives out there found the audio recording on your phone. It's pretty definitive. Your husband's confession is about as clear-cut as I've ever come across."

"Did you see the video too?" Jessie asked.

"Video?"

"I found camera footage from the boat where he killed the girl Natalia. It includes him laying her dead body next to me while I was unconscious in a bed, among other things."

"I did not see that," Hernandez said. "But I'll make the guys aware of it. That will help too."

"And yet, you still needed a pretense," Jessie reminded him.

"Right. It would be inappropriate for me to say too much. But I just wanted to make you aware that your husband is claiming that you were an accessory after the fact; that you were in on the plan to dump the girl's body. In fact, he suggests that it was your idea and that you told him where to do it."

Jessie looked at Hernandez closely. She wanted to believe that he was on her side, that he was trying to help her, maybe even warn her. But these days, she wasn't inclined to trust that anyone other than herself had her best interests at heart.

"And does any halfway-decent law enforcement professional buy that story?" she asked, making sure to sound as contemptuous as possible.

"I don't think so," Hernandez said. "He's spun so many different stories, including about four different ones on that audio you recorded, that it'd be hard to take much of anything he says seriously."

"So then why am I getting an unsettled vibe off you, Detective Hernandez?"

"It's just that I watched his interview a few times now," he said, not quite looking her in the eye. "And it's clear that he's a pathological liar, probably a sociopath."

"But...?"

"But when he talked about you knowing about the plan to dump the body and not opposing it, there was a slightly different inflection in his voice, something almost plaintive and borderline credible."

"So what are you saying?" Jessie asked, feeling a thread of fear crawl into her chest despite the happy drugs.

Detective Hernandez suddenly stopped avoiding eye contact and stared at her square in the eyes, unblinking. And in that moment, she knew he sensed that part of what Kyle said was true.

"It's probably nothing," he said after a moment of silence. "The guy tells lies like most people breathe. Just thought you should know. Anyway, your friend Melanie is in recovery. She has a concussion but is otherwise okay. Her husband is fine, though he can't seem to wrap his head around what happened. Not the brightest bulb, that one. I used your phone to check your last few

183

calls and reached your friend Lacey. She's in the waiting area and will be in when the detectives finish with you. My understanding is that you'll have to stay here overnight at least, maybe a couple of nights. But then you should be able to go home, or wherever you feel comfortable staying. In the meantime, I'll let you rest."

"Thanks, Detective. I appreciate it."

"No problem," he said as he walked out the door. "And call me Ryan."

She nodded and then he was gone. She closed her eyes, allowing herself a moment to rest before the other detectives came in. But her lids felt heavy and she didn't have much desire to open then again anytime soon. The other detectives would have to wait a bit longer.

## CHAPTER THIRTY THREE

A week later, Jessie stepped out of the elevator of Lacey's downtown LA condo building and walked slowly through the lobby, using her cane as sparingly as possible.

She nodded at the security guard, who held the door open for her. A cold blast of November air hit her hard and she dipped her head to avoid getting the full force of the wind in her face. She briefly considered just going back upstairs to Lacey's warm condo, where she had a spacious guest room all to herself.

But the doctors had told her that the more she got out and walked, the quicker she'd recover from her stab wound.

*I have a stab wound.*

She shook her head in disbelief at the thought, then thought better of it. After all, she'd dealt with a lot of unbelievable stuff in the last few weeks. She'd learned that her partner of nearly a decade was a sociopathic killer who had framed her for murder. Yet, she'd been clueless as to his true nature, putting into doubt how good a forensic psychologist she might make.

*Was he always like this? Was I that oblivious? Was he that good at hiding it from me? Or did it escalate over time?*

The questions gnawed at her constantly. Of course, in her session with Dr. Lemmon yesterday, the therapist had told her not to be too hard on herself; that we often have trouble seeing the clues in someone so close to us. It reminded her again of what Bolton Crutchfield had said in their last meeting when he'd told her to trust her gut.

"Maybe you ain't the one who should be twistin'," he'd said. Apparently he'd seen it all along.

She pressed on, shuffling down the street in the direction of the coffee shop on the corner, ignoring the wind whipping the loose strands of hair against her face. She didn't mind. Despite the wind tunnels created by the downtown skyscrapers, there was something comforting about being back in the old neighborhood.

Now that she was back in her familiar surroundings, her life in Westport Beach seemed almost like a bad dream. And yet, it had all been real. Wives put up with their husbands' indiscretions because they didn't have the financial freedom to say no. Women with

185

dreams shelved them to satisfy the demands of self-involved spouses.

And she was almost one of them. Only in her case it was worse. She'd been manipulated in that direction by a sociopath who was willing to kill for the life he wanted. But for a few things breaking her way, she might have obliviously lived a life beside him for years.

But that life was over. She would soon be single again. And though the pain of losing the baby still sometimes overwhelmed her with an aching sense of emptiness, she reminded herself that this was an opportunity to start fresh. Maybe one day she would be able to start a family on her own terms.

That thought buoyed her as she moved slowly down the street. This was where she wanted to be as she rebooted her life. As she navigated the crowded sidewalk, shielding her eyes from the sunlight shining off the glass from a nearby tower, she even found herself appreciating the stench emanating from a nearby sewer grate and the belch of exhaust from a passing delivery truck. She was home.

She didn't know how long she'd stay at Lacey's, though she had an open invitation. One way or another she was staying in the area. The house in Westport still needed to be sold and her lawyer had told her she wouldn't be able to do that until after Kyle was convicted, which he anticipated happening in the next six to nine months.

With all the evidence against him, everyone agreed it was an open-and-shut case. There was Jessie's audio recording, along with Teddy's testimony. No one other than Detective Hernandez (or Ryan, apparently) had even mentioned her husband's claim that she was in on the body-dumping plan. It would probably come up at trial, but maybe not. After all, it wasn't an alibi, just an excuse. And in light of him drugging her, leading to the miscarriage, even that excuse seemed dubious.

As a result, things were looking up. The authorities had busted up the prostitution ring being run out of Club Deseo, which was now rumored to be up for sale at a bargain price. Jessie's practicum was over and she'd passed Hosta's class, meaning she would get her graduate degree next month.

She was already getting offers to consult on cases from various local law enforcement agencies and was also toying with the idea of applying to the FBI's ten-week National Academy training program. She planned to review her options over the holidays.

When the house eventually sold, she'd be financially independent enough not to worry too much about picking the gig based on pay. And that didn't even account for what she would get in the pending divorce. She might even have the resources and spare time to dig into The Panel and find out, among other things, why they'd been so willing to let her interact with Bolton Crutchfield.

Otherwise, as long as she didn't think too much about Natalia—whose last name she'd learned was Urgova—dropping off the boat and sinking in the cold water of the Pacific Ocean, she was okay. The image came to her on occasion but she was usually able to shake it off. The truth was she'd had far worse images stuck in her head.

When she got out of the coffee shop, warm cup in hand, she debated whether to go back to the condo or wander a bit. Before she could make a decision, she sensed eyes on her and turned around.

To her surprise she found Officer Kat Gentry five feet away, staring at her. She was so startled that she stumbled back, losing her balance. Gentry moved quickly forward and grabbed her forearm, steadying her until she regained her equilibrium.

"Sorry," Gentry said. "Didn't mean to scare you."

"What are you doing here?" Jessie asked in astonishment. "Isn't this a little out of your jurisdiction?"

"A little," Gentry said. "But I'm not here on official business. We all heard about what happened to you and wanted to make sure you were okay. Cortez was especially concerned."

Gentry cracked a bit of a grin at that last line, which set Jessie somewhat at ease.

"That's very nice. But I get the distinct feeling that that's an excuse and you have another reason for looking me up."

Gentry gave her a long, hard look as if she was debating whether to come clean or just say goodbye.

"You know, you might end up being decent at your job. That is, as long as none of your other cases involve your ex. You seem to have a blind spot on that front."

"Officer Gentry," Jessie said, "I'm not sure we know each other well enough for you to be making such edgy quips at my expense."

"Probably not. Just stalling, I guess," Gentry said as she pulled an envelope out of her jacket pocket and handed it over. It was the cheap white kind and there was nothing written on it.

"What's this?" Jessie asked.

"I debated giving it to you for a long time. But ultimately I decided it was better to be safe than sorry."

"You're being a little cryptic," Jessie said, taking the envelope.

"It's from Bolton Crutchfield. He said you needed to be aware of something. He said you were in danger. And that this would convince you he was telling the truth."

"You believe him?" Jessie asked as she ripped open the envelope.

"I've worked around the guy for a while now. He hates me, has never said anything to or about me without a sneer or contempt in his voice. But when he asked me to give you this, for the only time since I've known him, he sounded sincere. I think he's fond of you, in a non-killing kind of way."

"He wrote this?" Jessie asked, pulling out the single sheet of paper inside and unfolding it.

"No. He said it was from the man who visited him that one day, his mentor, the Ozarks Executioner. He said this was the message the man left you."

Jessie unfolded the page and stared at it. She felt her blood turn cold. Gentry glanced at the words on the page:

*BE SEEING YOU, JUNEBUG.*

Gentry looked back at Jessie, who gulped hard and reminded herself to breathe.

"This is from the man who abducted you?" she asked. "The one who killed your mother and those other people?"

Jessie nodded.

"But how can you be sure it's not just Crutchfield messing with you?" Gentry asked. "How do you know it's really from the same guy?"

"Because he was the only one who ever said that phrase to me. He used to say it every night when he put me to bed, before everything fell apart."

"Wait, what?" Gentry said, confused. "He put you to bed? How is that possible?"

Jessie handed back the sheet of paper, her body pulsating with a fear she hadn't felt in years, and forced herself to say the words out loud.

"Because he's my father."

## THE PERFECT BLOCK
### (A Jessie Hunt Psychological Suspense Thriller—Book Two)

**In THE PERFECT BLOCK (Book #2), rookie criminal profiler Jessie Hunt, 29, picks up the pieces of her broken life and leaves suburbia to start a new life in downtown Los Angeles. But when a wealthy socialite is murdered, Jessie, assigned the case, finds herself back in the world of picture-perfect suburbia, hunting a deranged killer amidst the false facades of normalcy and sociopathic women.**

Jessie, thriving again in downtown LA, is sure she's moved on from her suburban nightmare. Ready to put her failed marriage behind her, she lands a job with the local police department, deferring her acceptance to the FBI's Academy.

She is assigned a straightforward murder in a wealthy neighborhood, a simple case to start her career. But little do her bosses know, there's more to the case than anyone suspected. Nothing can prepare her for her first case, one that will force her to probe the minds of the wealthy, suburban couples she'd thought she'd left behind. Behind their polished family pictures and manicured hedges, Jessie realizes, perfection is not what it seems.

A fast-paced psychological suspense thriller with unforgettable characters and heart-pounding suspense, THE PERFECT BLOCK is book #2 in a riveting new series that will leave you turning pages late into the night.

## Blake Pierce

Blake Pierce is author of the bestselling RILEY PAGE mystery series, which includes thirteen books (and counting). Blake Pierce is also the author of the MACKENZIE WHITE mystery series, comprising nine books (and counting); of the AVERY BLACK mystery series, comprising six books; of the KERI LOCKE mystery series, comprising five books; of the MAKING OF RILEY PAIGE mystery series, comprising two books (and counting); of the KATE WISE mystery series, comprising two books (and counting); of the CHLOE FINE psychological suspense mystery, comprising two books (and counting); and of the JESSE HUNT psychological suspense thriller series, comprising two books (and counting).

An avid reader and lifelong fan of the mystery and thriller genres, Blake loves to hear from you, so please feel free to visit www.blakepierceauthor.com to learn more and stay in touch.

# BOOKS BY BLAKE PIERCE

**A JESSIE HUNT PSYCHOLOGICAL SUSPENSE SERIES**
THE PERFECT WIFE (Book #1)
THE PERFECT BLOCK (Book #2)
THE PERFECT HOUSE (Book #3)

**CHLOE FINE PSYCHOLOGICAL SUSPENSE SERIES**
NEXT DOOR (Book #1)
A NEIGHBOR'S LIE (Book #2)

**KATE WISE MYSTERY SERIES**
IF SHE KNEW (Book #1)
IF SHE SAW (Book #2)

**THE MAKING OF RILEY PAIGE SERIES**
WATCHING (Book #1)
WAITING (Book #2)
LURING (Book #3)

**RILEY PAIGE MYSTERY SERIES**
ONCE GONE (Book #1)
ONCE TAKEN (Book #2)
ONCE CRAVED (Book #3)
ONCE LURED (Book #4)
ONCE HUNTED (Book #5)
ONCE PINED (Book #6)
ONCE FORSAKEN (Book #7)
ONCE COLD (Book #8)
ONCE STALKED (Book #9)
ONCE LOST (Book #10)
ONCE BURIED (Book #11)
ONCE BOUND (Book #12)
ONCE TRAPPED (Book #13)
ONCE DORMANT (book #14)

**MACKENZIE WHITE MYSTERY SERIES**
BEFORE HE KILLS (Book #1)
BEFORE HE SEES (Book #2)
BEFORE HE COVETS (Book #3)
BEFORE HE TAKES (Book #4)
BEFORE HE NEEDS (Book #5)

BEFORE HE FEELS (Book #6)
BEFORE HE SINS (Book #7)
BEFORE HE HUNTS (Book #8)
BEFORE HE PREYS (Book #9)
BEFORE HE LONGS (Book #10)

## AVERY BLACK MYSTERY SERIES
CAUSE TO KILL (Book #1)
CAUSE TO RUN (Book #2)
CAUSE TO HIDE (Book #3)
CAUSE TO FEAR (Book #4)
CAUSE TO SAVE (Book #5)
CAUSE TO DREAD (Book #6)

## KERI LOCKE MYSTERY SERIES
A TRACE OF DEATH (Book #1)
A TRACE OF MUDER (Book #2)
A TRACE OF VICE (Book #3)
A TRACE OF CRIME (Book #4)
A TRACE OF HOPE (Book #5)